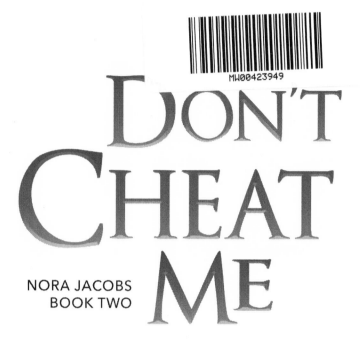

DON'T CHEAT ME

NORA JACOBS
BOOK TWO

JACKIE MAY

BLUEFIELDS

Published by Bluefields

Copyright © 2018 by Kelly Oram

Edition 1.1

Edited by Jennifer Henkes (www.literallyjen.com)

ISBN 978-1-9831555-4-3

For Heather. Because werewolves!

C H A P T E R
ONE

ONE MONTH AGO, I MOVED IN WITH A TROLL. IT'S BEEN surprisingly mundane, if you forget that first week where I helped find a dozen missing underworlders and consequently got kidnapped and stabbed by a crazy sorcerer. Other than *that*, it's been a very quiet month. Well, figuratively quiet. Literally, my troll roommate snores like a chainsaw on steroids, which is quite loud.

Terrance and I are on opposite sleep schedules, so we don't see each other much. He owns a nightclub, among a few other businesses in the not-so-lovely city of Detroit, Michigan, while I work in a motorcycle repair shop doing oil changes and tire repair. It's not bad work, now, but in a few weeks when the temperatures start to really drop, I'm going to wish I did anything else.

I get home just after four p.m. and head down the stairs into our underground house beneath the Ambassador

Bridge—yes, the troll lives under the bridge. It's okay to laugh. I did, when I found out. I shake off the chill of a cold and cloudy day. I need a new coat. My threadbare, old hoodie isn't going to cut it much longer.

Terrance is awake and eating pizza in front of the TV when I reach the main living room at the bottom of the stairs. At seven and a half feet tall, with a shiny, bald head, a face full of piercings, watermelon biceps, and tree trunk legs, most people find the surly man intimidating, but I adore him. He's got a weakness for me, too. He takes one look at my pink nose and cheeks and frowns. "You need a coat."

I smile as I snag a slice of his pizza. Meat Lover's, of course—trolls are on the carnivorous side. That works perfectly for me, since I love all things meat. "I was just thinking the same thing," I say around a mouthful of cheesy, greasy goodness. "Don't worry. I'll go get one this week."

"A good one," Terrance grumps, knowing—and hating—how I operate. "Not some used thrift store garbage."

I roll my eyes. "I've survived my entire life on *used thrift store garbage*. It'll be fine. And it's cheaper."

"It's poorer quality. You don't need to live on used things anymore. I'll leave you some cash. You can go get a new one tonight."

I try not to sigh. The thing about living with a troll— Terrance has claimed me as clan, and as head of the clan he feels responsible for me—he's always buying me stuff. I'm a foster kid from Detroit. To say I'm not used to people buying me things is a gross understatement.

"I don't need you to buy me a coat." I plop down on

the couch close enough to reach the pizza. "But speaking of cash..." I stick my pizza in my mouth and pull a wad of bills out of my front jeans pocket. I set it on the coffee table between Terrance and myself before grabbing my pizza from my mouth and taking a large bite. I wait until I swallow before saying, "I got paid today, so here's some rent." When he slants me a look, I add, "Don't worry. I kept enough to get myself a coat."

"Keep your money." Terrance gets up with a grunt, heading for the kitchen without picking up the cash. "And get yourself a good coat. A *new* coat."

I've never bought myself a new anything.

"If you don't, I will."

While he's shuffling around in the kitchen, my phone dings with an incoming text message.

Parker: Nora, please. Just give me a chance. One dinner. Not even dinner. Coffee. It doesn't have to be a date. I just miss you.

I miss him a little, too, but I still ignore the text and slip the phone back in my pocket.

Parker is the only decent vampire I've ever met. We went on a quasi dinner date last month, when we were both trying to find the missing underworlders. It went well, but I've been avoiding his texts and calls ever since. I fear him and don't entirely trust him, but at the same time, there's something about him that gets my blood pumping. I almost can't resist him. That's a recipe for disaster, so I've been ghosting him hard.

Terrance comes back with a beer for himself and a soda

for me. I stamp down my guilt for ignoring Parker and take the soda from Terrance.

"Thanks." I gulp down half of the Coke quickly, washing down that spicy sausage Terrance and I both love. "Don't buy me a coat. I'm not a mooch, Terrance."

"You're clan. Head of clan provides for those in his care. There's no need to pay rent, and if you need a coat, it's my job to get you one."

"That's nice of you, T-man, but—"

"*No buts.* This is how trolls live. You are my first clan member. Please let me do this my way. It is an honor."

I sigh. Terrance has a way of making it impossible to argue with him. "I guess." I chug the rest of my soda and grab a second slice of pizza. "It still doesn't feel right."

"I'm not saying you can't work and buy yourself things. Do whatever you want—work, go to college, learn a trade. Just let me provide for your basic necessities while you're under my roof."

College. Trade school. A real career. I shake my head, overwhelmed at the thought. Those are things I never dreamed I'd have the opportunity to experience. It's crazy how much my life has changed in the last month, how stable it's become for the first time ever. I'm still trying to process it. "Wow. That's...definitely something to think about, I guess."

I know Terrance is up to something when he starts fidgeting. I wait him out, finishing off my pizza. Finally, he clears his throat and mumbles, "I was thinking...you should come work at the club."

"Underworld? Doing what?"

"You'd make a great bartender." Terrance lifts a heavy shoulder and lets it drop, refusing to look at me. "You're friendly, chatty, pretty—plus, as a human, you'd be a bit of a novelty."

Did I mention the club Terrance owns is strictly an underworlder club? It's the main hub for all paranormal creatures in Detroit. I used to be terrified of it, and of all the monsters that frequent it, but I've learned they're not all bad. In fact, all of my friends now happen to be underworlders. Of course, I'm not your average human. I've got a few psychic abilities that give me more in common with the paranormal world than the human one I come from.

His smile tells me everything I need to know. He really wants me to do this. I'm not sure why. The underworld can be dangerous for a human like me. Maybe he wants to keep me close, or maybe he's lonely and wants us on the same schedule. From his sudden good mood, I almost suspect he wants to show me off. He's beaming like a proud dad.

"You think it'll be safe for me?" I hate to question his judgment, but after some of the stuff I've been through at the hands of underworlders, I've got to know.

His face turns serious. "I've thought a lot about that. I think it'll be safer for you than anything else. The underworlders in this city are curious about you after the whole mess you got into last month. I think having you around where they can meet you, and quench their curiosity under my watchful eye, will help ease some of the tension and dispel the rumors. It'll let people know that you're really under my protection." His smile turns wry. "Seems not many people believe I've claimed a human as clan."

I snort. "I wonder why." He's only the first troll in history to claim a human.

Terrance raises his brows, waiting, so I nod. "Okay, sure. Why not?"

Terrance beams at me. "Thanks. Wulf could really use the help."

"Wulf, the werewolf bartender?"

Terrance smirks. "Get your giggles out now, because he hates being asked about that."

"I'll try my best."

"Don't you go starting any trouble in my club now, Trouble."

I grin at the nickname. "No promises. You sure you want me there?"

Terrance tries not to laugh, but his lips twitch until he starts to chuckle. "Heaven help us all, but I really do."

.   .   .   .   .

UNDERWORLD PERFECTLY FITS ITS NAME. IT'S IN ONE OF the roughest parts of Detroit, in a large converted warehouse that's surrounded by abandoned buildings. It has a reputation among the humans for being dangerous and run by gangsters. Gangsters, no. But dangerous? Hell, yes. To humans, especially. Because they don't know that monsters exist and that they're walking into their den when they come to this place. I'll likely be the only human here most nights.

Like Terrance said, a novelty.

We come in through a back entrance off the employee parking lot. It brings us down a dim hallway past a few offices where Terrance makes me fill out all the proper paperwork before dragging me out into the club. He may be an underworlder, but he's still a law-abiding citizen. Underworlders don't like to call attention to themselves. Not paying taxes or running illegal businesses in the city would definitely raise a few eyebrows in the human world.

After I'm an official Underworld employee, Terrance gives me a tour of the place. We're early, so it's not open yet. There are three different dance halls that each play different styles of music, but the main one is where I'll be working with Wulf. (I'm to be by his side or Terrance's at all times.) It's a large room, with dance cages at the front on either side of the DJ stand. The room is black, with plush, red couches and chairs scattered around the dance floor. There are a few red booths, too, with black tables, but mostly the room is sparse, encouraging people to be out dancing.

Wulf is here early, getting things ready behind the long bar that spans the entire length of one wall in the room. He's not the only bartender, of course, but he's the manager of all of them. And he'll be my trainer, since he's the only guy in the joint Terrance trusts fully with my safety.

The ruggedly handsome man with the thick brown hair, light green eyes, a nice, deep tan, and a sexy five o'clock shadow smiles as we approach. "Ho! So your feisty little human decided to take you up on the offer," he teases Terrance while shooting me a friendly wink. "This should make the nights more interesting. Welcome to Underworld, Nora."

Wulf holds out a hand to me. I nod, opting not to shake hands. I don't touch people skin to skin, if I can help it. It's part of those psychic abilities I mentioned. I can read people's minds. It's really not as fun as you'd think, and I avoid doing it as much as possible.

"Make sure you keep a close eye on her." Terrance scowls at Wulf in warning, then looks at me. "You okay here? I've got some stuff to do."

I nod again. "I'm good. Go do your thing, T-Man."

When Terrance disappears, I turn back to my new supervisor. The smile he gives me is all wolf. It's toothy, shows his pointed canines, and screams predator. And it makes me laugh. "It's nice to officially meet you, Wulf. Thanks for being willing to watch the *feisty little human's* back."

"Eh." He shrugs, but it's a farce. "Things could stand to be a little livelier around here, and Terrance is right that you'll be a big draw." He eyes me from head to toe and shakes his head, huffing out a breath like I'm going to be trouble. I'm not dressed in anything spectacular—Terrance had me put on a black T-shirt and black yoga pants—but they're form fitting and make my tall, slender frame look curvier than it really is. I also have long, shiny brunette hair, pouty lips, and haunting green eyes. I tend to get looks.

"Every underworlder from here to Chicago is going to want to buy you a drink and take you home."

Unfortunately, he's right. I have a natural allure about me. It's got something to do with my weird powers, I think, but it's more than just my decent looks. Men are drawn to me. Some worse than others. It gets dangerous. I've had some horrible experiences because of it, and now I don't date. At all. Ever.

My anxiety kicks up, dissolving the playful atmosphere. I swallow hard as I look at Wulf, beseeching him with my eyes so that he knows how serious I am. "You'll be able to keep me safe, right? Because men *will* be a problem for me."

Wulf grows serious as well. From the storm in his eyes, I'm pretty sure Terrance has let him in on a little of my history. That's okay. The more he knows, the more he'll watch over me. I'm all for being a strong woman, but I'll never turn down a knight in shining armor, either. He clenches his jaw and glares fiercely at nothing in particular. "Anyone who touches you will answer to me," he growls. "And then Terrance will rip them to pieces."

He means that literally. I'm also fairly certain that Terrance would not be alone in the ripping-people-apart category. If I had any question about Wulf's alpha status as a werewolf, I don't now. He's so dominant that I'm shaking, and I don't have an inner wolf. If I did, I think I'd be belly up at his feet right now.

"Okay." I choke the word out. "Um, thanks."

Wulf takes a breath, and the glow of the animal in his eyes dims. "Just stick close to me, never sample the merchandise, and we should be fine. I mean that last part. We serve underworlder drinks here. Most of them would have severe consequences for humans."

"No worries. I don't even drink human alcohol. I've

been through too much shit in my life to ever want my judgment impaired."

"Good girl." He nods his head down the bar. "Come on, I'll give you a basic rundown before we open, and you can just watch me tonight until you learn how to mix the drinks."

"I know a lot of human ones already—had one foster father who was just better off plastered. I used to mix his drinks for him."

"That'll help. We do sell a lot of human drinks, and beer on tap isn't complicated. Still, I want you right by my side at all times until people get used to seeing you here."

I nod. "Not a problem. I've got no intention of wandering off on my own."

CHAPTER
TWO

TERRANCE, SMART MAN THAT HE IS, STARTS ME AT THE CLUB on a Monday. That gives me the week to get used to the place and to adjust to the really late nights before the weekend rush hits. Now, it's Saturday night, and the place is a madhouse.

Wulf is right that a lot of underworlders drink human drinks. It turns out some are just as susceptible to the funky drinks as humans. For instance, sorcerers and sorceresses are basically humans who can use magic. Their systems can't tolerate fey drinks any more than mine can. So there's a lot that I can do besides polishing glasses, even with it being only my fifth day on the job. Wulf keeps me busy, too. Terrance wasn't lying about him needing the help.

"Nora! Can I get a Blue Moon and a Guinness over here, pretty please?" Wulf calls from a few places down the bar.

"Pretty is right," one of the men ordering a beer says,

leering at me. "Is she human?"

"She's *Terrance's* human."

That's Wulf's go-to response when people ask about me. I hate how that makes me sound like some kind of pet, but it always makes the guys back off, so I let it go. I've even given that same response myself a few times. "You got it," I reply with a smile to Wulf.

I pour the beers, and by the time I head over to the waiting gentlemen, Wulf has moved on to the next customer. "Guinness and a Blue Moon," I say, sliding the glasses in front of the two guys. They both look human to me, but I know they aren't. Not in this place. I've mostly gotten past being curious about people's species—not enough time to dwell on it. But when I stop to talk to people, I always wonder.

"So, Terrance, huh?" the guy who called me pretty asks. "How does that work? A troll and a human?"

"Yeah," the other says after sipping his beer. "There's no way he can fit inside you. That must *hurt.*"

I roll my eyes. "We're not lovers, ass wipe. We're clan."

Both men snort. "Terrance took you in as clan?" Idiot One asks while Idiot Two laughs and says, "Yeah, right. You wish, pet."

"It's true," a silky voice interrupts.

Not that I care what these guys think, or feel the need to validate my claim, but I'm excited to see Cecile. She's a succubus, and the only female friend I've got. Her voice is so smooth that both men shiver. When she leans against the counter next to them, they both gulp and their pupils dilate—she has them completely in her thrall. "Nora is the first of Terrance's clan, and she's a close, personal friend of mine. I do hope you're both treating her with respect."

"Of course," Idiot One says.

"We were just having some fun." Idiot Two looks at me. "Weren't we? Who's your friend, Nora?"

I shake my head. Cecile is too good at her job. These guys are both gone. I can't resist having some fun with them. "This is Cecile. She's really friendly, but she likes guys who know how to have a good time…together. Maybe you two should go dance together for a bit, and she might be tempted to join you."

Both guys gulp down their beers and head out to the dance floor. My eyebrows hit the ceiling when they start grinding against one another. "Damn, Cecile, just what setting did you have the pheromones turned up to?"

Cecile laughs, the sound light and tinkling, and sucks in a deep breath as she watches the Idiot Twins on the dance floor. I'd been joking, but Cecile does have a preference for multiple partners at once. "Oh, sweet Nora, I do love having you here. You get all these men so hot I hardly have to do any work at all. As for those two, they deserve it for not believing you."

"Yeah," a new voice says. "Terrance should be in here with you, helping to spread the news. Not a damn one of the assholes in this place will believe just you."

I grin at the newcomer. Nick Gorgeous works for the FUA—Federal Underworld Agency—and gorgeous he is, even though his look is completely unconventional. If you mashed up a biker bad boy and a well-mannered cowboy, you'd have Nick Gorgeous. And if that's not enough of a picture, he's got smooth, ebony skin, warm chocolate eyes, a screw-me smile, and a cute baby face. He's quite the picture, but somehow it all works.

"Aw, but T-man's so much better at playing grumpy bouncer than friendly bartender," I say.

Snorting, Nick plops down on an open stool. Well, a stool that some other guy vacates after Nick gives him a look. (Nick is one scary badass when he wants to be.) "We meet again, little spitfire." He shoots me a wink. "I heard the rumors, but I had to come see it for myself, and, sure enough, here you are, serving drinks to rowdy underworlders. I swear you're the only human crazy enough to try it."

I laugh. "Have you come to warn me away, then?"

"Hell no. I came to watch the show. It's been a slow week for the FUA, and you're bound to stir up all kinds of trouble here. I could use a drink, too. How about some Demon's Brew?"

"Sure thing." That's one of the non-human beers on tap. The damn stuff smells so strong it practically knocks me on my ass just serving it. "How about you, Cecile? Can I get you anything?"

"Have you made a Sidhe Hurricane yet?"

"That's the one with the glowing blue, purple, and green, right?"

Cecile smiles. "That's the one. Two shots of the purple, dear."

"Coming right up."

I bring them their drinks and leave them to chat with each other while I fill other orders as fast as I can. Wulf constantly looks my direction to make sure I'm okay, but he already trusts me enough to let me do my thing. I ask him when someone orders a drink I'm unfamiliar with, but other than that, he gives me the freedom to work the bar on my own. I really like that about him. I can play nice with others, but I've always been independent, and I don't think I could handle a boss who hovers too much.

"Hey, sexy, how about you bring a shot of Angelfire and that pretty little ass over here."

I pour a shot of the fey alcohol and bring it to the tactless man with a forced smile. As I take the cash he lays out on the counter, he grabs my arm and pulls me close. "You know, I've never had a human before—they're not usually worth my time—but I'd make an exception for you."

I yank my arm back. "Not interested, thanks."

I start to walk away, so he quickly downs his shot and asks for another. "What's the matter? Think you're too good to bed an underworlder?"

I smirk as I fill his shot glass with another round of the light blue liquid. "Nope. Just too good for cocky assholes."

I don't have time to regret running my mouth off before the man has me by the throat and is pulling me across the counter to his seething face. "I'll show you manners, human. You're nothing but an insect in my world. A plaything. And now you'll be mine. I'll have you begging for death for all eternity."

His thoughts are scarier than his words. He plans to

follow through on his threat. He knows many fey in the winter court that keep human pets. He's never seen the appeal, but now he wants nothing more than to humiliate me and make me suffer. And maybe he'll eat me once he's bored of the torture.

His grip is so strong I can't breathe, but before I start to see spots in my vision, Wulf and Nick rip me apart from the psychotic winter faerie. Wulf has me behind him, using his body to physically shield me, while Nick has the faerie laid out on the bar by his throat. The man is wailing in pain, and it takes me a moment to figure out it's because Nick's buried a dagger in the man's shoulder, hilt deep. Judging from the screams of pain, the dagger is made of iron, which is poisonous to faeries. "What was that about begging for death for all eternity?" Nick asks. "Is that how you like to play?"

"But she's *human*," the faerie cries, as if that justifies his actions.

Wulf growls at this, and his whole body begins to shake. I place a hand on his shoulder in an attempt to calm him down. I've heard that werewolves like physical touch, and a gesture to tell him I'm all right should help with his protective instincts. I've never seen a werewolf shift, and I don't really want to see one now while he's pissed and I'm trapped behind a bar with him. I want to say something soothing, but honestly, I'm too scared to get any words out. That faerie has a dark, twisted mind.

"She is an employee of this club and Terrance's only *clan*," Nick says.

The fey's eyes pop wide open. "She's his *clan?*"

"His first." Nick nods. "And he's especially fond of her. So I would advise you to leave her alone. In fact, I bet you're a dead man walking once Terrance figures out you're the asshole who put the bruises around her neck."

Nick's eyes do that thing they do when he gets really pissed. The pupils turn into vertical slits. It's freaky looking. He also emits some kind of power. I can't really explain it. I don't know what kind of underworlder Nick is. It's rude to ask, and he's never offered the information up. But it's something totally badass that scares even the nastiest underworlders. Mr. Creepy Fey Man is squirming under his grip, looking like he's about to piss himself. "I'm sorry," he whines. "I didn't know who she was. I'll leave. Just let me up before Terrance comes."

"Maybe we should leave him pinned to the bar for a while," Wulf says, making the fey's eyes go wide again. "That'll send the message that Nora is off limits, which might appease Terrance."

I can't help the way my mouth falls open. "You're not serious."

Wulf gives me a grim look. "This man disrespected Terrance's staff. That won't go unpunished—house rules."

"Terrance will kill him for touching you, unless we punish him first," Nick adds, backing up Wulf's claims.

They're not kidding. They plan to keep this guy staked to the counter the way he is. The underworld runs on a different set of rules. It's brutal and dangerous. If I want to survive it, I need to learn to stomach the darker side of it and trust those who have my well-being at heart.

"Okay," I say, since both Wulf and Nick seem to be waiting for my approval. It's not that hard to agree, considering how evil the man's thoughts were. "Let's leave him for a while."

"Put a sign on him so everyone knows," Nick says.

Wulf writes a note on a pad that says *I touched the human girl.* He puts it on the faerie's chest. "Hold this, and don't drop it."

The man grips the message and holds it against his chest where everyone who gets close can read it. But he's squirming, swearing, sweating, and hollering about the pain. I have no doubt it hurts. Nick has no sympathy for him. "Shut your mouth," he says, touching the dagger's hilt and twisting it ever so slightly, causing the faerie to scream in real agony. "This is a tender mercy. Stop whining, or I'll put this dagger through your heart to shut you up."

I'm not surprised when the faerie shuts his mouth and keeps his discomfort to mild whimpers from then on. If Nick had looked at me the same way he looked at that guy just now, I'd find a way to forget about the pain, too.

The next hour goes by torturously slow. Wulf keeps me glued to his side as we work, and we stay close to the guy pinned to the counter the entire time. Terrance nearly kills the faerie anyway when he finally comes inside and sees the bruises on my neck. Wulf talks him out of murder, but Terrance decides the faerie has to stay put until closing time so that everyone who comes to the bar tonight knows I'm under his protection.

He also stands behind the bar, shadowing me like he's

my own personal bodyguard. And let me tell you, a pissed off troll makes one hell of an intimidating guard. Word is definitely spreading that I'm untouchable. Is it horrible that I think maybe tonight's gruesome events are worth it? People will definitely think twice about messing with me now.

Last call is at two a.m., but it takes over an hour to get all of the club patrons out the doors. The faerie is the last to leave, just after three. He looks pale and slumps as he exits, but both Wulf and Terrance assure me he'll feel right as rain by tomorrow.

I try not to think about it as I set to work cleaning the mess behind the bar, but I can't help the way my body shakes. A hand comes down on my shoulder, and I whirl around with a startled yelp. My heart is in my throat, but it's only Wulf, gazing at me with concern. "That guy really scared you tonight, didn't he?"

I hate to show my weakness, but hell yeah, that guy scared me. I have his fingers imprinted around my neck, and that was the least scary part of the ordeal. My head is a mess right now, so I shrug and own it. "It's not easy having a front row seat to people's worst fantasies. Sick men have even sicker minds. His thoughts were very clear, and I can't get them out of my head. Plus, he moved so fast I didn't even see him. His hand was just suddenly there, squeezing the life out of me. I've never been strangled before."

I shiver again and nearly drop the tray of dirty glasses in my hands. I'm not in the mood to talk about this anymore, so I turn to head back to the kitchen to drop these last dirty dishes off. Wulf stops me, calling out softly to me. "Would it help if you knew some self-defense?"

I slowly turn back around to face him. "You offering to teach me?"

He shrugs. He's trying to look nonchalant, but there's tension beneath the casual appearance. Tonight shook him a little, too. "Werewolves love a good tussle. I know how to hold my own in a fight. Yeah, I'll teach you, if you're willing to learn. You'll always be human and female, so size and strength won't be your allies, but I could teach you how to work around that to give yourself at least a chance."

He has no idea how badly I want this. I've spent my entire life wishing I knew how to fight. I've had too many attackers not to want to know how to protect myself. I know I'll still be human, but any leg up is a blessing, no matter how small. Still, I can't just accept it right away. "Why would you do that?" I ask, letting my wariness ring out in my voice. "What do you expect to get out of it?"

"Peace of mind." He shakes his head at my frown. "You're not the only one with images stuck in your head right now. I'm going to see that bastard's hand around your throat in my sleep all night tonight."

I'm touched by the admission.

"I've been an anxious mess all week. Terrance trusts me with your safety, and I'll always do my best, but I'm just one man, and things can get rowdy here. I'd like to know that if a real bar fight ever breaks out, you'll be able to at least hold out for a few minutes until Terrance or I can get to you. I'll teach you, simply because you need to know it."

He seems sincere. And he hasn't hit on me at all this

week. He's been friendly, but he treats me like a little sister, if anything. I'm a kid he's fond of, but that he's babysitting all the same. That's what makes me think he could train me without it becoming a problem.

I've never gotten self-defense lessons before, as badly as I've wanted them, because I've been too afraid of all the physical contact necessary. Teaching someone to fight and defend themselves requires a lot of touching, high energy, and intense situations. With my uncontrollable allure, I've never felt an instructor would be able to resist taking advantage of me before. For the first time, I'm not worried about that. Well, not too worried. "Would we be in public?" I ask.

Wulf knows exactly what I'm asking and why. He knows all about my problem with people. After that first night working with him, he said I was a hundred times worse than Cecile, so I had to break down and tell him about my problem. After a week working together, he knows it's not in my head.

His face falls sympathetically, and he says, "We can go to the training gym out at my old pack's compound, if you'd like. There's always a steady flow of both men and women in there, so we'll never be alone. It wouldn't hurt me to put in an appearance there. My old alpha's always trying to get me to come home for a visit."

I feel bad making him go back to the pack grounds if he really doesn't want to be there, but I don't want to spend any time alone with him, either. "Are you sure you don't mind?"

He shakes his head and grins. "Only if the females start sniffing around too much. Then I'm out."

I raise an eyebrow, and he laughs. "She-wolves are the worst. Always trying to tie you down with that whole mate bonding thing, and they can't resist a dominant wolf. I'm not ready to settle down, move to the compound, and have some woman constantly nagging me and trying to change my lone-wolf ways."

He's not joking. He's happy as a lone wolf and is a hopeless flirt with all women, except for with other werewolves and me. I've wondered what his deal was with his own kind. I can believe it's as simple as him not wanting a pack or a mate. "Okay, that's fair," I decide. I wouldn't want to be chased like that, either. "As soon as the females start hounding you, we'll bring it back here—as long as it's going okay. If my problem gives you any trouble, though, will you let me know?"

He nods. "Of course."

"Great. In that case, when do we start?"

CHAPTER
THREE

Wulf drives us about half an hour south of Detroit to a city called Flat Rock. Flat Rock has a much more spread out feel to it than Detroit, with lots of trees everywhere. Very suburban. We drive through town, cross over a river, and hit the edge of civilization. Buildings give way to trees and water. Then, about ten minutes later, we reach what looks like a random planned community on the edge of a large park. The place is gated and looks newer than anything I saw in the actual town of Flat Rock. It's pretty fancy. I've stepped into upper middle class suburbia, and I feel a bit out of place.

I squirm as we stop at the gate, and Wulf speaks to the guy in the little guard shack. They murmur in low voices, so I only catch my name and the word *human* before the guard shakes his head in surprise, checks his list, and opens the gate. The man's eyes stay glued to me until we're out of his sight.

"Are humans not usually allowed?" I ask.

Wulf glances sideways at me. "It doesn't happen too often, but it's not frowned on or anything. Wolves like humans just fine. It's the humans that are usually shy of us."

I can fully understand that.

We drive through the stunning neighborhood full of beautiful homes, groomed yards, and kids running around, and come up to a large building that looks to be a clubhouse of sorts. It's obviously the pack headquarters as well. When Wulf parks, he looks around warily at all of the people now staring at us.

"Been a while since you've been home?" I ask when I realize they're not staring at *us*, they're looking at *him*. "Or do you just not bring home many human girls?"

Wulf blows out a big breath and rakes a hand through his hair as he eyes one woman specifically. She's stopped jogging along a path and is openly staring at Wulf. Even I can see the hungry gleam in her eyes. "It's been a few years since I visited the compound." He breaks the lady's stare and smirks at me. "And I've never brought a girl with me, much less a human one."

"Well, this should be interesting. You sure we shouldn't turn back and forget this whole thing?"

He hesitates and then shakes his head. "No. You need to learn, and this is the best, safest place to teach you. Come on. Gym's in there." He points to the building.

People don't realize I'm human until they can smell my scent, because when I get out of the car and meet Wulf in front of the hood, there is a collective gasp from everyone around us. All eyes move from Wulf to me, and mouths drop. "Right," I grumble. "This was definitely a smart idea."

Next to me, Wulf chuckles quietly. "Just don't be afraid, Nora. Our kind can smell fear, and we can't resist preying on the weak."

I shoot him a sideways glare. "If you'd just show me to the gym already, I won't be weak anymore."

I get another laugh. At least one of us is in a better mood now.

Like Wulf promised, there are plenty of other people using the gym's training facilities. There are people training all the way from pre-teens to guys that could pass for grand-parents. All of them seem in stellar shape. My friend Ren, a gay incubus from the FUA office, is going to kill me for not bringing him when I give him the details of all the bare muscle I'm seeing.

Thankfully, Wulf leaves his T-shirt on with his sweat-pants. It's still skintight and shows all his muscles, but that's not what I'm worried about. Less skin means less risk of read-ing his thoughts while he's teaching me to defend myself. Wulf's one of the few people that knows about my abilities. I appreciate his attempt to respect my boundaries.

"Okay, first things first. We need to warm up. Start with a couple laps around the gym to get your blood pumping, and then we'll stretch and get loose."

Ugh. I hate running. But I'm not going to complain about the first order my new trainer gives me, so I head over to the small track around the edge of the gym and start into a slow jog. Wulf joins me but takes off at a much more aggressive speed. At least he's not one of those trainers that stands around barking orders but doesn't participate. Those kinds of coaches annoy me.

After one loop around the gym—in which Wulf has already lapped me once—Wulf falls into step beside me. When he speaks, he doesn't sound winded at all. "Is this the fastest you go?"

I'm embarrassed, but at least my cheeks are already red from the exercise. "I'm not much of a runner. Never had a treadmill, and I'm not stupid enough to try to jog on the streets of Detroit—day or night."

Wulf sighs. "Okay, we'll need to work on conditioning first. The most important part of self-defense is being able to get away. You're human and female. Most times your opponent is going to be larger and stronger than you. Your best bet will always be to run, if you can. You need speed and endurance training."

"Understandable." I'm not one of those girls that's too proud to accept my reality. I want to know how to fight if I need it, but I'm completely okay with running when the situation allows it. Better to run than die.

"I'll talk to Terrance about getting you a good treadmill. I want you to get up to six a day as quickly as possible."

"Six laps at one time?" My eyes bulge. "I'm not even going to last three right now."

I know I'm in trouble when Wulf smirks. "Miles, Nora. Six miles a day. These laps are only a quarter mile. I want you to do four today, even if you have to walk some of it."

"Six miles a day..." I'm already huffing, and I haven't

even completed a half-mile yet. "I knew this was a bad idea. You're going to kill me."

"This is a better idea than I first thought. You need this, Nora. It's your lack of being in shape that might get you killed someday. Not me."

"If you say so."

Wulf chuckles. "It won't be as bad as you think. Now pick up your pace, run your third lap as fast as you can, and then you can walk the last one."

At that, Wulf winks at me and takes off at a sprint. Well, I think it's a sprint. It's probably only a jog to him. Six miles a day... Yeah right, he's not trying to kill me.

I'm a good sport, though, and I did tell him I was eager to learn. I don't want to prove myself wrong on the first day, so I do as I'm told and run a lap as fast as I can. I can hardly breathe by the time I hit the last lap. I've never been more grateful to walk in my life. Wulf is there again as soon as I slow down. "Put your hands on the back of your head. It'll make it easier to breathe."

I startle at the voice, because it isn't Wulf's. Looking closer, I realize this man looks very similar to Wulf but is a little older and friendlier looking, and his eyes are blue instead of green. Otherwise, they could be identical.

Still, Wulf or not, I do as he suggested and put my hands behind my head. He's right—my lungs open up. I greedily suck in huge gulps of air. A sharp pain lances my side, and I groan. "Damn. I'm the most out of shape girl on the planet," I pant between gasps.

Wulf's look-alike doesn't argue. Instead, he frowns as he

studies me head-to-toe with a critical eye. "We do have our work cut out for us, but don't get too discouraged. Everyone starts somewhere."

"We?" I ask, then state the obvious. "You're not Wulf."

The man grins at me. It's a gorgeous smile. "Rook Winters. I'm Wulf's grumpy older brother." He winks to let me know he's kidding. "And yes, we. If you got my brother here, then it must be serious. And if my baby brother's finally found a female, you bet your ass I want to get to know her."

I blush and look at the ground as I keep walking. Where the hell is Wulf? A glance across the room tells me he's busy talking to some man. They're standing close, speaking quietly, and they're both looking my direction.

"That's Alpha Toth," Rook says, following my gaze. "He'd like to meet you, too, as soon as your training session is over."

The alpha? No pressure, huh? Oddly enough, though, he doesn't seem as intimidating as either Wulf or Rook. If I had to guess, I'd say both the brothers are dominant over the alpha, but that doesn't make any sense.

"So, how did you and Wulf meet?"

Rook's smile has me blushing again, even though my relationship with Wulf is completely innocent. "It's not what you think," I say. "There's nothing going on between Wulf and me. He's my boss at the club."

"*You* work at Underworld?"

His surprise, though understandable and expected, is still insulting. "Yes. I just started last week. Terrance took me in as clan and thought my working there would be safe for me because he and Wulf could keep an eye on me."

"Ah." Rook's smile turns to one of understanding. "You're *that* human."

I roll my eyes. "Yes. I'm that one. And I'm not dating your brother. I just work with him."

"But he offered to train you. He brought you to the compound. He's never done that for anyone before. *I* can't even get him to come home."

I try to hold my poker face. Wulf hadn't told me that. Now I feel bad. Not enough to stop training, unless he asks me to. But I do feel a little guilty making him come home if he really hates it so much. I shrug. "He probably just feels bad that I was attacked on his watch last night." I point out the bruises around my neck and watch, with mild satisfaction, as Rook's eyes widen. "I was pretty shaken up after being strangled over the bar, so Wulf offered to teach me a little self-defense. That's it. Nothing else is going on." I smirk when he frowns. "Sorry to disappoint you."

"Me too," Rook says. "My baby brother could really use a good woman to make him settle down."

"Ha!" I doubt that's going to happen any time soon.

Rook startles at my laugh, but then chuckles. He understands his brother better than I do. He's wishful thinking, and he knows it. He decides to change the subject instead of arguing the point any further. "So you were attacked over the bar last night? How'd that happen?"

We reach the end of my laps, and I look around for Wulf again. He's still talking to his alpha now, but the conversation looks more relaxed. Both men are watching me still, but this time their focus isn't just on me. It's on Rook and me together. They both seem curious about Rook's interest in me. I realize, now, that Wulf is giving his brother and me space, and I barely suppress a groan. Geez. Bunch of meddling busybodies!

"Nora?"

I turn my attention back to Rook and try to remember his question... Oh, the attack, right. "Yeah, it was just this stupid winter faerie. He grabbed me when I poured him a drink last night. I got a little colorful with my rejection. Guess I pissed him off, because he snapped and tried to strangle me."

Rook's eyes narrow, and a faint glow begins to shine from them. "Does that happen often?" His voice lowers and gets all growly like his brother's does when he's pissed. "Guys trying to grab you when you pour them drinks?"

"Often enough. Hence the reason I jumped at the self-defense lessons."

The noise that escapes Rook next is a flat-out werewolf growl. No other way to describe it. "Whoa, dude. Relax."

Rook blinks and shakes his head, as if startled he'd almost wolfed out right in front of me. "Sorry."

"It's all good. I just don't need to witness my first werewolf shift right now."

That reclaims his attention, and he smiles at me. "You haven't seen a wolf shift before?"

"No. I was raised in the human world. I knew about the underworld, but no one was sharing their secrets with me, if you know what I mean. So really, I'm a newbie to all of it."

"Oh. Well, allow me to give you a tour of the compound and explain a little more about my kind after I show you a few moves."

He wants to teach me about werewolves? I won't say no to that. "Yeah, sure. I'd like that. I might be allowed to be part of the underworld now, but so far most of the underworlders I've met have been close-lipped about everything."

"Habit," Rook says, stripping off his hoodie to reveal the most muscled body I've ever seen. The thin material of his black tank top does nothing to hide his ripped body. It's hard not to drool. "Most underworlders are really wary around humans, even the ones who know about our world—which there aren't many of. Wolves are different. We blend better."

Honey, I've got news for you. In no way would you blend in a human crowd, I think as I try to tear my gaze from his amazing body. I may not date, but just because I don't want to get involved with guys doesn't mean I don't notice them. Rook is impossible to not notice.

"All right," he says, moving to stand directly in front of me. "How did this guy grab you?"

Forcing myself to get my hormones under control, I grip my wrist where the faerie jerk grabbed my arm the night before. There are a few bruises there, too. Rook's jaw clenches when he sees them, but he doesn't growl again. He reaches for my other wrist and says, "Okay, there are a couple of ways you can escape this grip, even if you're not as strong as your opponent."

For the next half hour, Rook takes me through a handful of different moves to break a hold. Skin-to-skin contact is unavoidable. At first, I worry because I don't know Rook, but he keeps his thoughts pretty focused on training me. He thinks I'm gorgeous, but my beauty worries him. I'm too vulnerable to be so stunning, so he dives headfirst into teaching me to protect myself from predators.

Wulf never once interrupts us. When we're finished, and Rook asks again if he can give me a tour of the compound, Wulf sits down at a weight machine and waves me off. "Go look around. I'll wait here until you're done." The man has his shirt off now and is all sweaty. I guess hotness isn't the only thing to run in the Winters family. Muscles do, too. Hot *damn*.

The first stop on the "tour" happens to be the alpha's office. I'm not really surprised, but I don't feel prepared to meet the pack alpha, either.

Alpha Toth is a large, formidable-looking man, though, again, I get the feeling both Rook and Wulf are more dominant than he is. I'm not sure how I can tell; I just know. That puts me at ease a little as the bulky, dark-haired, dark-eyed werewolf stands up and comes around his large desk to greet me. "Miss Jacobs, I'm Alpha Peter Toth. Welcome to the Huron River pack compound. It's wonderful to meet you."

"It's nice to meet you, too. And, please, call me Nora." I can't refuse when he offers a hand to shake. Luckily, he gives me a quick, firm pump and then lets go. I still catch a single odd thought. *I hope I don't regret this.*

CHAPTER
FOUR

ROOK SHUTS THE DOOR TO THE OFFICE ABOUT THE SAME
time as Alpha Toth says, "Please have a seat."

He waves to a set of wingback chairs in front of his desk
and moves to sit back down in his own chair. Rook encour-
ages me to sit in one of the guest chairs and takes the other.
There's a grave tension in the air. "I'm sorry," I say, my heart
kicking up with anxiety. "What's this about? Was I not supposed to come here? Wulf said it would be all right."

Rook chuckles. "You're not in trouble, Nora."

Alpha Toth is still wearing a grim face, so I'm skeptical
of Rook's reassurances. Not that I don't want to believe I'm
safe with Wulf's brother—he obviously thought I would be,
or he wouldn't have let me go off with him—but my track
record with underworlders isn't the best.

"I'm not being kidnapped, am I?" I ask. "Or being
forced into a mate bonding of some kind?"

Both men's jaws fall open when they realize I'm serious.

"Of course not," Alpha Toth sputters. "Why on earth would you assume something like that?"

"Um, because that's usually what happens when I find myself unexpectedly alone with strange underworlders."

Neither man has a response to that.

"Well…" Alpha Toth continues to gape at me, open-mouthed like a fish, unsure how to proceed. He clears his throat and shakes off his shock. "I assure you, you are safe here on my lands. We mean you no harm. In fact…"

He shoots Rook an unsure look and grimaces when Rook nods. "Miss Jacobs," Alpha Toth begins, "the pack needs your help."

That is so not what I'm expecting that I sit back, blinking at both men. "I'm sorry, what?"

Toth and Rook exchange another glance. The alpha rakes a hand through his hair and then meets my eyes with a grim look of determination. "One of my wolves, Maya Forsythe, was one of the underworlders you rescued last month."

I nod, remembering the name, and can't help my smile. "That's right. Maya said she was part of the Huron River pack."

"My third in command, actually."

My eyebrows hit the ceiling. I knew wolves weren't a sexist lot—their hierarchy is purely based on dominance—but I hadn't realized Maya was such a strong wolf. Though, she'd been weak at the time from all the magic and silver used to keep her subdued. "Awesome. I like her. Tell her *hello* for me."

My comment breaks the tension, and Alpha Toth chuckles. "I'm sure she'll find you before you leave here today. She's been wanting to thank you personally."

I nod. "I'll make sure I find her, then, but…what does she have to do with me now?" Maybe it's rude to cut straight to the chase, but I can't help it. I hate not knowing what's going on.

Alpha Toth sighs. "She told me about you. She mentioned you were an extraordinary human, though she didn't know exactly how you're different. But she knows you have strong power and unique gifts. I'm hoping…that since you used those gifts to find Maya and the others, you might be able to use those gifts to help me with a different problem as well."

I sit up in my chair. "Are you missing more pack members?"

"Money, actually." He grimaces. "Someone in my pack is ripping me off."

The anger in his expression tells me this isn't about the actual missing money. He's glaring when he looks at me again, but he's not glaring at me. He's just pissed. Supremely pissed. "Miss Jacobs, if this is something you can help with, I'd like to hire you to find the wolf or wolves who would dare betray their pack."

I'm stunned. I can't believe he's asking for my help. I know I've garnered a bit of a reputation in the underworld, but I had no idea it was as some kind of supernatural detective. "Mr. Toth—Alpha Toth…I don't know what to say."

"What are these powers you have? Is this something you could help me with?"

I think about it. I'd have to mentally vet the pack members somehow, which would be difficult without admitting what I can do, but not impossible. And I might be able to pick up imprints if they have some kind of accounting office.

I don't necessarily want to get involved in pack business—that could be hazardous to my health. But it felt good last time to be able to use my gifts to help people. And Maya and Wulf, and even Rook, all seem like very good people. Wulf is a great boss, he's loyal to Terrance, and he offered to help me, even though he hates coming home. Of course I'd want to help his pack.

"I might be able to help," I finally say. "But it's not a guarantee."

"What are your gifts?" Alpha Toth asks, leaning forward in his chair. His eyes are hopeful. "What powers do you have? How can you help?"

I cringe. "I like to keep my gifts to myself as much as possible. I'd become a target if people knew what I can do, but just know that they're a sort of psychic-based set of gifts. It's not an exact science, but it can be helpful. If we could handle this very discreetly, I wouldn't mind doing what I can for you. I'm talking *it-can't-leave-this-room*, secret. I'm not exactly Supergirl. If your pack were to find out I was investigating them, and getting all up in their business, well, that could get ugly very quickly."

Rook and Alpha Toth share another grim look. "Agreed,

Miss Jacobs. It won't leave this room. You have my word."

I'm surprised he agreed to that one so quickly. Reading the suspicion on my face, Alpha Toth grimaces again. "We'd prefer discretion as well. Having a traitor in our pack is a dangerous thing. It'll be seen as a huge weakness. Not only would that cause trouble within our own ranks that could lead to mutiny, but it would catch the attention of neighboring packs as well. Unfortunately, a hostile takeover isn't outside the realm of possibility for something like this."

Damn. And I thought I had problems. No wonder he was reluctant to ask for my help. He's putting a shitload of trust in me right now. I can't leave him hanging. "Okay. I'm in, then. I'll do everything I can to help."

"As far as compensation, you can have the money you recover, and if you don't find—"

I hold up a hand. "I don't need compensation. I don't want to be paid for helping out a friend. I'd feel skeezy."

Alpha Toth sits up in his chair and arches a single brow. It's the first truly alpha-looking move I've seen him make. "I didn't realize you considered us friends."

My lips twitch, but I fight my smile. "I don't. But Wulf is my friend, and you're his pack."

Surprise lights up Alpha Toth's face, and Rook grins a huge, knowing smile that makes me groan. "Stop, dude. Stop right there. Wulf helped me get free from Henry a month ago when the vampire asshole tried to keep me as a pet. He's also giving me self-defense lessons. I owe him. I told you there's nothing romantic going on between us."

Rook's smile grows even more annoying. "So *you* say."

"Ugh. I do say. You do realize that this guy right here"—I point to Alpha Toth—"and Wulf were watching you teach me those moves in the gym earlier with that same shit-eating grin, right? And that Wulf only let you take me on a tour because he thinks *you're* interested in me, and he was letting you make your move?"

Rook's smile drops into a frown as he thinks back on what I'm saying. When he realizes I'm right, he looks to his alpha to confirm it. The man gives him a sheepish shrug that makes Rook curse. "Aw, man. I really thought there was a chance. I mean, he brought you home."

I laugh. "Yeah, he really didn't want to do that. But, look, I swear, stop planning my wedding to your brother."

"Mating ceremony," Alpha Toth corrects with a smile.

I roll my eyes. "Mating ceremony, then. Whatever. It's not happening. I don't date. Sorry." I think about the task I need to do and add, "I do need to snoop a little, though, so I will still take you up on that tour of the compound, especially if you have, like, a specific financial office where someone is most likely to steal the money from you."

"We have an accounting office," Rook offers while Alpha Toth cringes again. "I'm sorry, Miss Jacobs, that's confidential pack informa—"

"Alpha Toth. Dude. I don't want to learn your financial situation. I don't even care what it is. Obviously, your pack isn't strapped for cash. But I do my thing by touching stuff. If you want me to help, you'll have to give me some trust."

Alpha Toth turns his frown to Rook. "Did…she just… call me…*dude?*"

Rook's lips twitch as he says, "I think so, sir."

"Sorry. Alpha Toth, sir, whatever. Can I poke around in the accounting office or not? You can both come with me if you need to."

Alpha Toth blinks at me several times before making the decision to trust me. "Very well, let's take a field trip."

Our field trip ends two doors down and across the hall at a room aptly labeled *accounting*. Alpha Toth raises his hand to knock, but I stop him. He pauses, watching with curiosity. "Before we barge in and make your accountant suspicious, when's the last time someone took money?"

"There was another payment moved last night."

"Oh, perfect." I grin at their curious looks and grab the handle of the door.

My guess is that if someone was sneaking into this office to steal from the pack, they'd be pretty worked up while breaking in. I might be able to pick up an imprint off the handle. "Catch me if I fall," I whisper as I'm sucked into a vision.

The only lights on in the building are the nighttime emergency lights. It's hard to see much, but a tall, muscular man with brown hair and shifty brown eyes glances both directions down the hallway as he pushes a key into the lock on this door. When the lock turns, he wipes sweat from his brow and holds his breath as he slips into the office, immediately relocking the door behind him.

"Whoa." I sway on my feet as I come out of the vision, and immediately Rook's arms are around me, holding me steady.

"You okay?" he asks.

"I'm fine. Nasty side effect. It'll get a little worse the more I use my gift, but it's worth it." I pull myself out of his grip and lower my voice just in case there's a wolf with exceptionally good hearing on the other side of that door. "What does your accountant look like?"

Alpha Toth's eyebrows raise, but he answers the question. "Short blonde woman."

"Voluptuous curves," Rook adds, earning a look from his alpha. He lifts his shoulders. "What? It's hard not to notice a shape like that."

I laugh to myself and stay on task. "Okay, not her, then. I don't know if it was last night," I say, so low both men have to lean in close, "but it was dark, and I never pick up clues more than two or three days in the past. Ever. So...sometime in the last couple nights, a man snuck into this office. It was dark. Everyone was gone. Place was empty. He had a key, but this guy was really nervous. Sweating, twitching, shifty eyes...the whole bit."

"What did he look like?" Alpha Toth demanded, getting angry.

I place a finger to my lips, reminding him to be quiet. I look over my shoulder to make sure no one is coming down the hall, and both men seem to remember we're currently sneaking. "He was tallish, had a bit of muscle. Kind of cute.

Brown hair, brown eyes."

Rook sighs. "Well, you just described half the pack."

I shrug. "I could point him out on sight." Both men perk up again. "But first, I need to get into that office. We don't know what our guy was doing in there. We don't know if he's the man you're looking for."

I wait for Alpha Toth and Rook to make a decision. I'm not sure what they're debating, until Rook says, "I could pull the fire alarm."

"No, I think we can be more subtle," Alpha Toth says, staring at the door. "I have something I could discuss with her. I'll call her into my office." He looks at me. "Will ten minutes be enough?"

I shrug. "It should, but I can't be certain once I get sucked in how long it'll take to come out again."

"We'll come knock on your door when we're done," Rook says to Alpha Toth. "Stall, if you need to."

Alpha Toth nods my direction. "Work quickly, Miss Jacobs."

I'm a little surprised he's giving me the trust to snoop. "As fast as I can," I assure him.

Rook and I back down the hall and duck out of sight to wait for the accountant to leave her office.

"So, you see visions?" Rook asks as he peeks around the corner.

"Sort of. I call them psychic imprints, but it's basically glimpses of the past, yes."

"That's got to be convenient."

I shake my head. "Not always. I can't control when I pick up an imprint, and I can't help what I see. I can't always pull myself out of the visions, either. The stronger the imprint, the more I'm stuck waiting until it's over, and the sicker it makes me."

Down the hall, a door opens and closes. When we hear a knock on another door, Rook peeks around the corner again. "Come on. Time to do your thing."

I shake my head, chuckling as Rook lets me into the office. The room is tiny compared to Alpha Toth's office, and overcrowded with filing cabinets along the back wall. It has a small desk crammed into one corner, but at least it's neat. Toth's accountant is meticulously organized. I swipe my hand across the filing cabinets on my way to the desk and immediately get pulled into a really strong vision. I groan as I settle in to watch Ms. Accountant get banged up against her filing cabinets.

My knees buckle when the vision ends, letting me get back to reality. Rook catches me and helps me sit in the desk chair. I lean over, moaning lightly and willing myself not to puke.

"What'd you see?"

"A lot more than I'd have liked to." He waits for me to expand. "Let's just say you aren't the only one who's noticed Ms. Thang's voluptuous curves."

Rook rears his head back, blinking at me in disbelief. "Holly's getting it on in her office? *Up against the filing cabinets?*" He eyes the cabinets in question with newfound respect. "Whoa. That's hot."

I snort. "Not really. What was that? Four minutes total? Five? She totally faked it. I hope her lover is better between the sheets."

Rook moves to sit on the edge of Holly's desk, smirking. "So, you get sex visions?"

I roll my eyes. Of course he'd focus on that. "Unfortunately, those are what I get most. Imprints are like emotional residue. The higher the emotions flying, the stronger the imprint. I try to get out of them, but again, the stronger the imprint the more I get stuck."

"Oh, come on, you don't like it at least a little?"

"No," I say flatly. "Now shut up, and let me work."

Rook frowns, but he moves off the desk and goes to stand silently against the office door. I look around and figure my best bet is the computer. *Mouse and keyboard, it is.* Moving one hand over each, I instantly know I've found what I'm looking for.

Mr. Slim Shady's hands shake as he slides the mouse over the pad. He clicks on a locked file. When it asks for a password, he unfurls a small paper and types in a long, complicated password. It seems to pull up a list of bank accounts. He clicks the first one on the list and transfers one hundred dollars from that account into one that was also written on his paper. Once the transfer is complete, he continues to go down the list of accounts, doing the same thing with each one. There must be thirty or forty accounts. When he's finished the whole list, he logs out of the computer and leaves the office.

"Oh, man," I moan, leaning my head down on the desk. "I'm gonna hurl."

"Are you okay? You've been under for a good twelve minutes."

"Seriously? No wonder I feel like shit. Damn, that was so boring."

"Can you move? We need to get out of here."

"You might need to help me walk, and I might puke on you, but yeah. Let's get out of here. We've got exactly what we need."

CHAPTER
FIVE

ROOK WALKS ME OUT THE BACK DOOR OF THE CLUBHOUSE, toward the Huron River. The fresh air helps clear my nausea and headache. I crash down on a bench on the water's edge with another moan. My eyes fall closed while Rook texts Alpha Toth. "Are you okay? Do I need to get you help or anything?"

"No." I grunt. "It'll pass. Just give me a couple minutes."

"Alpha Toth is on his way."

We sit in silence a couple more minutes, until Alpha Toth's gruff voice says, "What's wrong? Is she okay?"

"I'm good," I promise. "It's passing already."

"What is it?"

"My body's natural reaction to sucking up psychic imprints. It's a bitch, but we got what we needed. Sneaky McSneakerson is our guy. I just watched him skim one hundred bucks from every different pack account you have and deposit it into one personal account."

Alpha Toth growls. "That fits."

"Fits what?"

"The money's been disappearing in such small amounts, it took us almost a year to notice."

"A year? That's a nice little chunk of money, then."

"The money's not the issue. He's been robbing the pack for a year. He's going to pay."

"They," I say. "I'm assuming he has an accomplice. He got that key from somewhere, and he was relieved when it worked…like he was nervous it wouldn't. Then he got the password to Holly's computer from somewhere—had it written down on a piece of paper. The personal account number, too. And overall, he was just too nervous to be the brains behind this scheme. My guess is this was the first time he's had to be the one moving the funds. He's got someone helping him. It could be Holly, but I wouldn't know unless spending some time with one or the other, or both of them. Though, I doubt it's her, considering she's polishing the filing cabinets with a different man."

When I quit talking, I wait for a reply but am met with silence. I open my eyes and rub my temples. "What?"

"What do you mean, you could get more if you spent time with them?" Rook asks.

I blush. I don't want to tell them I can read minds. Them knowing about the visions is bad enough, but mind reading makes people really uneasy. No one ever trusts a mind reader. "I can pick some things up from people, too, not just objects. But it has to be skin-to-skin contact, which could be hard to do if we're going for discreet."

Rook and the alpha share a look. "The pack social?" Rook asks.

Alpha Toth nods. "Could be hard to get her there without raising suspicion, though."

Rook shakes his head. "She saved Maya. She could be an honored guest."

"Oh, yes, that'll work perfectly."

I'm falling behind. "What will work? Honored guest at a what?"

They ignore me, of course. Alpha Toth nods, as if everything is settled. "You'll have to keep a close eye on her, but make sure you aren't stepping on your brother's toes. I know what she said, but she got him here for the first time in thirty years."

My brain stalls at that. "Thirty years!" I cry. "He said it's been a few, but *thirty?*"

Rook sighs. "Werewolves live a long time. Thirty years isn't as long to us as it is to you. Still, it's a long time to go without a pack. You accomplished something big, Nora. I didn't think anything would ever bring Wulf back."

I'm stunned, but I feel awful at the same time. Why did Wulf agree to come here after so long? Was it my whacked out allure that had him jumping through hoops for me? I don't get it, but he and I are going to have a long chat. "Oh, that little liar," I grumble, getting to my feet. I'm ready to stalk back into the gym despite my headache and upset stomach. "Excuse me, gentlemen, I need to go kill myself a Wulf."

I get one good stomp in before Rook grips me by the shoulder. "Hang on there, little lady. Wait until you're well away from the compound to lay into him, huh?" He chuckles. "Coming here was hard enough for him. He doesn't need the humiliation of getting disciplined by a human female on top of it."

All of my anger deflates, and I'm back to feeling guilty. I just don't get why he'd make the exception for me. I didn't even have to push. It was his idea to come here. "Fine. It can wait." I won't really do it now, though. I'll probably just ask him about it nicely. "So, what is this social you guys were talking about?"

"Our monthly pack social is next weekend," Alpha Toth says, puffing up his chest and smiling proudly. "It's a dance."

"And a dinner," Rook adds. "Usually a cookout with a big bonfire. It's a hell of a party."

"Would a dance work for you?" Alpha Toth looks at me.

It takes me a moment to understand what he's asking. "Oh!" I said I needed reasons for skin-to-skin contact. "Actually, yes, your social sounds perfect, as long as our thief shows up."

"Oh, he will," Rook promises.

"The monthly socials are mandatory," Alpha Toth adds.

Huh. "A mandatory monthly party? Wow. Pack life sounds interesting."

Rook laughs and places a hand at the small of my back, urging me toward the clubhouse. "It's a blast, most of the time. No better life than that of a werewolf in a stable pack."

"That's why it's so important we find these thieves and

stop them quietly," Alpha Toth mutters, walking up the path behind us.

"No problem," I say. "I already know who one of them is. Pointing him out and finding the other next weekend shouldn't be too hard. Seems like an open-and-shut case."

"I hope you're right, Miss Jacobs. I really—"

He stops talking to frown at a text, and then he sighs. After the dark look he gives Rook, I know I'm missing something important again. I look to Rook for the answer. He echoes Alpha Toth's sigh. "Jeffrey's challenged Wulf."

Challenged? I don't like the sound of that. "Who's Jeffrey?"

"Jeffrey Bean is my second-in-command, my beta," Alpha Toth explains in a tired voice.

He picks up the pace a little, and Rook grabs my hand, dragging me through the clubhouse. I'm surprised by his thoughts. He's not worried about his brother getting hurt, but he is worried about his brother killing the pack's beta. He'll never be allowed back again if he does that. Not that he'll want to come back after this. Rook's angry—no, he's *furious*—at Jeffrey. Jeffrey's too hotheaded. This dumb power play was completely unnecessary, and all it's going to do is complicate something that didn't need to be difficult.

We hurry out the front doors of the clubhouse to find a ring of people crowded around two wolves on the front lawn. I gasp, unprepared for the sight. The fight looks so vicious.

The two wolves are huge, and they're snarling and drooling everywhere as they circle and pounce on each other. Both of them are showing red, but one wolf is a lot bloodier than the other.

The people standing around aren't cheering or screaming or stepping in to help. They're simply looking on with fascination and morbid curiosity. It's a very controlled, if one-sided, fight. Still, Rook puts his arm around me and pulls me tightly to his side in a protective manner, and it's clear he's not going to let me go until he hands me over to his brother. Thank heavens Wulf didn't make me take my T-shirt off to train today. I'm totally gross after my workout, but at least I'm not hearing Rook's thoughts.

The bloody wolf gets a good slice of his claws into the side of the bigger wolf. The bigger wolf howls, and the air in the fight shifts. The bigger wolf has just been putting up with his attacker thus far, but he's done messing around now. He bucks the bloodier wolf away and waits. The second the smaller wolf lunges again, the big wolf dodges the strike and goes for the kill. He grabs the smaller wolf by the throat and slams him to the ground. He doesn't let go of his hold. The smaller wolf is beaten, but he's refusing to submit, so the larger wolf pinches his throat a little harder. He'll kill the smaller one if he doesn't let go soon.

"Enough!" Alpha Toth's voice booms across the scene. "Jeffrey, you're beaten. And you're an idiot for picking that fight. Both of you, change back. Now."

I barely have time to register what he means by "change back" before the bigger wolf lets go of the smaller one and the wolves morph into men. Wulf and a short, stocky blond are both standing butt naked in the middle of the circle.

Both are bloody, though Jeffrey is a mess and Wulf only has four long gouges in his side.

I can't look away, and it's totally not the blood I'm looking at. I feel bad for perving, but Wulf is beautiful in all his natural glory. I don't breathe, or even blink, until someone hands Wulf his jeans and Rook quietly clears his throat beside me. My face flames, and I glare at a smiling Rook. "I've never seen a wolf change before."

"You look like you've never seen a naked man before," he teases.

I roll my eyes, but my gaze drifts back to Wulf. "I haven't seen one like him before," I admit. I was caught staring. May as well own it. It's not like Wulf isn't drool worthy.

Rook chuckles.

When the two fighters are dressed from the waist down, the circle of spectators opens to let Alpha Toth, Rook, and myself through. Rook still has his arm tightly around me, as if he expects someone to challenge me next. The way some of the people are gaping at us, and especially some of the females are glaring, I wonder if that's a possibility.

Alpha Toth steps forward, and though he talks directly to Wulf and Jeffrey, he's speaking to the entire group. "Wulf, you have won the challenge. The position of my new beta is yours."

The group looks as if they expected this, but Wulf sighs and Jeffrey snarls. "But, sir! He's not even pack! He shouldn't have been here!"

"You lost the challenge!" Alpha Toth snaps. I think he's throwing some alpha mojo around now, too, because people are squirming and my heart is hammering in my chest in a way it wasn't before. "You know pack law. Wulf has always been welcome to join this pack, and the spot of beta is rightfully his now. You shouldn't have challenged him."

"I respectfully decline the position," Wulf says calmly.

Alpha Toth frowns, disappointed, but not the least bit surprised. "You won the challenge, Wulf. The position is yours automatically."

Wulf groans, as if he's being inconvenienced in the worst possible way. "I have no interest in being a pack beta."

"Then you shouldn't have fought—"

"I had no choice. The asshole jumped me without warning."

Alpha Toth's jaw clenches, and he glares at Jeffrey. Jeffrey glares back, standing proud and puffing up his chest. "He's not pack! He wasn't supposed to be here."

Alpha Toth sighs and throws a hand over his face, rubbing his eyes. "He had permission," he says tiredly. "He was bringing someone dear to our pack to visit." He removes his hand from his face and waves it my direction. "Everyone, meet Nora Jacobs, the brave human who rescued Maya and the others last month."

The crowd gasps and erupts into cheers, clapping and whistling for me. I'm a bit shocked by the reception, and flash an awkward wave.

"I had hoped to introduce her as an honored guest at the pack social next weekend, but now that we've bloodied her escort, I'm not sure she'll want to come."

"A little fight isn't going to scare her off," calls a familiar voice.

I scan the crowd for the face I know is out there, and grin when I spot it. "Hey, Maya."

"Hey, girl!" Maya flashes me a wolfish grin. She looks a lot healthier than the last time I saw her. I almost don't recognize her. "Welcome to the compound. It's good to see you again."

"You too."

"You're still going to come to the social, right?"

"Sure. Sounds like a hell of a party. I'm not so sure Wulf will want to come now, though."

Maya grins, but this time she's looking at Wulf. She slings her arm over his shoulder and says to me, "He'll have to. It's mandatory for the pack. They'll introduce him officially as our new beta. There's a little ceremony for it and everything."

"No!" Wulf groans again. "No ceremony. I'm not joining the pack. I have no desire to be anyone's beta." He casts Alpha Toth a serious gaze and adds, "Or anyone's alpha. Which is what my wolf would demand, if I rejoined."

The crowd gasps, and Alpha Toth stiffens. "Is that a challenge?" he growls. I'm surprised he's so angry. I got the impression he really liked Wulf.

"*No!* It's not a damn challenge. I hate werewolf politics. GAH." Wulf fists his hair with both hands as he groans at the sky. "You see?" he says to me. "This is why I never come back. I'm a lone wolf, Nora. I'd be a crappy leader, only my wolf is too dominant to be anything but." He gives Alpha Toth what is meant to be a pleading expression. "I'm sorry. I have to decline the position of beta. I mean no disrespect, but I can't join your pack. I only came today because Nora needs training."

Alpha Toth looks at me, then back at Wulf, before sighing helplessly. "I'm sorry, friend. Your cause is noble, but we can't have a lone wolf in pack territory. It'll cause too many problems within the pack. Thank you for introducing me to Nora, but I'm afraid if you don't join, you can't be allowed back."

My heart sinks. I understand where Alpha Toth is coming from—we've been here an hour, and Wulf's already been in a fight with the pack's beta—but I'm still disappointed. Wulf, on the other hand, is beaming. "That's okay," he says, smiling bigger than I've ever seen him. He nods his head toward his brother. "Rook can train her."

"What?" I shout. "You're passing me off after one lesson?"

"I won't, if you don't want me to," he says, still grinning, "but the only other place I have to work with you is my place, and we'd be alone there, which I know you don't want." I blush, because he's right, but I didn't need the whole pack hearing that and assuming things. "Besides," he continues, "Rook is much better at fighting in human form than me. I'm more of a go-at-it-on-all-fours kind of guy."

"I noticed," I say flatly. "Fine. But did you even ask Rook? Are you sure he would even want to help me?"

"Oh, he doesn't mind. Do you, big brother?"

When he grins at Rook, it's so devious I almost laugh. I don't know why, but he did this on purpose. He wanted Rook to teach me from the start. Rook knows it, too, and though he's both shocked and annoyed, he's also trying not to laugh. "*That's* what you're up to?" Rook asks, shaking his head. "*Thirty years?* You don't come home for thirty years, and when you do, it's to bring me a *girl?*"

My mouth falls open. No freaking way. This is about me? And his brother? Like, as in, together?

"Nora's not just a girl," Wulf says. He winks at me and adds, "And I'm right, anyway, aren't I? I mean, you stole her from me like five minutes after I got here, and you still haven't let her go."

He means that literally, because Rook's arm is still around me. I know he was only protecting me during the fight, but now it looks like he's holding me, or staking a claim on me. My eyes bulge, and I scramble out of Rook's grip. "You were setting me up?" I shout at Wulf. "Are you freaking kidding me? You brought me here to *set me up?*"

The crowd laughs, making my cheeks flame again. I glare at Wulf, but he doesn't look the least bit repentant. In fact, when he shrugs at me, it's the cockiest I've ever seen him. "You'd be good for each other, since you both refuse to date."

Rook's head whips in my direction. His brows are raised in a question. "It's true," I tell him. "I don't date."

"Neither does Rook," Wulf promises. "So just give the

friends thing a try for a while. Let him train you, Nora. Talk. Hang out." He steps closer to me and lowers his voice to barely a whisper. "You both have traumatic pasts," he says softly. "Maybe you two can help each other heal."

I want to kill him, but he's being so sweet. He's really just looking out for his brother. And, I have to admit, I'm a lot more intrigued now that I know Rook doesn't date and that he has some kind of traumatic past.

Wulf smiles when he sees he's won me over. I sigh and glance at Rook to find him eyeing me just as curiously. "You don't have to train me, if you don't want to," I say. "I'm sorry Wulf put you on the spot like this." I step back and fold my arms across my chest. I give Wulf a stink-eye and add, "I had no idea he was so meddlesome."

Every wolf within earshot cracks up laughing.

"That's a werewolf trait, girl," Maya calls to me. "We're all that way. Better get used to it."

"Yeah, I don't think so," I mutter under my breath.

This time, only Rook laughs. I look at him, and he raises a brow at me. "I don't mind training you. If you think you can handle hanging out here with us meddling wolves three times a week."

"There's nothing to meddle in—I truly don't date—so as long as you keep your paws to yourself, then yes, thank you, I'd love to train with you."

The crowd laughs again, and Rook grins. He holds his hand out to me. "Deal." I give it a quick shake and laugh when his only thought is something about needing to kill his damned meddling brother.

"Great," I say, and then force a smile at my rather large audience. "Well, as awesome as this visit has been, I need to get to work pretty soon. So I think it's time I take my lone wolf back to the city."

CHAPTER
SIX

Sunday night at the club isn't quite as busy as Saturday was, but it's still loud, chaotic, and exhausting. I'm glad for it, because it doesn't give Wulf much time to hound me about Rook. Oh, he finds time when he can, just not as much. "Honey, I'm not saying you have to mate with the guy. Just hang out with him. He needs to not be scared of women anymore, and you, pip-squeak, are the least scary woman on the planet."

I punch him in the arm for that, as hard as I can. He laughs at my efforts and winks at me before turning his flirty smile on some woman at the bar, showing more cleavage than the Swiss have Alps.

I roll my eyes and pour a small, grumpy dwarf his fourth shot of absinthe. "If you're so worried about Rook," I call down the bar to Wulf, "why not just find him a good she-wolf to date?"

"Because all she-wolves are just trying to snag mates." Wulf shivers in horror. "Rook would never give one the chance to get close."

"So I'm supposed to go in all undercover-like, disguised as a nonthreatening female who just wants to be friends?"

"And then win his heart without him realizing it? Yeah. Basically."

"Human! Hey, human! Girl! What's a guy have to do to get a drink around here?"

I shake my head at Wulf one more time and then smile at the elf man waiting to be served. The condescending asshole—elves are the worst when it comes to respecting my human status—orders his drink, and as he saunters off, that intuition of mine hits me like lightning, nearly making my knees buckle. Tingles shoot down my neck and into my whole body, making me feel alive and alert, and yet paralyzing me at the same time. Dread washes over me so strong that I gasp and grip the counter to keep from falling. Whoever my gift is warning me about is close by, and they mean business. Death is on my doorstep. "Wulf!"

Even though it's loud and busy, Wulf is at my side in an instant. "What's wrong?"

"Someone here is going to try and kill me."

Wulf doesn't like that comment. He snarls, and his eyes glow as he lets his wolf come to the surface. "How do you know?"

"How do I do any of the things I do?" I glare at him, but it's mostly my anxiety making me lose control. "I just *know*. I can *feel* it."

Wulf shoves me behind him and glares at the crowd around us. "Who? Where?"

"I don't know. It's only a warning."

"Well, that's helpful."

"It's better than nothing."

He harrumphs and pulls out his cell phone, ignoring all the annoyed customers shouting for drinks. "I'm texting Terrance. Tell me if you see anyone suspicious."

I'm in a club full of supernatural monsters. Right now, they *all* look suspicious. It's especially impossible to tell if anyone means me harm right now, because both Wulf and I have stopped serving drinks and people are starting to get pissed.

"Come on." Wulf grunts, gruffly grabbing my arm and dragging me toward the end of the bar. "Terrance says to take you to his private suite. It doubles as a panic room."

He refuses to let go of me as he drags me away from the bar, yelling at his other bartender to hold down the fort until he gets back. We push through the crowd toward the back of the club, where a stairway leads to a set of rooms on the second floor. The hallway is open to the large room, but Terrance's suite is toward the end of the row.

I can't help feeling like heading upstairs is a mistake. The dread in my stomach is getting heavier, not lighter. "Are you sure we should be going upstairs? Have you ever seen a horror movie, Wulf?"

"It's a panic room, Nora. It's the safest place for you in the club while Terrance and I figure out who wants to hurt you."

"You're going to leave me alone, too? You *really* don't watch horror."

"You'll be fine."

We reach Terrance's office, and as Wulf pulls out his keys, a tall, skinny woman arrives out of nowhere and grabs Wulf's face. "Go back to the bar," she says, staring into his eyes. "Nora is fine."

Oh. Nora is so *not* fine. The woman is a vampire, and she's just compelled Wulf. He actually smiles as he passes me, heading back for the stairs. I scream his name and grab his arm, but he keeps walking. I try to run after him, but the vampire lady grabs me. I scream Terrance's name at the top of my lungs, while the woman drags me into the nearest room and throws me to the ground.

Stars burst in my vision as my head hits the ground, but the woman slams my head again for good measure. "Shut up!" she hisses.

When I scream for Terrance again, she hits me so hard across the mouth that my jaw shatters. Pain explodes through me like roaring fire. I can't scream now. I whimper, and tears leak from the corners of my eyes.

"I don't know how you bewitched my sire," she says, "but I'm going to save him from your wretched curse."

The woman is a stranger to me, but I know she's talking about Henry Stadther. Henry is the master of the largest vampire clan in Michigan. He's also completely obsessed with me. The FUA warned him to leave me alone, but he doesn't do a good job of it. I guess his vampire whores are getting as tired of his infatuation as I am.

This crazy vamp-bitch is out for blood. Her eyes are red, and her fangs are on full display. Hopefully Terrance heard me and gets up here fast, otherwise I'm dead.

"I used to be Henry's favorite, you know. He was *mine* until you came along, and now he doesn't even remember I exist. All he cares about is his precious Nora." She gives me an evil smile. "We'll see how long he cares about you once you're dead. I'm going to enjoy drinking you dry."

"NNNOOOORRRAAA!" Terrance bellows, shaking the entire club. His voice is completely guttural. I've only heard it like that once before—when I'd been kidnapped and he found me chained and bleeding on a sorcerer's altar. He's totally in raging troll mode.

I can't speak, or smirk, so I narrow my eyes at the shocked woman. *That's right, bitch. You've done it now. I'm his clan, and you're a dead woman.*

As if she can see the smugness in my eyes, the woman growls at me. "I was planning to make you hurt for a bit first, but I guess I'll just have to make this quick." She lifts my wrist but pauses before biting me and smiles again. "Still. I can make you suffer a little." She looks into my eyes and whispers, "Fear me."

Immediately, I'm overcome with terror so strong I can't breathe or think. I try to squirm and thrash to escape, even though every move causes my jaw more pain. I get one more command before she begins to drink. "You will feel pain instead of pleasure."

Agony tears through my whole body when her fangs pierce my skin, and she begins to pull the blood from me one swallow at a time. I'm on fire from the inside out. I thrash, but it does me no good. Pain and fear, that's all I know. It's all I feel. There is nothing else.

I can't tell how long it goes on. It feels like an eternity. And then it stops. Just as my vision fades, my massive angry troll friend rips the woman away from me. He grabs her and tears her head from her body. Blood flies everywhere, splattering us both, and that's the last thing I remember.

. . . . .

WHEN I COME TO, MY MIND IS FOGGY, BUT NOT ENOUGH that I don't remember what happened. I'm still lying on the floor where I passed out, and I'm still a bloody mess. My jaw is healed but really stiff, and I know I must have been drained nearly dry of blood because I'm so weak I can't move.

The shaman kneeling over me is one I recognize. He's a freelance healer that is usually on call for the FUA. He's healed me several times before. "Enzo," I croak. "We've got to stop meeting like this."

He gives me a pained smile. "Just lie still, Miss Nora."

I pass out again, and I'm kind of glad, because I still hurt like a bitch.

When I wake up the second time, I feel a lot better—weak still, but not like I'm on death's door. I'm also not still lying on the floor splattered in vamp blood, which is nice. I've been moved to a large, comfortable bed in a smallish but lavishly decorated room. I've also been wiped down, and someone has changed my clothes. Enzo is sitting by my side in a folding chair, looking pale as a ghost and exhausted, but he smiles when he notices I'm awake. "How are you feeling?"

"Much better. Thank you."

I try to sit up and quickly rethink that decision. "Okay, only a little better. But still, thank you."

He gives me a humble bow. "You're welcome, Miss Nora. I'm sorry I couldn't do more."

Is he kidding? "Hey. I'm alive. I'm sure that's thanks to you. You are, once again, my favorite underworlder."

I love making him blush. It's so easy.

Over half a dozen other faces cram into the room when they hear us talking. Wulf, my best friend Oliver, Nick Gorgeous, Parker, Cecile, two unfamiliar men, and Terrance all crowd into the small room, hovering behind Enzo with worried expressions.

Terrance pushes everyone out of the way and crashes to his knees beside my bed with a thump that rattles the room. "Hey," I say softly, recognizing that while he might not still be lost to his rage, he's not entirely calm yet, either. "You saved my life. Thanks, T-man."

Terrance grumbles something unintelligible while he rakes his thick fingers through my hair.

"I'm okay now, Terrance. Promise."

He grunts and walks out of the room to resume his furious pacing in the hall. So…he's going to brood a while, then. "All right. Where am I?" I ask everyone else in the room. "Whose clothes are these? Please tell me Cecile changed me. And what are you all doing here?"

Cecile flashes me a smile. "You're still in the club. This is my private suite. Those are my clothes, and don't worry, I cleaned you up and changed you. I even kicked all the men out first—Terrance excluded. I couldn't get him to go anywhere, but he turned his back."

I let out a breath of relief. "Thanks." Again, my gaze circles the room. "And you guys?"

Oliver makes a face like *duh*. "I was worried about you. I left work as soon as I heard what happened."

I give him a smile to let him know I'm grateful.

"I'm just checking in on my favorite human," Nick says. His favorite human? I'm probably his only human. Not that I'm his. You know what I mean. As if he can tell what I'm thinking, he flashes me a grin that could light up a room and shows me his badge. "I'm also here on official business. When stuff happens between the different factions, they send in the FUA. I'll need to get a statement from you." He points a thumb at Parker and the two strangers. "Since the vamp was a member of Henry's clan, his enforcers were also called in as a courtesy to him."

My blood turns cold in my veins, and my stomach churns. I may trust Parker some, but I don't like that those other guys are vampires. And enforcers from Henry's clan, no less. I wish they would leave. Hell, after tonight, I wish even Parker would leave. I could go forever never seeing another vampire again, and it would be too soon.

As if he can read my thoughts, Parker's face crumples. He steps toward me, longing in his expression. My heart speeds up as he comes closer, only it's not stemmed from my fear of vampires. There's a physical connection between us that ignites like wildfire when we get close.

"It's good to finally see you again, Nora," he murmurs. "I'm sorry it's under these circumstances."

He takes my hand in his and softly rubs his thumb over the back of it. I shiver at the contact, and heat flares in his eyes. I get caught in his gaze and can't look away. My mouth dries up, and I swallow thickly.

I focus on his thoughts in an attempt to get my body under control. Parker's relieved that I still react this way to him. I've been avoiding him since the Henry thing a month ago. He thinks it's because I fear his kind. I do fear vampires, but that's not why I've been ignoring his calls. I'm afraid of my attraction to him. The feelings he stirs in me are intense and dangerous, and I'm not ready to feel those things.

"Nora, this wasn't Henry's fault," he says, loyal to his master to a fault. "He didn't know about Josephine's insta-bility. In fact, if she weren't already dead, he'd have killed her himself for this. He's devastated that you were hurt because of him. Our whole clan is upset."

He's not going to convince me that his clan is full of wonderful people tonight. I pull my hand from his, because he's making it hard for me to think straight. "Just forget it, Parker. Damage done."

Parker steps back, disappointment bleeding from his eyes. I look away, hating that I'm hurting him. If I knew how to give him what he wants, I would.

I try to sit up again, and this time I almost succeed. Oli-ver moves forward and puts a few pillows behind my back to help me stay sitting up. After I'm situated, I look to Nick. "Is Terrance going to get into trouble for killing her?"

"Nah. She had it coming."

I smirk. Justice in the underworld takes some getting used to.

"Do you know why Josephine attacked you?" one of the nameless enforcers asks.

I flinch at the sound of his voice and give Nick a pleading glance. I may not fear Parker, but I want the other vampires out of this room and far away from me. Both Nick and the vampire who spoke frown.

"I understand your history with vampires isn't pleasant," Enforcer Dude says, "but you need to overcome your fear of us. We can sense it, and it sets off all of our instincts. Perhaps that's why Josephine lost control and attacked you tonight."

I scoff. "Seriously? You think she lost control? No way. She came here for no other reason than to kill me tonight. She even said so. She monologued as she tortured me. She kept ranting about how she used to be Henry's favorite and how he didn't pay her any attention anymore because of me. She thought he'd love her again if I were dead, or something like that. Real nice lady. A lot in common with Henry, actually. They both broke my face."

Enforcer Dude sighs but doesn't argue. He doesn't really look surprised, either. I bet poor, jilted Josephine complained a lot before she went off the deep end of the crazy pool tonight.

"Still," the other enforcer says, his voice haughty as if I've insulted him, "I'm sorry about Josephine, but you can't be so afraid of us. We are predators. You are tempting to us for many reasons."

Parker places a hand on the guy's shoulder when I glare at him. "We aren't all monsters, Nora," Parker murmurs.

"So you keep telling me. And yet…your kind keep hurting me. Over and over again." I sigh. "Look, I don't have the energy for this conversation. The bitch was jealous of Henry's obsession with me and wanted me out of the picture, so she tried to drain me. End of story. Can we be done now?"

"I've got what I need," Nick says. He glances at Parker and his cronies. "You?"

Parker sighs. "I think we're good." He nods to his two enforcers, gesturing for them to head out. They both look back at me, but the less rude one stops when he reaches the door. "Henry really cares about you, you know. You should give him a second chance to prove himself."

I want to laugh—no way in hell is that happening—but I don't want to piss off another vampire by rejecting his sire, so I shrug noncommittally and look away. Parker waits until I meet his gaze again before he follows his enforcers out. "Please call me when you're feeling better," he murmurs, then leaves.

Once he's gone, I shiver. "Henry's not going to stop obsessing over me. If his vampires are going to start going crazy because of it, I might have to quit the club."

Terrance stops pacing the hall and storms back into the room to glare at me. *"No."*

"He's right," Wulf says, crossing his arms and frowning at me. "You don't run. You never run. They will chase. You stay, and you pretend like they don't terrify you."

"That's not enough," Nick says. His eyes fall on mine. "Those guys were right. You need to get over your fear of vampires. Maybe your fear is justified, but it's also tempting to all predators—which most underworlders are. If you're going to be a part of this world now, Nora, you can't fear it anymore. Find a way. Hate them, fine. But get over your fear."

Great. How am I supposed to do that? I'm making headway with most underworld species, but it seems like every vampire I meet tries to kill me. They're the monsters that murdered my mother in front of me when I was six. It's hard to let go of a lifetime of nightmares and fear.

"I'll host a party!" Cecile blurts, seemingly out of nowhere. "A party for Nora." The smile she gives me is both sincere and full of wicked delight. I'm pretty sure I have another meddler on my hands. As if my werewolf boss isn't enough.

"I'll invite lots of decent vampire friends of mine for you to get to know. There are some wonderful ones out there, Nora. If you meet a few who aren't assholes, like Henry, you'll learn to love them as much as you like the rest of us."

"A *party?* Full of *vampires?*" I groan and close my eyes as I sink back into the pillows behind my head. "I must be really out of it right now, because I can't believe I'm about to say yes to that."

Cecile claps her hands. "Yay! Don't you worry about a thing, darling. I'll keep it small, with an exclusive guest list."

"I better be invited," Nick says. He's smiling now, as if

he approves of this plan.

"Gorgeous, darling, it wouldn't be a party without you," Cecile purrs, making the man shiver when she runs a finger up his arm. I get the feeling she only affects him because he lets her, but she's definitely stirring feelings in him now. He closes his eyes and lets out a long, satisfied breath. "All right, enough of this." He looks at me. "Go home and get some sleep. Lots of sleep and protein. Enzo worked a miracle, but you're still really low on blood. Rest for a week. I'm not kidding. A full week. At least."

I roll my eyes. "Yes, Mother."

He winks, then turns his fierce gaze back to Cecile. "And you. Keep the guest list small, and have Nora in mind when you plan it. She needs this."

"Of course!" Cecile chirps. "It'll be like the good old days back in England. It'll be a coming-out party for Nora into underworld society. I'll only invite the best of the best."

"Small!" Terrance orders, while I groan again.

I'm in trouble. Someone has unleashed a monster.

CHAPTER
SEVEN

TERRANCE, CECILE, AND WULF ALL GO BACK TO WORK.
They'd kicked everyone out—or maybe everyone ran screaming when the body parts started flying—but everything still
needs to be closed out and cleaned up. I don't envy them
that job. The vampires took the remains of their dead clan
member away, but the blood left behind has to be... Ugh.
Nasty. Hopefully magic will be involved.

"You got her?" Nick asks Oliver, referring to me. "I've
got to head out. Got to go babysit some stupid Washington
yahoo about some demon business."

I smirk. He sounds *thrilled* about that.

Oliver nods and gives me a grin. "Yeah. I'll get her in
bed. Don't worry."

I choke on a laugh, and Nick snorts. Oliver has to think
back on his words, and then he chuckles and shakes his head.
"That's not what I meant."

"Better not be," Nick teases. "At least not for a week. Then I say go for it."

I groan. "Oh, shut up, Nick."

"Nora. I've told you a hundred times. It's Gorgeous. GORGEOUS. Not Nick."

I smile a big, toothy grin. "You got it, Nick."

Nick rolls his eyes and heads out the door, grumbling about beautiful smartass women. I laugh to myself and then call him back. I've got one last question for him before he leaves. "Hey, Gorgeous?" I humor him just this once.

He spins around, giving me a sly grin. "Yes, beautiful?"

I groan internally. He's incorrigible. "Does the FUA keep old records?"

The question catches him off guard. His brain flips into work mode, and he answers professionally, for once. "How far back?"

"About fifteen to twenty years?" I suck in a breath as if it might give me the courage I need to say my next sentence. "My mother and I were attacked by vampires when I was six. They nearly drained me and left me for dead, but they were brutal to my mom before they killed her."

Nick's eyes bulge, and his mouth pops open. Oliver, however, gives me a sympathetic smile. He's heard this story before. I gulp and hedge on. "That's how I found out about the underworld, and it's the main reason I'm so scared of vampires. I've always been terrified of them—long before Henry. He and Josephine were both just affirming my fear."

Nick's response is earnest. "No kidding. I'm sorry, Nora."

I shrug, not knowing how to respond to that. "I was

thinking it might help to know what happened to those vamps that attacked us. Do you think you still have it on record? My mom's case?"

Nick's brow furrows, and he shakes his head. "Your case wasn't known. No way. If what you're saying is true about the two of you, we wouldn't have left a witness alive."

Meaning they'd have killed me to keep the secret of the underworld safe. I cringe, and Nick shrugs. "Sorry. It's harsh, but true. You and your mother slipped through the cracks somehow."

Of course. A dead end. My entire life has always felt like one giant dead end. "But there had to have been other victims who didn't," I say. "Henry told me they were rogues. He said regular vampires would never do what they did to us. They must have had other victims around the same time that didn't fall through the cracks. I could give you a time and a place. I could even identify them by face. Henry got in my head and made me relive the memory, so I know what they look like. If you arrested them or something—it'd give me peace of mind to know."

Nick scratches the back of his head and slowly nods. "Yeah, that sounds doable. Though, to be honest, something like that is way more Ren's department than mine."

"Okay, I'll ask him about it."

"If you want to search for your mother's killers, I could do that, too," Oliver offers. "It would be pretty easy to look up." He gives me a small smile that's a little sad. "I'd be happy to help you."

Of course he would. He's the sweetest, kindest man that

ever existed. He's also the most adorable. He's tall and slim, with wavy light brown hair and beautiful amber eyes. He doesn't wear glasses, but his look screams geek that doesn't know he's hot. I love that about him, because I'm usually surrounded by too many cocky, testosterone-filled men who love to peacock around. My sweet, humble best friend is a breath of fresh air.

"I'd love your help. Thanks, Ollie. My hero, as usual."

Oliver grins while Nick snorts. "Aw, how sweet."

Oliver and I both flip Nick off, and he laughs his way out the door. "Night, guys. Nora, do me a favor and try not to get attacked for at least the next twenty-four hours."

"I will. Good-bye, Nicky!" I grin at Oliver when Nick grunts curses down the hall.

Once we're alone, Oliver sits down on the edge of my bed as if he's been patiently waiting his turn for my attention. He's always so quiet when others are around. He's a big-time introvert and a little shy, but more than that, he's just the type of guy who knows I appreciate him no matter what. He's happy to stand in the background while all of the other more dominant personalities monopolize my time. I like that, because it means, in the end, I get more one-on-one time with him, and alone time with men is not something I get a lot of. Aside from Terrance, Oliver is the only man I trust enough for that.

"I think you're the only person in Detroit who dares tease Nick Gorgeous," Oliver says, still chuckling a little.

"Aw, he's a big softy. It's Cecile who scares me. Did I really just agree to a *coming-out* party?"

Oliver laughs. "I think so. And Cecile is known for throwing exclusive, swanky parties, so have fun with that."

"I will. I'll be hiding in the corner with my best friend, mocking all the stuffy rich people pretending they're in some Jane Austen novel."

"What?" Oliver gasps with mock outrage. "Who is this imposter best friend that'll go to parties with you?"

I lightly punch Oliver's arm, but he's got me laughing. I'm so grateful for him. "Seriously, though, you'll come, won't you? I'll need a wingman to keep me sane."

Oliver grimaces, and then when I make a pouty face, gives me an over-the-top sigh. "Of course I'll come with you. I'll hate every second of it, but I'll come anyway."

I grin. "And that's why you're my best friend. You'll dive into exciting trouble with me, but you'll also suffer miserable, boring parties with me. Thanks, Ollie."

Oliver pulls a Nick Gorgeous move and mutters something under his breath about cute nicknames and not being able to refuse me. My grin grows even bigger, and I close the small gap between us, leaning against him and resting my head on his shoulder. He gives my leg a quick pat to let me know he's thrilled with the rare gesture, but otherwise holds still and doesn't touch me. Oliver is one of the few people in my life who really understands my aversion to physical touch and is very careful to give me space.

After a minute, my eyes start to droop, and Oliver breaks the silence. "All right. Time to get you home."

I try to stand up, but I simply don't have the energy. With a defeated sigh, I hold my arms out to him. He scoops me up with surprisingly little effort, making me wonder what kind of muscles he's hiding beneath his dress shirt. I'm surprised that I want to know. Oliver is my best friend, and that's how I've always seen him, but being in his arms like this is surprisingly exciting. "Do you work out?" I blurt suddenly, then cringe, because I sound so stupid.

Oliver laughs. "You're a lightweight. And I swim a lot."

A swimmer. That explains it. It also fits him. I can totally picture him calmly doing laps in a quiet pool. I wouldn't mind seeing him in a swimsuit.

Without the fear I normally have around men, I allow myself a moment of indulgence to explore this new interest. I bury my face in the crook of his neck and inhale deeply. A faint hint of aftershave floods my senses and makes me shiver.

Oliver freezes, and his whole body stiffens. All those swimmer muscles I was thinking about suddenly flex to life. Hope washes through me from Oliver, along with his thoughts. *Did she just smell me? Is it possible she's attracted to me? Is she just exhausted, or could she feel the same way I feel about her? What do I do? Do I ignore it? Do I say something?*

His nervous rambling touches my heart, and out of nowhere, I press my lips lightly against the side of his neck before pulling away from his skin. Both of us suck in sharp breaths. "Nora..." he rasps.

"Sorry," I mumble, not knowing what else to say. I'm as shocked by my actions as he is.

He swallows and slowly relaxes his body. "I'm not sorry," he murmurs with a tiny chuckle. "Feel free to kiss me whenever you want."

I relax. He's so good at making me feel comfortable. I consider his offer and surprise myself when I realize I wouldn't mind a kiss from Oliver. The thought scares me a little, but thrills me more. Maybe Oliver is the key to getting over my issues with intimacy. "I'll work on it," I finally say.

He chuckles again and squeezes me a little tighter to him as he starts walking. He carries me all the way to my car, which is parked right out front, waiting for us. Leave it to Terrance to think of something as small as my car, even after I've just been nearly murdered. I'm not even surprised to learn that Oliver already has my keys. He helps me get settled in the passenger seat, and then he climbs behind the wheel.

I fall asleep in the car on the way to my place and don't wake up again until I'm lying on my own bed, Oliver removing my shoes. "Sorry. Go back to sleep," he says softly as he sets my shoes neatly on the floor at the foot of my bed. He then proceeds to help me pull the covers back and tucks me in. My heart melts a little at the sweet gesture. I haven't been tucked into bed since my mom died. I'm surprised that I love being taken care of this way.

He perches on the side of my bed, and his face becomes serious as he looks down at me. "You okay?"

I want to be strong and tell him I'm fine, but I can't lie to him. "Not really. Physically, yeah, I'm just exhausted. Emotionally...?" I bite my lip and will myself not to cry as I say, "Can you—would you mind staying? I really don't want to be alone tonight."

Oliver's mouth falls open, and he sucks in a silent breath. "You would trust me like that?"

Instead of blushing and feeling vulnerable, a sense of surety washes over me, forcing me to calm down. "There are exactly two people in this world I trust with my life—you and Terrance. I'd feel safer with you here."

Oliver responds by smiling softly and taking off his shoes. He turns out the light and then lies down on the other side of my bed on top of the covers. I'm grateful he's staying, but I'm even gladder that he knows me well enough to know exactly how to make me comfortable without me having to say it.

"Thanks, Ollie," I whisper into the dark.

There's a smile in his reply. "Good night, Nora."

.   .   .   .   .

I WAKE UP THE NEXT AFTERNOON TO OLIVER BRINGING ME breakfast in bed. Well, breakfast food, anyway. Technically, it's more like lunch in bed. "My hero," I say as I sit up with a big stretch and a yawn.

"What? This is mine," Oliver teases as he sits down on the side of the bed he slept on with the tray of food in his lap. "Go get your own."

He sticks a crispy piece of bacon in his mouth before he finally sets the tray on the bed between us. There are two plates piled high with food on the tray. My mouth waters as the smell of strawberry pancakes, eggs, ham, and bacon hit my nose. The man really is my hero.

While I go to town on all the delicious food, Oliver props himself up against the headboard, crosses his feet at his ankles, and grabs the TV remote from the night table. "I called in sick from work this evening, so we have a full twenty-four hours to lay in bed like slugs, binge watching every episode of *Stranger Things*."

I laugh at that. You'd think with fantasy being reality for us, we'd prefer normal television, but we're both paranormal geeks at heart.

Ollie doesn't turn the TV on right away. Instead, we eat in silence until he clears his throat and says, "So...Parker was awfully worried about you last night."

I cast him a sideways glance to let him know I'm not thrilled with the direction of this conversation. "Parker is a worrier. He's like that with everyone."

Oliver snorts. "Nice try. He may care about his clan, but he's Henry's chief enforcer because he has the ability to be cold and ruthless when he needs to be. I've seen it. The concern he shows you is different."

"Yeah, because he feels guilty since it's his clan always trying to hurt me, and he's the one responsible for bringing me fully into the underworld."

Oliver rolls his eyes. "It's more than that, and you know it. I've never seen someone look at a woman the way he looks at you."

I glare at Oliver, but he's right, and he holds my gaze steady in his. I break first. "Fine." I sigh. "Parker has an infatuation. I know it, but nothing's going to come of it, so there's no point in talking about it."

Oliver is quiet for a long minute, then quietly asks what's been on his mind since last night. "So, you're not interested?"

That's a question I've been skirting since I met Parker, because the answer is too complicated, but Oliver's not going to let me off the hook with some bogus crap this time. I throw my head back against the headboard and groan at the ceiling. "It wouldn't matter even if I was, which I'm not sure I am. He's attractive and nice, but I'm too screwed up to get into a relationship, and his feelings for me aren't real. He's just affected by my curse."

Oliver frowns, but I'm not sure which part of that he's frowning at, so I say nothing. He moves the empty breakfast tray out of the way and turns to face me. "What curse?"

Okay, so I knew which part of that he was frowning at. I was just hoping I wouldn't have to explain it to him. I cringe beneath the weight of his stare and give in. "There's something different about me that draws people in."

Oliver smiles wryly. "Could it be that you're beautiful, smart, friendly, compassionate, loyal, and brave?"

I resist the urge to deny all of his compliments. I know he means them, even if I don't feel deserving of his praise. "That's not it. I mean, I put men under some kind of spell, until their fascination with me becomes obsession. Like with Henry. It's happened all my life."

I shake my head and interrupt Oliver when he starts to argue. "Think about it. Henry, Parker, Wulf, and Rook. Nick. *Terrance*."

Oliver frowns again, this time seeing my point and

having a hard time denying it.

"I think it has something to do with what I am."

"What you are?"

I shrug. "Everyone's always talking about me having underworlder blood. I have gifts that humans don't have. Maybe I'm some weird human/underworlder hybrid. But whatever it is, I can't get into a relationship when I know the guy only likes me because of my curse."

Oliver's face falls flat. "I don't think that's the only reason Parker likes you."

"Parker doesn't know me. He can't like me. Parker *wants* me. There's a difference. And with my history, there's no way I'm getting involved with someone who's only interested in sex. I can't. If I'm ever able to go there with someone, and that's a pretty big if, it's going to have to be someone I trust implicitly and who I know isn't going to lose control of themselves—which is what people tend to do when I return their attraction. My weird allure kicks into overdrive. It's like when Cecile or Ren turns up their sex mojo. People can't help themselves. They *aren't* themselves."

Oliver sits there for a minute, processing what I've just told him. Eventually, he nods. "Perhaps there's something there. Maybe you do have some kind of unknown power of attraction. But I'm sure that's not always the case. It *is* possible for someone to like you, not because of some supernatural power, but because of *you*. There's so much about you for people to like."

A lump forms in my throat. He's talking about himself, and we both know it. I don't know what to say. I adore him, but he's just as influenced as anyone. "Oliver…"

He gives me a crooked smile and shakes his head, denying the thoughts he knows I'm thinking. "I know you, Nora. I've known you for years. And I was never around you, so it couldn't have been some curse affecting me. You're just special. You're so strong. You're beautiful and smart. You're a survivor."

He takes a risk and pushes my hair behind my ear, letting his fingers graze my cheek. The rare skin-to-skin contact raises goose bumps on my arms and makes me shiver. The thought I catch when he touches me is tender. *I wish I could make her see. She deserves so much more than she allows herself.*

My eyes start to sting, and I press my hand against the burning in my chest. *"Ollie,"* I murmur.

He gives me a soft smile and takes my hand in his. *I love you.* The thought is so direct I wonder if he's just thinking it or if he's sending it to me on purpose. My stomach flips, and a half-crazed sob bubbles up from my chest. For once I don't pull away. I don't want to let go. His feelings aren't lust-filled. They're tender and comforting. They feel sincere.

"The things I think about you—feel for you—it's because of who you are," he insists softly. "And I think, deep down, you believe that, or you'd never be able to trust me the way you do."

Tears spill from my eyes. I quickly swipe them away and take a deep breath to get control of myself. I'm so not a crier, but I've never felt such pure feelings or heard such beautiful, sincere thoughts. "I do believe you," I promise, sniffling. "I just can't…I don't know how to…I'm too broken."

The loving smile never leaves his face. "I know, Nora." In a rather bold move, he pulls me into his lap and cradles me against his chest, resting his chin on the top of my head. I close my eyes and soak up the affection being offered to me. I've never been held before. Not since my mother used to comfort me when I was little.

He wraps his arms around me tightly and leans us back against the headboard. I can still hear his thoughts, but they're absentminded. He's simply enjoying this moment, the same as I am. His sorcerer community was cruel to him for years because he wouldn't use his magic. His family disowned him, kicked him out as soon as he turned eighteen, and turned their backs on him. He's as alone as me and loves our unique relationship as much as I do. He doesn't need more than this right now. He's healing from his own experiences as much as I am.

I let out a deep breath and relax against him. "I love you, too, Ollie."

He drops a small kiss on the top of my head in response and reaches for the remote. "What do you think? *Stranger Things*, *The Walking Dead*, or *Game of Thrones?*"

I grin and snuggle deeper into his hold. "You choose."

CHAPTER
EIGHT

I GET A NICE GLARE FROM ROOK WHEN I SHOW UP TO THE compound clubhouse on Wednesday afternoon. He wasn't expecting me, so I start my warm-up without him, knowing that the gossiping wolves will tell him I'm here. I get one slow lap in before the angry werewolf plants himself in front of me. "What are you doing here?"

I knew he wouldn't be happy, but I don't care. "I came for training," I say stubbornly. "You said three times a week. Monday, Wednesday, and Saturday. It's Wednesday. I'm ready for my first session."

He's not amused. "No," he growls. "No way. You were nearly *drained* Sunday night. Wulf told me. You're supposed to rest for a whole week. We are not training today."

"But Enzo healed me, and I feel fine. I've done nothing but lie around for almost three days now. Can't we just do a little?"

Rook crosses his arms over his chest and keeps up his glare. "No."

I go for a pout. It's low, but I can't help it. "Aw, come on, Rook. I had to get out of the house. I was going crazy. And besides, my attackers aren't going to wait for me to recover, so neither should I."

He growls at me—a real snarl—then scrubs a hand over his face, muttering unintelligible things to himself. He sucks in a sharp breath, then lets it out in a huff, eyeing me as if measuring my determination. "You use that move I showed you when you were attacked?" he asks.

"I couldn't. I was attacked from behind this time."

He sighs. "Fine. We'll work on that next." When I clap, he glares again. "Next week."

"But—"

"NO BUTS, NORA. You are not training this week. Do you want to kill yourself? You may think you feel fine, but your body needs time to recover and regenerate."

I get what he's saying, but I honestly *do* feel fine. I'm not just saying that. I feel like I've been speed healing. I'm stronger today, recovered. I can't explain it, but I *swear* I've healed. Still, there will be no convincing Rook.

"Fine. No training. I guess I'll see you next week."

I stomp out of the gym. I'm being a brat, but I can't help it. I was almost killed twice, and I couldn't do a damn thing about it. That's not a great feeling.

I don't get far before Rook calls out to me. "Nora, wait."

I whirl around, hopeful. "Yes?"

Rook is staring at me, rubbing the back of his neck.

"Well, you're already here," he says. I think this means he's giving in, and my face lights up. "Damn it, woman, don't look at me like that. We're not training." And cue my face fall...and his sigh. "I was just going to say that since you're here, you might as well stay for a while. If you want, we can walk—slowly—over to my place, and I'll cook you a steak."

Every wolf in the gym—and there are a large handful—gasps. I frown at all their gawking. Why is that so weird? Is it because I'm human? Wulf said shifters generally like humans. And it's true they aren't glaring—well, one woman is—but the other men aren't. They're just shocked. I decide to ignore them, and I pat my stomach. "Thanks. I could use the walk, but you don't have to cook for me. I already ate lunch."

Rook smiles, seeing that I've given up my pouting. "You need the protein. Think you can eat more?"

Well, if he's going to continue to offer... I grin. "I can always eat more. Especially if it's a nice, juicy steak."

He matches my smile and cocks his head toward the gym exit. I fall into step beside him, and we both ignore the stares as we head out of the clubhouse at a casual stroll.

Rook passes me his track jacket the second we set foot outside. He'd told me to come for my sessions in shorts and a sports bra so that I could move easier and he could see the way I was moving my body. He swore it was a training thing. But I flat-out refused, and we compromised on stretchy yoga pants and a clingy T-shirt, so that's what I'm wearing right now. I accept his jacket happily and zip it up to my chin.

It's a nice day—sunny—but it's a little chilly. Fall is in full swing, and if Michigan has a best quality, it's fall. The air is crisp, and the trees are in full autumn bloom. The entire compound is a canvas of vibrant greens, oranges, yellows, and reds.

The walk is revitalizing, and just what I need. Rook must see how much I'm enjoying myself, because he walks in silence, allowing me to take it all in. He's a very comfortable walking companion.

In the silence, my phone chimes at me. I have a feeling I know who it is, and I don't want to talk to him, so I ignore it. Rook cuts me a sideways glance, and I just shrug. He lets it go without comment.

We pass through most of the community, and the gasps, stares, and whispers keep coming from every wolf we pass. You'd think they've never seen Rook with a girl before, but the guy is freaking hot. And nice. And dominant. Which I know is big in the werewolf world. Wulf claimed Rook doesn't date, but I have a hard time believing he *never* dates.

Rook lives on the very outskirts of the community next to the river and up against the park. His home is a modest one-story, light gray with blue trim and shutters, and he has a sprawling lawn. There are no fenced yards in the compound, so I can see a giant wooden deck built off the back of the house that wraps around the side.

Instead of going inside, he leads me around the side of the house and up the steps onto the deck. I whistle. The deck is huge and has a view of both the river and the park. He's got a grill and a patio table in one corner and a set of couches around a built-in fire pit. It's a *nice* deck. "Wow. You've got quite the spread here."

He grins, not a shred of humility. "Thanks. I built it myself. I don't like to be indoors much."

"You *built* this?"

Now he does shrug modestly. "I'm good with tools."

He turns on the grill and then disappears into the house through a wide sliding glass door. I take a seat on one of the couches, and seconds later he calls out, "I have red wine, beer, Coke, milk, and water."

"Water or Coke is fine, thanks!"

"The fire pit's gas. There's a switch on the side, if you want a fire."

I've never seen an actual gas fireplace, so I turn on the fire. I can't believe it dances to life literally as easy as the flip of a switch. It's somehow not warm the way a wood fire is, and it doesn't smell like one, but it's still pretty, so I sit back and stare into the flames.

My phone dings again. I break down and look at the messages. Sure enough, they're both from Parker.

Parker: I understand you're angry with my clan, but I really need to speak with you. Will you at least call me?

Parker: If you're ignoring me because of Josephine, please remember she was one vampire out of many. Nora, what can I do to make this right? Please tell me.

I sigh. He doesn't deserve to be ignored like this. Losing the battle with my conscience, I respond.

Nora: I'm sorry. It has nothing to do with Henry or Josephine. I don't blame you for their actions. I just don't think us seeing each other is a good idea. You want more from me than I can give you.

He answers immediately.

Parker: You want it, too; you're just scared. You don't need to be afraid of me. I would never hurt you.

I'm not afraid of him hurting me. Not exactly. I'm afraid of losing control with him.

A long whistle over my shoulder makes me nearly jump out of my skin. "Rook!" I drop my phone in my lap and quickly scoop it back up. "Shit! You scared the crap out of me!"

The man is leaning over the couch behind me, shamelessly reading my texts. He's got a couple of Cokes in one hand and a plate with two steaks on it in the other. I pull my phone to my chest and glare at him. "Nosy much?"

Rook laughs. "Yes." He hands me one of the Cokes and cheerfully says, "Who's Parker? I thought you didn't date," as he makes his way to the grill.

"He's a vampire in the Detroit clan. And I *don't* date. Hence, the slightly desperate texts. I don't think he's ever been turned down before. He doesn't seem to know how to give up."

"Parker…Parker…" After placing the steaks on the grill, he turns around to face me with wide eyes and a gaping jaw. "Parker *Reed?* Henry Stadther's chief enforcer?"

I nod. "That would be the one."

He whistles again.

"Tell me about it."

While he's still blinking in disbelief, I finally notice the apron he's wearing. It says *All this…and I can cook, too.* I laugh, and when I point at the apron, Rook looks down at his chest and rolls his eyes. He stares me down for a minute, as if debating whether to let me change the subject, but then, thankfully, lets the topic of Parker drop. "It was a Christmas gift from Wulf one year. That man is worse than a meddlesome old lady. He's determined to see me mated off. Never mind that he's so scared of pack females he'd rather live as a lone wolf in the city."

I smile at that. True, Wulf often rants about the pushiness and clinginess of pack females, but it seemed to me the last time I was here that romance isn't the only thing Wulf dislikes about pack living. "Aw, I think Wulf's happy living the way he does. He really does strike me as a bit of a lone wolf. You should have seen him on the drive here the other day."

"I'm sure." Rook shakes his head with a chuckle. "I can't believe he came back."

Rook snaps his mouth shut and turns to the grill, as if suddenly remembering that setting him up with me was the reason for Wulf's return. I try to break the awkward silence.

"So, can I ask you something?"

"Shoot." His word is friendly, but he sounds wary and keeps his face to the grill instead of me.

"Okay, so packs are ranked, right? Like the alpha is the most dominant, and the second strongest is his beta, and so on...?"

His whole body sags with relief at the change of topic, and he gives me a cheerful, "Yup. The books get that part right."

"But you're more dominant than Alpha Toth, aren't you?

Wulf is, too, right? If I ranked you all, I'd place you first, Wulf second, and Alpha Toth third. What am I missing?"

Rook closes the lid on the grill and turns to gape at me, slack-jawed and bug-eyed. "You can feel dominance?"

"I didn't realize I wasn't supposed to."

Rook comes over to sit on the couch near me. "Most non-shifters can't, and humans never."

I shrug, vulnerability washing over me. "I'm a bit of a psychic. Maybe that's why. I can feel magic, too, and Terrance told me humans don't feel that, either."

"They don't." Rook shakes his head, eyeing me like I'm something special.

I squirm under his gaze, hating that I'm different, yet again, and turn the conversation back on him once more. "So, I'm right? You're the strongest? How come you aren't alpha, then? What's your place in the pack?"

Rook sighs and then goes back to the grill to flip the steaks. "It's a long story. How do you like your steak?"

"Medium rare. And we have to have something to talk about while we eat, right?"

Rook slides me a wry glance.

When the steaks are done, we move to the patio table and I give him a look. I'm still waiting. "You are relentless, aren't you, woman?"

I just grin.

"Oh, all right. I used to be alpha."

My brows shoot up. I hadn't expected that.

Rook grimaces at my look and shrugs. "Our father—Wulf's and mine—was the previous alpha of the pack.

Our great-grandfather was the one who started it when the Detroit area pack split into two. Wulf and I were both groomed from the time we were born. Wulf always hated the leadership, but I was good at it. I think everyone was relieved when I turned out to be more dominant. Just before I was ready to take over for my father, I found my mate."

I almost spit my drink out. "You were *mated?*"

Rook chuckles. "Is it really so hard to believe?"

I blush and shake my head. "No, of course not, but… you just seem so adamant about not dating."

His face crumples, and I know immediately what happened. "Rook…I'm so sorry."

He forces a pained smile at me. "Lilly was everything to me. We were mated for nearly forty years."

I choke on my food. "*Forty years!* How old are you? You look thirty, at best!"

Rook rears back, startled by my outburst, then throws his head back and laughs so loudly we catch the attention of all the wolves using the park or enjoying the river. Then again, the number of wolves in view has nearly doubled since we got here, so they may have already been spying on us. But now they're openly staring.

"Sorry," Rook says, trying to calm his laughter. "I thought you knew about shifters' life spans."

"Hu-uh. Just how long is it?"

"Wolves live to be around three hundred."

"Whoa."

"Yeah. I'm one hundred fourteen, so that'd be closer to thirty-five, in human terms."

The man was one hundred fourteen years old. It took everything in me to play it cool. "Huh." I blatantly ogled him for a moment, then said, "Well, you look great for your age, old man."

Rook burst into laughter again.

When he quieted down, he seemed ready to talk about his mate without falling apart, because he continued his story without my having to ask. "So, like I said, Lilly and I were mated for forty years, and though that's not necessarily a long time to a werewolf, we were mated young, and we were happy together. Soon after we were mated, my parents stepped down, and Lilly and I became the alpha pair. Thirty years ago, there was a vampire uprising in Detroit. A couple different clans who were having trouble with rogue shifters decided they were going to rid the area of all shifters. My pack was the largest and the strongest, so they attacked us first.

"We had no warning, and we were massively outnumbered. It was a slaughter. Over half of my pack was killed before we stopped them, including my parents and Lilly."

I gasp, completely caught up in the story.

He swallows, and it takes him a moment to speak again. His voice falls to a mere whisper. "I was devastated after the battle. Completely broken."

"I can imagine," I murmur.

"I blamed myself. I was Alpha. I was supposed to protect my pack. Instead, my pack was torn apart, and three of the people I cared for most in the world were dead."

"It wasn't your fault. You had no reason to think that

vampires wanted to wipe out your pack. It was completely unprovoked and without warning."

Rook looks at me for a long time but says nothing to my comment. After eating a few more bites of his steak in silence, he finally says, "I couldn't be in charge anymore after that. Back then, I couldn't live with myself. I was going to go off on my own, like Wulf had years before. Toth was my beta at the time. I handed the pack over to him and tried to leave.

"I roomed with Wulf for a year or so, but Peter came looking for me. He'd always been my best friend. He knew how much I still needed the pack. I'm not like my brother. I'm a social creature. Being a lone wolf was turning me dark. I would have eventually gone rogue. I'm not sure if Wulf called Peter for help, or if Peter came looking for me on his own, but he convinced me to come back.

"I refused to take the alpha position from him, but I swore my loyalty to him as alpha, so he let me stay despite my dominance over him. I don't really fit into the pack now. I'm a bit of a misfit."

I snort. If anyone knows about being a misfit, it's me. Rook smiles, knowing exactly what I'm thinking. "People still like me well enough, though," he says. "I'm basically the pack handyman now, and Peter uses me as a special advisor. He's still my best friend. He tries to convince me to take the pack back every now and then—says I'm better suited for the job than he is—but I haven't been able to bring myself to do it. Can't seem to get back in the saddle after Lilly, either. No matter how much Wulf tries to push me back up on the horse."

Conversation dies until we finish our dinner. I help him with the dishes and notice a couple of women growl and glare at me when I enter Rook's house. Again, I wonder if it's because I'm human. Is hanging out with me some kind of werewolf faux pas, and Wulf just lied to me so I'd spend time with Rook and let him train me?

Rook washes and I dry. As he hands me a dish, I finally bring it up, because people are trying to spy on us from the park through Rook's sliding glass door. I throw as much sarcasm into my voice as I can and say, "Don't look now, but I think we're being watched."

When we both glance out the window, our lookie-loos scamper off. Rook chuckles as he hands me a plate. "I was wondering if you would notice."

"Oh, I noticed the second we left the gym. Is it because I'm human? Wulf says you guys are friendly toward humans, but after I learned he was only trying to hook us up, I'm not sure I want to believe anything the meddlesome bastard says."

Rook laughs again. He does that a lot for a guy who's been through so much. He's a lot like Wulf that way. For a loner, Wulf is one cheerful werewolf. "It's not because you're human," he finally admits. "It's because you're hanging out with me. I may be well liked in the pack, but I'm not the most social. I'm polite and friendly to everyone, but I keep to myself as much as possible. Peter's really my only friend."

"Huh. I wouldn't have expected that."

He shrugs. "It's awkward not having a real rank within the pack. Guys are on edge around me because I used to be their alpha, and the women…" He shakes his head and shudders. It's the exact same gesture Wulf does whenever he talks about pack females. "They can't help themselves. They have an instinct to mate, and their wolves are attracted to power."

"Then that must make you the pack's most eligible bachelor."

When Rook grimaces, I snicker. "So, werewolves are the jealous type?" I ask, realizing that all the glares came from females, while the men only looked curious.

"Jealous," Rook agrees, "and possessive."

"So I should watch my back on the walk to my car, then?"

"No. I'll walk you, but you'd be fine even if I didn't. No one could challenge you unless I turned you and announced a mate pairing. Come on, the kitchen's clean enough. Let's get you back so you can go home and rest."

I groan but follow him good-naturedly back toward the clubhouse and my car. "What do you mean, no one could challenge me? Do you mean fight me? Like your beta fought Wulf?"

Rook nods, like it's no big deal. "It's a werewolf thing. Once a mate pairing is announced, wolves can challenge the mated pair—the females for the right to take the female's place, and males to challenge the male's place."

I stumble to a stop. "Wait. Two people announce they essentially want to get married, and other people can fight them for the right to marry their lover instead?" Rook nods. "That's awful. Why would anyone want to mate with someone who hurt their lover in a fight?"

"They proved they're stronger—a better match."

"That's messed up. What about love?"

Rook sighs. "It's hard to explain, but shifters have two different personalities—the human and the wolf. When it comes to mates, the wolf instinct is stronger than the human desires. Wolves mate with the strongest eligible pack member. If your wolf doesn't agree to the pairing…" He shrugs again, a helpless gesture. "The pairing won't work out."

That's insane, and I shake my head to let him know I think so. "Still, that sounds whacked."

"It doesn't happen often," Rook agrees a bit sheepishly. "Most werewolves want their human side to be as happy as their wolves. But it's always a possibility. Peter and his luna are that way. Marie was the next strongest female after my Lilly. When I gave up the alpha spot, Marie challenged Peter's girlfriend for the luna spot and won. Peter accepted the pairing because an alpha needs the strongest female to be his luna, but it was hard for all of them for a while. Peter's lover eventually left the pack when Peter and Marie were mated."

"Wow. So Alpha Toth just let his girlfriend go and mated the luna, even though they don't love each other?"

Rook shrugs. "I think they do, now. When wolves accept each other, they can have a strong influence on their human sides."

"Huh." I blink a few times and shove my hands into the pockets of Rook's jacket. It's hard to imagine having another spirit inside me and having to reconcile with its instincts.

"Learn something new every day. Werewolves are strange creatures."

Rook laughs. "I guess it's a good thing we're not dating."

I smirk. "I guess so."

We finish our walk in companionable silence. When we get to my car, I shrug awkwardly. "Well…this is my stop."

I start to take off his jacket, but he stops me. "Keep it. Give the busybodies around here some good rumors to spread," he says with a wink.

I snort, but push the zipper back up. "As if they don't have enough gossip fodder already?" I slide into my car. "Thanks for making me lunch. Well, second lunch. I feel like a hobbit, but it tasted great."

Rook grins. "You're welcome. Now, go home and take it easy. I don't want to see you back here until Sunday for the pack social. We're *not* training this week." He means business, so I don't argue. His jaw relaxes when I nod. "Meet me at my house, and we'll walk over to the social together." I cock a brow at him, and he shakes his head. "Trust me, you don't want to show up to the social alone. They'll swarm you."

Yeah, I don't want to be swarmed by werewolves, no matter how friendly—or not so friendly, in the women's cases—they may be. "Your place it is. See you Sunday."

CHAPTER
NINE

SUNDAY COMES TOO QUICKLY. I'M A LITTLE NERVOUS FOR MY first werewolf party. So far, as a whole, I've really liked werewolves, but it's like they're all extreme extroverts. Haven't met one yet that wasn't energetic, outgoing, fun, flirty, and intense. Even Wulf—the lone wolf—is still extroverted. He just doesn't like other wolves. Get him around anyone else, and he's the life of the party.

I'm not shy, but nor am I an extrovert. Little wallflower me is going to be strung out by the end of the night. I can just sense it. Even the guy in the guard shack as I enter the compound tells me his name is John and asks me to save him a dance tonight.

The party is held in the large multipurpose room in the pack's clubhouse. There're no decorations, just a stage at one end where a DJ has a nice setup, and there's room to dance on the floor in front of the stage. The other half of the room is filled with tables and chairs, where families and friends are eating and socializing. There are buffet tables lining the back wall piled with food. The party seems to be potluck style, with the exception of the hot dogs and cheeseburgers they're bringing inside from some sliding glass doors that open to an outside picnic area.

I'm glad I meet Rook at his house instead of showing up to the social alone, because when we get there, the party is in full swing and every pair of eyes looks my way when we walk in. There are almost five hundred wolves here, from babies to elderly, and every single one of them stops what they're doing to openly gawk at me. That they're all smiling doesn't make me feel better about the staring.

Maya dissolves the awkward tension by breaking away from the group of people she was talking to and shooting straight for me, squealing my name. "Nooooorrrrraaaa!"

I brace for the tackle hug, but Maya is so strong that if Rook didn't reach out and steady me when he did, we would tumble to the ground. "Easy on the human, Maya," he growls.

Maya blushes under the reprimand and lets me go. "Sorry. I keep forgetting you're so fragile," she says to me. Her grin quickly comes back. "I'm so glad you made it. I've got a ton of people to introduce you to." She elbows me and winks. "Everyone's interested in the woman who saved my life and got Wulf to come home, even if temporarily."

She grabs my hand, and her thoughts immediately swarm me. She doesn't just have a list of people to introduce me to; she's been talking me up to all of the pack's single males. She likes me—likes how brave I was when we were captured last month—and hopes to find me a mate within the pack so that I'll join. I hate to burst her bubble, but that's not going to happen, for several reasons. Still, for this job, I do need to be social, and I couldn't have thought up a better plan than to have someone else throwing me at a number of dance partners.

"Hang on a minute, Maya," Rook says, grabbing the hood of my jacket before Maya can successfully sweep me away. "Alpha Toth wants to introduce her to the luna, and *I* get the first dance."

Maya pouts, but it's playful, and she hands me back over to my escort. "Oh, all right. But don't hog her all night. She's my friend, too, and I promised I'd introduce her to a few people."

Rook snorts, as if he knows Maya's plan without needing to read her mind. He drags me away without promising her anything. "I don't know whether I should thank you or yell at you for acting like you own me," I tease Rook as we make our way to the stage, where Alpha Toth is standing with his mate.

Alpha Toth is talking to someone who has a clipboard and is saying something while pointing toward the food. He's wearing designer jeans and a nice button-down shirt, and is holding hands with a beautiful blonde woman wearing a warm smile and a short black cocktail dress. The handsome couple makes me feel underdressed in my jeans and hoodie. "You said this was casual," I mutter to Rook, who's got my hand tucked in his arm like some old-fashioned gentleman.

Rook chuckles. "I said casual, not sloppy."

I scoff, but he has a point. "For your information, I have on a nice halter-top blouse that Cecile picked out for me under the hoodie. And my hair is down, for once, *thank you very much.*"

Rook looks at me with an envy-worthy cocked eyebrow that I immediately find annoying. "And you're wearing the hoodie because…?" he asks.

"Hello. It was cold outside. We humans don't have the same inner heater you werewolves do."

He sighs as he leads me up onto the stage beside the alpha and the luna. "All right, fine, you're excused, but hand it over." He holds out his hand to me, waiting for me to give up the hoodie, and my stomach drops. I know I need to glean some thoughts from these people, and I can only do that by skin-to-skin contact, but knowing that and being ready to do it are completely different.

"Come on, take it off." Rook shocks me by leaning in so close to me that his lips brush my ear. He rubs his cheek against mine and says, "You were the one who said you'd need to show a little skin to get good reads on people, or whatever."

I gasp when he lifts the bottom of my hoodie up, forcing my arms into the air. He slowly raises the hoodie over my head, caressing my sides as he works it off, and tosses it aside, all while giving me a heated gaze, as if we're in a bedroom about to get naughty. The move is sensual and so full of tension that it makes my body shiver and my face flush.

My eyes grow so wide they begin to hurt. Rook has

just marked me with his scent and sort of undressed me in front of the entire pack. Rook's mouth twitches, snapping me out of my shock, and I immediately punch him on the arm. "Rook!" Everyone in the room laughs—Rook most of all. I hadn't realized they were all still watching us. My face turns bright red. I lean in and hiss at him. "I can't believe you just did that! That is *beyond* giving them something to gossip about."

Rook nods, unrepentant. "That was the point."

"What? Since when are you a possessive douche?"

That earns me another laugh—from the crowd and Rook. "Sweetheart, I'm a werewolf. We're all cavemen when it comes to women." The room chuckles again, and Rook lowers his voice a little. "Sorry. My wolf is close to the surface with you around so many unmated males. That was all him."

I stand back and eye him skeptically. "I thought you don't date."

"I don't. But my wolf senses your dominance. He can't help himself. And it doesn't help that even my human side feels protective of you. Wulf told me how you're very wary around men. *With good reason*, he said." Rook looks out over the crowd, narrowing his eyes at a few people. "Wolves can be…enthusiastic. I just want to make sure any man interested in you is a little more reserved than normal. Trust me, with my scent on you and a public display of intimacy, any man who wants you will think twice before making a move on you now. They'll be too afraid of the competition."

"Too afraid you'll rip them apart for touching me, you mean."

Rook gives me a proud smile that is all wolf. "Exactly."

Inside, I'm really grateful, but I can't say that to him with everyone in the room subtly listening to our conversation. "Well," I say, huffing a little in exasperation, "I appreciate the thought, but isn't the point of being here tonight to get to know people? No one is going to come near me at all now."

Rook laughs again, waving his hand to point out several men hovering nearby with curiosity written all over their faces. "Oh, that's not true at all," he says. "I haven't deterred most of them, I just sort of slowed them down. Besides, Maya seems determined to mate you off by the end of the night."

I cringe, and am caught by the alpha and luna who have finally come over to join our conversation. "Would that be so terrible," Alpha Toth asks, his expression not quite offended, but almost, "being mated to one of my wolves? Joining the pack?"

I force a smile. "Not necessarily. The joining the pack part, anyway. You wolves are a fun, friendly lot. But I don't know if I'm ready to sprout fur—no offense—and I'm definitely not ready for a mate. I don't date for a reason, Alpha Toth, but rest assured it has nothing to do with your wolves."

Alpha Toth eyes me a moment before relenting. "Well, stick around and have some fun. We may convince you eventually. If you do find a man who catches your eye"—his gaze darts, embarrassingly, to Rook—"just know that such a union would be most welcome."

He winks and puts his arm proudly around his mate.

"Nora, I'd like you to meet Marie. The pack's luna, and my mate."

Unlike some of the single female pack members I've seen so far, the luna smiles at me with genuine kindness. She seems pleased that I'm here. When she shakes my hand, I confirm her sincerity. *Such a pretty little thing, and so dominant. She would be a higher-ranking wolf. Peter is right; she would make a fine addition to the pack.*

After quick introductions are made, and some small talk, Rook pulls me away, claiming I owe him a dance. The second he does, the DJ stops the song that's playing and starts a slow song. It can't be coincidence. The DJ is smiling playfully my way. He gives me a wink before sending a subtle nod to his ex-alpha, Rook.

I groan, and Rook laughs before hoping off the stage and holding his hands out, offering to help me down. I let him lift me to the floor, but I complain the whole time, so it isn't exactly romantic. "Is everyone in your pack determined to embarrass me?"

Rook moves me onto the small dance floor and begins waltzing me around in slow circles. People stop to watch us like we're the bride and groom at a wedding. "Nah, werewolves are just hopeless matchmakers, and I think a lot of them hope I'll find another mate again someday."

"That's sweet of them, really, but don't any of them care that we both said we didn't plan to date?"

"And yet, here we are on the dance floor."

Rook smirks, spins me in a circle, and then pulls me close, tightening his grip on me. If I couldn't hear his thoughts, and they weren't completely focused on wondering how I could point out the man from my vision without giving us away, I'd be worried by how flirty he's being. But the truth is, Rook's just a good actor. He's also enjoying being able to dance with a woman and not having to worry that she's expecting a mate bond at the end. I laugh at that thought and relax, allowing him to twirl me around the dance floor. The man's right, after all. I never get to enjoy a worry-free dance, either.

"So," I say, after our dance is over, "why don't you introduce me to a few people before Maya steals me away? I happen to like tall, muscular men with brown hair and brown eyes." I scan the crowd and spot the man from my vision. I don't just want to single him out, so I point at several men who meet my description. "Like that guy, or him, or…*him*."

Rook shoots me a sharp glance, and I give him a subtle nod. *Yes. That's our guy.*

"Him?" Rook asks incredulously.

I'm surprised by his shock. "Definitely. What's wrong with that guy?"

Rook shakes his head. "Nothing. He's just…"

"Just one of the most submissive wolves in the pack," Maya says, shamelessly butting into our conversation.

"What's wrong with a submissive wolf?" I ask, offended on the guy's behalf. "He's probably sweet, and he'd probably do anything for the woman he loves."

"He's a big pushover," Maya corrects.

"Whatever." I wave at Rook as I let Maya drag me off. "I think he's gorgeous."

Maya huffs. "Woman, you'd be wasted on a guy like that. You're too dominant for him. You're a fighter. I've seen you in action, remember? You need a real man. Come on, I've got a few in mind."

The next hour is exhausting. Maya pushes me into the arms of what feels like half the pack. The number of men that want to dance with me even though I'm human surprises me. I guess Wulf really wasn't kidding about them not having a problem with my kind. Several of them even ask if I'm considering applying for transformation. I leave it vague but tell them Alpha Toth already gave me permission, if I should decide I want to.

Dancing and keeping up conversation with them all is hard to do while listening to all of their thoughts. It's the hardest task I've ever tried to do with my powers yet. If helping people out like this is going to become a thing, I need more practice using and controlling my powers. I'm going to have to stop being afraid of them.

I barely finish a song, and am going to try and make my way to the food, when Alpha Toth's beta catches me by the elbow. "Well, little human, seems you've danced with everyone else. How about you give me the honor next?"

This is the man who challenged Wulf. I can tell without touching him that he likes me just as much as he likes Wulf—whom he attacked. Either that, or he's just a condescending asshole to everyone. That's a good possibility. "I suppose." I force a sugary sweet smile and take his offered hand. "If you really want to."

"Of course I do."

He takes me into his arms just in time for me to hear him think, *Time to see what all the hype is about.* The music morphs into another slow song, so Jeffrey begins to move me around the floor with as much expertise as the others—werewolves sure can dance. "Are you enjoying the party so far?"

"Sure. I usually prefer things quiet, but your pack has been very friendly."

She's as dominant as everyone says. Probably stronger than Maya. She'd be an alpha female. Just what the hell is Rook up to? Or is it Wulf she's working with? Maybe the three of them are working together. "Especially Rook, eh? He seems *very* friendly."

The smile on his face turns hard, as if he's clenching his jaw beneath it and trying not to glare at me. What a lovely man. I've received questions about Rook all night, and I've been quick to explain we're only friends, but I keep it vague this time, hoping to draw out his thoughts and figure out why he's suspicious of Rook and me. He can't know what we're really up to…unless he's Mr. McSneaky's accomplice. That's a good possibility. He'd have all the right access to the accounts and stuff as Toth's second. "Rook's been great."

His jaw definitely clenches this time. "So you like him?"

"What's not to like?"

He's a coward, for one. He deserted his clan when they needed him the most and left us in Peter's hands. Peter, who is also a coward because he wouldn't take care of Rook and Wulf properly, and who isn't strong enough to lead this pack the way it should be led. "You could do better."

I hate this man's thoughts. Rook was broken after the

battle and after losing his parents and mate. Stepping down when he knew he needed to wasn't cowardly; it was brave. I could tell from our one conversation that it had been hard for him to do.

I'm also shocked by his words. I could do better? Than Rook? Is he talking about himself? Is he flirting with me? "Let me guess," I say dryly. Jeffrey pushes me out, spins me, and pulls me close again. I give him my best smirk when he wraps his arm around me again. "I could do better with *you*?"

"Rook may be dominant, but he doesn't have a real place in the pack. He's a glorified handyman. I'm the pack's beta." *For now.* "I could give you a good life." *And you could make a strong luna when I finally take over the pack. Much stronger than that stuck-up bitch Maya.*

Whoa. Wait. WHAT? He plans to take over the pack? Could the missing money have something to do with that? Could he be planning to hire help for his hostile takeover? And what about the other guy? Is he a willing partner in this crime, or someone being coerced? It would fit the vision I had. The guy was so nervous, after all.

It takes everything in my power to hold my smile and not let him know I'm onto his thoughts, but I can't concentrate the rest of the dance. Our conversation dies, and he assumes my silence is because I'm considering his offer. He pulls me uncomfortably close, as if we're already lovers, and when the song ends, he grabs my hand before I can escape.

His eyes turn toward the doors, and his thoughts race. *I can't claim her without her consent. Rook would challenge me on principal. But if I could convince her to choose me, Rook is honorable… Perhaps she's been telling the truth all night, and they aren't romantically involved. Maybe he wouldn't challenge me if she didn't want him. I just need to win her over. I could use someone so well liked by the pack on my side. She's a hero to them. They would follow her.* "Would you like to go outside and take a break for a bit—get some fresh air?"

That sounds heavenly, but not with you, I think. I pull my hand from his and give him a smile I hope he can't tell is fake. "I'd love to, but I'd freeze outside right now, and I'm technically Rook's date to this party. I wouldn't want to hurt his feelings by sneaking off with another guy. Thank you for the dance, though. It was nice meeting you."

I take off before he can say anything. I don't think I'd be able to keep myself from telling him off if he tried to argue. Rook isn't hard to find. In fact, he's so easy to find, I have a feeling he's been subtly hovering all night. "How's it going?" he asks. His smile is pleasant, but his question is loaded. His eyes keep drifting to Jeffrey, as if I've given something away of my thoughts. Or perhaps Rook was already suspicious of Jeffrey.

"I'm exhausted. Is there someplace quiet we could go hang out for a bit? I need a breather."

"Of course. Follow me." He holds out his arm to me, and once again we start strolling about like a couple in a Jane Austen novel.

Instead of leading me outside where I would freeze and there are other wolves mingling about, Rook takes me through the empty clubhouse, down a dark hall past Alpha Toth's office, and then past the accounting office, until finally we come to a door marked MAINTENANCE. Rook unlocks the door, and before me is either a small office or a large supply closet. It's probably the same size as the accounting office, but it's so cluttered with tools and random parts to things that saying it's cozy inside is being generous. "This is your office?" I ask as he clears a pile of junk off the desk chair.

He pats the chair, gesturing for me to have a seat. "Home, sweet home."

I sit in the chair, and he rests his butt against the desk that's also cluttered to high heaven. "I suppose it's a good thing you're the handyman and not the janitor."

Rook snorts. "I keep it like this so people are afraid to come in here. A lot of the wolves around here still think of me as their alpha and come to me with problems they should take to Peter. Having an office like this reminds them I'm not the alpha anymore. And hey, soundproof walls, so speak freely."

I smirk. "Thought I just did."

He shakes his head and chuckles again. "I can see why Wulf likes you. He's always had a thing for sass."

"Then why'd he try to pawn me off on you?"

Rook's mouth twitches at the corners. "Because I like sass even more."

I roll my eyes. "So about Jeffrey..."

Rook laughs at my obvious subject change.

There's a quick knock on the office door, and then Alpha

Toth slides in. "I can't stay long."

"We shouldn't, either," Rook says, indicating himself and me.

Both men look to me. I don't have great news, so I take a deep breath and just blurt it out. No sense beating around the bush. "So Jeffrey's planning to take over the pack."

I don't get the response I expect. Rook rolls his eyes, and Alpha Toth sighs.

"Are we not taking this seriously, then?" I ask.

Rook lets his alpha explain. "Jeffrey is ambitious. He's always wanted to lead the pack. He's challenged me twice before. Don't worry, he can't beat me, or he would have by now."

I shake my head. "That's fine and dandy and all, but this felt different. He was suspicious of Rook and me. He thinks we're up to something. And I don't know how to describe it exactly, but his thoughts felt solid. He felt like he had a plan."

Rook pulls his shoulders back, blinking at me. "His *thoughts?*"

My face turns red as I cringe. "Busted."

"You're a mind reader?" Alpha Toth asks, eyes wide. "You hear actual thoughts?"

I sigh. "When I make skin-to-skin contact, yes, I hear thoughts and sense feelings. But that is very dangerous information, so I appreciate you both forgetting you know it."

Both men frown at me. I raise my hands in surrender. "I know you won't tell anyone. I just hate people knowing that.

It's not a talent people are fond of."

"It's a helpful one, though," Alpha Toth says.

"Yes and no. I only get surface thoughts and feelings. I can't just dig around in someone's head. So I can't necessarily find out if Jeffrey is Hottie McMoney Thief's accomplice unless I straight up ask, and I can't do that without raising suspicions. More suspicions. All I can tell you is that he is planning to take over the pack, and that he feels very confident it's going to happen."

"Hottie McMoney Thief?" Rook snorts. "Really?"

I groan. "Again, focusing on the wrong information here. I need to find out more. I may need to talk to Jeffrey again, though he gives me the creeps. And I really need to spend some time with—"

"Hottie McMoney Thief," Rook supplies with a grin.

"Yes."

"His name is Daniel McCrary."

"Well. I had the Mc part right, then." I stick my tongue out at Rook, and he laughs. "Fine. I need to talk to Daniel, but that means you have to keep Maya and the other wolves away from me for a while. No offense to your pack or anything, Alpha Toth, but those guys are acting like they've never seen a woman before, and they're starting to annoy me and piss off all your pack females."

Alpha Toth chuckles. "Ever heard the term *fresh meat?*"

"Gee, how charming."

Alpha Toth shrugs. "You're a novelty, and everyone's curious. Can't blame them for being interested in a beautiful, dominant, brave, sassy, confident woman who is rumored to be very powerful and saved the life of one of our pack's favorite females."

"Well, shit, when you say it like that, I feel like I need to be paraded around the complex on a float."

"Don't tempt me."

"We're getting off topic again. Have either of you considered that Jeffrey could be using the stolen money to buy help if he's not capable of taking you down himself? Or that Daniel may not be acting of his own free will? He did look scared shitless in my vision."

"Daniel always looks scared shitless," Rook says. "The man is spineless."

"Spineless enough to steal from the pack if he's being threatened by someone like Jeffrey?"

Alpha Toth's eyes flash, and he stands up straight. He's finally taking this theory seriously. "Possibly. As possible as Jeffrey stealing the money to pay mercenaries to take me out and using Daniel as a fall guy."

I scoff. "If Jeffrey is such a disloyal bastard, why is he your second?"

"He's the strongest wolf below me. That's pack way. Besides, having him close, I can keep my eye on him." His hands clench into fists, and he growls. His eyes start to glow faintly as his wolf rises to the surface. "Obviously, I'm not watching him closely enough."

"Hey, we'll get him," I say, trying to calm him down before he shifts in this tiny cluttered room and accidentally rips me up. "I'll help you guys with this until we know for sure, and then you can tear him apart, or whatever it is you wolves do."

Alpha Toth takes a deep breath, pushing his wolf back and calming his temper. His eyes focus on me, and his face softens. "Thank you for doing this, Nora."

I hold up a hand. "Hey. No worries. We've already been through the thanking. No need to do it again. I just want to help bring the creep down."

Alpha Toth nods. "Very well. I'll let you get back out there to do just that. Rook. Keep a close eye on her. If Jeffrey is suspicious of the two of you already, I don't want him getting too close to her where he can do something stupid."

Rook growls. "If he touches her, I'll kill him."

CHAPTER
TEN

WHEN WE GET BACK, THE PARTY IS STILL GOING STRONG. Some of the people with babies have gone home, but there are now more people dancing than before, and the laughter is louder.

I spot Daniel quickly. He's sitting at a table alone, watching the couples on the dance floor. I motion in his direction, and Rook nods subtly. We head for the buffet, and Maya stops us halfway there. "There you are!" she says. "I've been looking all over for you!"

"I took her out to rest someplace quiet," Rook says, thankfully not making it sound like innuendo. "You wore her out with all the dancing. I, however…" He grabs Maya's hand when she reaches for my arm to drag me away again. "…have not danced enough. Would you give me the honor, lovely Maya?"

Maya looks at me, torn, but then smiles at Rook.

"Absolutely. Let's go cut a rug, handyman."

I laugh. Maya is fun. My chuckle catches her attention, and she points at me with a warning glare. "Don't go anywhere."

"I'm just going to grab something to eat."

As soon as she and Rook turn their backs on me, I hightail it over to the buffet table. This is a bonus, because I'm starving. I quickly fill a plate with food—a double bacon cheeseburger and homemade mac 'n' cheese, with a couple of cookies on the side—and then sit down right next to Daniel. "Hey! Mind if I sit here?"

He looks startled to have company. Then again, maybe he's just surprised I sat so close to him. I'm practically touching him. I'm hoping for the opportunity to rub elbows—literally—with the guy while I eat. I laugh at the way he eyes the mound of food on my plate and shrug sheepishly. "You wolves sure know how to cook. This is delicious."

He loosens up at my friendliness and chuckles a little. "You eat like a wolf."

"I do when it tastes good."

He grins. "It always tastes good at a werewolf party. We like our food."

I shove another bite in my mouth and chew a bit while nodding. "I can tell. I may have to come to more of these things. As long as I can chill a little more next time. I'm exhausted."

Daniel's eyes move back to the dance floor. His gaze locks on Maya and Rook. I wait for the question about Rook and me, but it doesn't come. He says, "I've seen you dancing.

What's it been, an hour straight?"

I groan. "At least. I swear I've been through all the single males in the pack by now." I eye him with a raised brow. "Except you, it seems." I hold my hand out to him. "Hi. I'm Nora."

"Daniel. It's a pleasure to meet you." He smiles and shakes my hand. *Why is she talking to me?*

The thought isn't rude. His mental voice is laced with confusion and a hint of worry. I find the concern very interesting. Why would he be scared that I'm talking to him? He can't know what I'm up to. No one in the pack besides Rook and Alpha Toth knows what I can do.

"So, Daniel, what is it that you do for the pack?"

"Technically, my degree is in computer programming. I'd like to be a software developer, but there aren't any jobs like that available within our pack's territory—we're pretty rural out here. I've ended up being sort of an IT guy for the pack. I fix their computers, help them with new software, or viruses, or just whatever problems they're having. It's not glorious, but it's better than working at a fast food place or something."

Pack life never stops surprising me. "You can't commute out of pack territory for a job?"

Daniel cringes. "It's dangerous for someone as submissive as me. My wolf is pretty weak. If I came across a rogue, he'd attack just because he could. I couldn't really hold my own against a vampire, either, and they own the cities where the good paying programmer jobs would be."

He shrugs, as if it doesn't matter, but he sounds

disappointed. It's written on his face, too. I feel bad for the guy. I know how it feels to be a target, and to be the weak link in the world. "That's rough. What if you went to work for the FUA? They're always asking me to come work for them, and I'm basically useless. I'm sure they'd have need for a guy like you, and they'd be able to keep you safe there."

He perks up and falls deep into thought. I want to know what he's thinking, so I lean toward him enough to brush arms with him. The action is so subtle, and he's so lost in his own mind that he doesn't notice.

...great idea. As soon as we leave, I could apply at the Agency. If she doesn't kill me for talking to Nora, anyway. But I'm not flirting. We're just talking. And it's for our benefit. Nora sounds like she knows people at the FUA. Maybe she could get me an interview, or at least put in a good word for me.

I'm so shocked over the direction of his thoughts that I don't notice when he turns toward me to say something, and I forget to lean back in my own space. Daniel practically falls out of his chair when he realizes we're so close to each other. When he scrambles a few inches away, blushing and apologizing, I sigh. There go my chances to read his mind anymore. But I did glean a piece of the puzzle. I just don't know exactly what it means.

He's planning to leave the pack, and he's not going alone. I knew he had to have an accomplice, but what if it's not Jeffrey? Jeffrey wouldn't leave the pack. He wants to take it over. Maybe Daniel wants to leave because Jeffrey's using him. Or maybe it's unrelated. It sounded like he has a secret girlfriend. What if they're planning to leave together, and she's his accomplice? There's no way to know without asking.

Time to get my flirt on. I lean closer to Daniel, placing my hand on his arm, and say, "So how come such a smart, good-looking man is sitting alone tonight when there are so many single females in your pack?"

I wink at him, and his jaw drops. He looks around the room, as if he wonders who's playing the practical joke. "I'm serious," I say, letting my hand fall on top of his. "You seem nice, and you're friendly, and you look like you'd be quite a catch. Why don't you have a girlfriend?"

I do have a girlfriend. She's just too dominant for me, so our relationship has to stay secret. I wish it didn't. I'm sick of hiding it. When we leave, things will be different. If she doesn't kill me for this conversation first. I can't believe Nora is flirting with me. Out of all the guys she's had throwing themselves at her tonight. What's she doing here? How do I get her to go away without hurting her feelings?

He forces a smile at me and gently pulls his arm away from me. "It's because I'm too submissive," he says. "I'm one of the weakest wolves in the pack, and most of our females are strong. There's not anyone close to my dominance level."

I frown, suddenly grateful to his girlfriend for not being shallow even if she is making him keep the relationship secret. "So what?" I say. "My best friend is the shyest, sweetest guy on Earth. He's totally submissive, and I love the hell out of him. If you ask me, a submissive but considerate man is way better than a guy chock-full of dominance and ego. I'd date you over half the guys I just danced with in a heartbeat."

Several wolves growl. I look up, startled by the sound,

and am shocked to see that a few of the wolves I've danced with are hovering nearby and are now glaring at Daniel as if it's his fault I just insulted them. Daniel ducks his head a little, and his face pales with fear. This pisses me off so much. It's bad enough that all those cocky wolves don't respect Daniel just because he's not as dominant. But to try and scare him away from the one girl who's spoken to him all night? That's just rude.

"You know what?" I push my plate away. "I suddenly feel like dancing again." I glare at all the scowling werewolves as I grab Daniel's hand. "Come on, hot stuff. Let's dance."

My new plan is to flush out the girlfriend. If I've learned anything about werewolves, it's that they're all possessive and jealous. No female werewolf is going to stand around while I flirt with her man. And maybe if I can get him and the girl-friend together, I can figure out if their plan involves taking the money themselves, or if maybe Jeffrey is blackmailing them.

I grab Daniel's hand and drag him onto the dance floor. His thoughts are a conflicted mess running a mile a minute. *I can't say no. It'll offend the pack's honorary guest for the night. Do I even want to say no? I don't want to date Nora, but I've never been asked to dance at a social before. I don't have any feasible reason to say no, anyway. Not that anyone knows about. No one knows we're together. But she's going to kill me. She's going to kill Nora first, and then she's going to kill me.*

This is perfect...unless it's the stupidest thing I've ever done. It'll draw out Daniel's girlfriend, but it sounds like she's not a weak wolf, and she's not going to be happy with me. Strike that. She wants to murder me. I know I'm in danger, because the second I put Daniel's arms around me and start to sway, those warning tingles shoot up my spine like fire licking up tapestries. My skin explodes with goose bumps, and my gut rolls, until I'm forced to gasp.

"Nora? Are you all right?"

My knees buckle, which is actually good, sort of, because Daniel has to catch me and cradle me against him to keep me upright. But the feeling of foreboding is so strong I can't run. Not that I could outrun a pissed off werewolf anyway, but, you know, I'd at least like to try. "My hero," I tease Daniel, sagging my body against his. "Sorry. I guess I've done a little too much dancing this evening. Maybe you could take me someplace quiet, instead? We could get to know each other better?"

And that does it. Suddenly Daniel's arms clamp around me. "No! Wait!" he shouts, as a giant wolf parts the crowd heading straight for us—for me. His girlfriend does not feel like listening. She jumps at us, teeth first, and Daniel whirls us around, blocking me from the snapping jaw and taking the claws. "Maya, stop!"

Maya?

Daniel pushes me away, yelling, "Run, Nora!" as he turns around and tries to grab Maya to keep her from coming at me again.

I don't have time to run. Rook sweeps me away from the trouble at the same time Alpha Toth shifts and attacks the wolf that attacked me. Alpha Toth quickly subdues his out-of-control third. When he's got her in an obvious

I-could-kill-you-right-now position, he lets go of his grip on her throat and transforms back to human. "Shift!" he orders.

The command is so strong several people whimper, and a couple of the young teens actually turn into wolves. Maya shifts and jumps to her feet, as naked as Alpha Toth and just as unconcerned about it. She ignores her pissed off alpha and glares at me. "You bitch!" she screams. "I can't believe you! I introduced you to every available alpha male our pack has, and you had to go after the one man I told you to stay away from! I thought you were cooler than that."

I know it's ridiculous, because I'd been doing it on purpose to draw her out, but I feel the need to defend myself. "I *am* cooler than that. It's not like you told me you were dating him. I specifically said I was interested in him, and all you did was call him weak. What kind of a girlfriend does that?"

"I'm not his girlfriend, I'm his *mate!*"

I ignore the gasps of the shocked pack members, but Maya doesn't. She's at Daniel's side in a blink, looking for all her worth like she'd kill anyone who came near him. I don't get it, until the room erupts into growls and several men call out, "I challenge!"

And then I understand why they had to keep their relationship secret. It's like what Rook was saying might happen to me if I were turned and tried to mate with him. Only this is a hundred times worse, because Maya is third in the pack. She's the strongest female other than the luna, and she's mated to one of the weakest males.

Daniel is standing there, shoulders hunched, face pale and looking hopeless. But Maya shouts at all the men now gathering around her and Daniel. "NO!" she growls. "My wolf has accepted that I love him. We are happy. I will not choose another mate!"

"Challenge!"

"I challenge!"

The men in the crowd don't seem to care that Maya loves Daniel. Wolves may be a friendly lot, but they definitely have their issues.

Jeffrey, the creep, steps forward, glaring at Maya. He waves a hand at Daniel and sneers. "This is why you keep refusing me? *Him?* You can't say no once a challenge has been offered, and I was first. He has to fight me, and when I win, you're finally mine."

"No," Daniel says, shocking the entire pack. His voice and hands are shaking, but he squares his shoulders and says to Alpha Toth, "We choose to leave the pack."

Daniel and Maya share a look that tells me everything. Forget Jeffrey. Daniel and Maya stole the money together. They're confident that they'll be fine if they leave. More than that, they're ready. Daniel had thought they were leaving soon anyway. They couldn't do that without the proper funding to get them safely away from here.

They link hands, and Maya nods to Alpha Toth. "We choose to leave the pack. We'll go to the free territory and live as lone wolves."

"They can't do that!" Jeffrey roars. "I issued a challenge! He has to fight me!"

He pushes Daniel in the chest, and Maya steps between the two, as if she plans to rip Jeffrey apart.

Alpha Toth finally explodes. "ENOUGH! Maya and Daniel, in my office, *now*."

Everyone starts to move, but stops when Luna Marie says, "No. Let them enjoy their disgrace in front of the entire pack. We'll set an example to those who might consider going behind their alpha's and luna's backs in the future."

Alpha Toth looks annoyed, but he won't go against his luna in front of everyone. He sighs, as if the weight of the world is on his shoulders. And it is, really, or at least, the weight of his small world. He looks back and forth between Daniel and Maya and finally says, "All of this because you forged a mate pairing without my permission?"

Maya looks around the crowd, hating the public display as much as Alpha Toth, but she squares her shoulders and nods once. "Alpha, I'm sorry, but we had to. You saw what happened. I love him, sir. He's a good man. I don't want him hurt, and I have no desire to mate with anyone else, but the pack never would have let us be. I'm too strong."

"And you didn't think you could come to us for help?" Luna Marie asks, sounding devastated by the betrayal. "You're Peter's third-in-command, my right-hand woman. Do you know what kind of example this sets when our third sneaks around behind our backs? How weak of a leader it makes your alpha seem?"

Jeffrey scoffs, and Rook snarls at him for the disrespect. Alpha Toth silences them both with a glare.

"We're sorry, sir," Daniel says quietly, staring at his shoes. "We didn't know what else to do. You would have encouraged Maya to leave me."

Alpha Toth nods. "I would have, but only because I care about you both." When Daniel looks up, Alpha Toth adds, "You have a hard, dangerous road ahead of you." His eyes flash with anger. "If I let the two of you live, that is."

Maya and Daniel both stiffen. So do Jeffrey and Luna Marie. So does the whole room of onlookers, for that matter. Only Rook and I are completely at ease. But then, we know the real reason Alpha Toth is so pissed.

Luna Marie steps forward and places a comforting hand on Maya's shoulder, while I move slightly to stand beside Jeffrey. I get close enough to rub arms with him. He notices the touch and frowns at me. I just shrug and crane my neck, acting like I'm trying to see around him to get a better view. He smirks and, with a smarmy smile, moves me right in front of him where I can see everything and he can keep his hands on my bare shoulders. I want to slug him, but I've also accomplished my goal—I can hear his thoughts. He's seething at Maya and thinks she's despicable for wasting herself on Daniel. But now he's done wasting his time on her and has a new target—me. He's confident he can win my affections. The fact that I'm not pulling away from his touch right now is helping that sudden ego boost.

"Honey," Luna Marie says to Alpha Toth while I'm trying to listen to Jeffrey's thoughts, "I understand the slight they've caused you, but a secret mate pairing is hardly a capital offense. Perhaps banishment would be more appropriate?"

Maya sags, letting out a giant breath she's been holding. She gives Luna Marie a grateful smile, and the luna returns it with a sad one full of affection. Alpha Toth allows them their moment before nodding. "Yes, banishment would be appropriate if their *only* crime was a secret mate pairing."

Maya and Daniel both stiffen again. It's easy to see the truth. They've both gone pale and probably reek of fear. They know they've been caught and believe they're dead already. Daniel starts to tremble.

It's clear that Jeffrey isn't in on it, either. His thoughts are curious, not nervous. He's not worried they'll tattle on him; he's wondering what they've done.

Luna Marie frowns at her mate, and Alpha Toth sighs. He's come to the same conclusion I have about Maya and Daniel, but he looks to me with a question in his eyes. He's asking about Jeffrey. I shake my head once, and he nods his understanding.

Both Jeffrey and Luna Marie shoot me sharp looks. Jeffrey's wondering what the hell that look was for and how I'm involved with Alpha Toth. Luna Marie is probably thinking the same. I have a feeling their questions will be answered right now.

"I have evidence," Alpha Toth says to Daniel, "that you've been siphoning money out of pack funds for over a year." His wolf rises again, and he growls at Luna Marie through a clenched jaw. "What's the punishment for stealing from the pack?"

CHAPTER
ELEVEN

THERE'S NO SOUND IN THE LARGE MULTIPURPOSE ROOM filled with werewolves. Not even breathing. Everyone is watching the drama unfold, shocked and waiting to see what the alpha will do. But it's the luna who moves. Gone is her calm, sweet composure. In its place is outrage. She marches right up to Maya, looking as if the betrayal was personal, and slaps her sharply across the face. The hit is a hard one. Maya's head rocks from it and immediately begins to bruise.

Maya takes the beating in silence, her shoulders back and her head held high. Her eyes gloss over and her chin quivers, but no tears fall. Luna Marie is unmoved. "You were mine," she hisses. "You were my wolf, and you betrayed me first for this disgusting excuse for a wolf, and then you have the nerve to steal from me, too?" She surprises Maya with a hard punch to the gut that has her doubling over, gasping for breath. "How *dare* you!"

"Luna, *please*," Daniel whimpers. When the luna's attention whips his direction, his face drains of all color. His eyes flick to Maya, and he mumbles, "Have mercy."

"Mercy?" The luna laughs. It's a chilling sound that sends goose bumps down my spine. "Why don't you get on your knees and beg me for it?"

"Marie," Alpha Toth whispers in response to the luna's utter coldness.

"Daniel, no," Maya whispers.

She shakes her head frantically, but Daniel drops to the floor anyway. "Have mercy, Luna Marie. I beg of you." His fearful face becomes desperate. "You *have* to help us. Please. You are—"

Luna Marie lunges toward him with a roar and twists his head, snapping his neck before he can finish his plea. His body falls to the ground to the sound of Maya's scream. Her cry is so anguished. I feel sorry for her, even though she just tried to attack me. And even though she stole money from the pack.

"Damn it, Marie!" Alpha Toth snaps.

She whirls on him next. "Justice had to be carried out, and you weren't going to do it!"

"I would not have acted so brash, no. The alpha pair can't just go around killing their pack at will. That is not good leadership!"

Marie bristles at the reproach. "Neither is letting those that lie to and betray you and steal from you go unpunished. You would have banished them. That's what they wanted anyway. That is not punishment. Man up, Peter, and have the balls to do what needs to be done to rule your pack."

Alpha Toth growls, his wolf rising to the challenge, and he clamps his mate around the neck with one hand. Her eyes widen with shock. "We do not *rule* our pack; we lead it. With justice, but also with mercy when needed. And *I* am alpha. *I* decide when mercy is needed. Do you understand me?"

Luna Marie holds onto her defiance until Alpha Toth squeezes her neck even harder. "DO YOU UNDERSTAND ME?" he roars.

Luna Marie closes her eyes and nods once, showing submission, and Alpha Toth releases her immediately. "Forgive me, my alpha," she says. I'm shocked to see lust in her eyes. She was excited by his display of dominance, and now she looks like she's going to jump his body right here in front of her entire pack.

Alpha Toth doesn't share her lust. He's disappointed in her right now and ignores her physical reaction, turning his attention back to Maya.

Maya looks devastated, and I don't blame her. Daniel didn't deserve to die. The money-stealing ploy so they could leave together had probably been Maya's plan. She'd probably been the one doing the stealing most of the time. Daniel had looked too new at it, too scared. His death is on Maya's shoulders.

Tears stream down her face, but still she stands, back straight, chin up like a good soldier. She glares at her luna with pure hatred, while Luna Marie looks back at her with disappointment and heartbreak.

"I'm sorry, Maya," Alpha Toth says. "The punishment was harsh, but so were the crimes. You've made our pack weak. Others will hear of this and think I am incapable of keeping control of my wolves. Your actions will make our pack vulnerable to attack. Even still, enough blood has been shed this night. If you can pay back the money, every cent, then I will spare your life. You will have to leave my territory and never return, but you will live. Do you understand?"

Maya clenches her jaw, and her entire body shakes with rage. "I understand this pack's true weakness," she growls. Her bloodshot, tear-filled, rage-filled eyes turn to her luna again. "Luna Marie," she calls out loud and clear. "I challenge you! I challenge you for the position of luna."

Cries of outrage and shock ring out in the crowd, but Luna Marie quiets them all. "Very well," she says with a strange smile that makes me wonder if this wasn't her plan all along. "But you'll have to kill me, because I will never submit to you."

Maya growls. Her eyes glow, and her body shakes, ready for the change. "I'm going to enjoy ripping you apart."

The change is fast. Maya gets a head start, but Luna Marie's change is almost instantaneous, and she's a bigger wolf. The two crash together at the same time, each taking swipes from the other that draws blood.

That's all I see before Rook whisks me away from Jeffrey and throws me up onto the stage. He hops up with me and stands in front of me like it would take a bulldozer to move him. I have to peek around his shoulder in order to see what's happening.

The fight doesn't take long. It's a brutal frenzy of claws and teeth. These women aren't fighting like Jeffrey and Wulf had been. Wulf toyed with Jeffrey until he got bored, and then he quickly subdued him. These wolves are much more evenly matched, and they aren't messing around. They're trying to kill each other. Both are bloody messes, but Maya's wolf is losing too much blood from her right hind leg, and she's limping badly.

She slows down just enough for Luna Marie to get a good jump on her. The luna slams into her side, knocking her over, and jumps on her. I look away just as she goes for Maya's throat. I don't need to see that. But I still hear the sound of ripping flesh. My entire body stiffens, and Rook pulls me into a tight hug just as Luna Marie releases a long howl, declaring herself the victor. His arms touch mine, and so I hear his foremost thoughts before I can pull myself from his grip. *Poor woman. She's only seeing the worst parts of our culture. I wanted her to love wolves, not think us savage.*

I scramble out of his hug and force a smile. I want to tell him that I don't consider their culture savage, but the words don't come. Knowing what I do about the mate challenges, and now seeing the swift and harsh justice done tonight, I understand that's how wolves are, and that they need a bit of strong discipline to be kept in line, but two women just fought to the death in front of me and no one tried to stop them. If that's not savage, I don't know what is. I don't hate Rook and Wulf, and I don't blame Alpha Toth, but I definitely have no desire to ever join the pack.

"If you don't mind, Rook," I say quietly into the solemn

atmosphere, "I think I'd like to go home now."

Rook nods his head in both answer to my request and understanding of my feelings. His small smile is sympathetic with a hint of disappointment. I hate to let him down, but I can't help it. I feel like Daniel's and Maya's deaths are my fault.

"I'll walk you to your car."

He jumps down from the stage and once again offers to help me down. All eyes in the room are on me as I hop down. I wonder if I'm not the only one who holds me responsible for what happened. I've been getting glares from the single women all night, but now there are a few from mated women as well. And there are plenty from the men, too. Mostly the men I'd danced with.

"Hold on, Nora," Jeffrey calls, approaching Rook and me with a smug grin on his face. "Just what was your part in all of this?"

I feign innocence. "I don't know what you mean. I just danced with Daniel and Maya freaked out, that's all."

The room erupts into growls. Rook responds with a louder one and shoves me behind him, pressing my back against the stage. At the same time, that prickling sensation of impending danger crawls up my neck. My gift is telling me that someone close to me means me harm. Looking at the few dozen snarling werewolves, I want to laugh. *Someone wants to harm me? Really? You think?*

There's only one way out of this, even though I really don't want to do it. I'm going to have to come clean and give up my anonymity. I sigh and murmur into Rook's back.

"So…that bit about werewolves smelling lies is true, then?"

Again, wrong thing to say. The pissed off wolves not only hear my mumbled comment, they move closer. Rook's body begins to shake as he resists the change. My intuition is screaming at me now. My body explodes into goose bumps, and I gasp at the rolling sensation in my stomach.

"Nora?" Rook asks over his shoulder, his eyes never leaving the threat in front of him.

"It's nothing. I'm okay. It's just my gift warning me that someone nearby means me harm."

Rook snorts. "Multiple someones, and they mean to kill you, most likely. Don't move. No matter what happens." He raises his voice and says, "Nora has my protection. I will kill anyone who attacks."

Alpha Toth steps in before there's a bloodbath. "Now, hold on. Everyone calm down. There is no need for anyone to attack. It's not what you think." He looks at me again. I'm surprised to see he's asking permission to tell the truth, and then I remember that I was the one who swore *him* to secrecy. I give him a small nod. *Yes. Please tell them, and stop them from ripping me to shreds.* "Nora is here at my request. I asked her to help me figure out who was stealing money from the pack."

Gasps sweep through the crowd, but the feeling that I'm about to be psychic toast calms down from *your-death-is-imminent* mode to the less severe *someone-means-you-harm* setting. It's a start.

Jeffrey glowers at Alpha Toth. "You involved an outsider in pack business?"

Several grumbles of agreement ring out in the crowd. Alpha Toth holds his hands up, trying to settle everyone down. "It was with great consideration and reluctance, but yes, I went to an outsider for help. Daniel and Maya have been stealing from the pack for over a year, that we know of. We've been trying to discover them for months and found nothing leading us to the thieves. Nora has unique gifts that help her in these specific situations and had already proven herself a friend to this pack."

Most of the pack calms down at this and even looks on me with approval, though there are a few scowls still, and my intuition hasn't quit warning me of danger yet.

"What gifts does she have?" one of the men I danced with calls out.

Jeffrey—who has gone from scowling to calculating—smiles at me. "Yes, Nora, what power do you have? You're such a dominant female. What else are you capable of?"

His leer makes me feel dirty enough that if Rook weren't standing in front of me, blocking my way, I might just march over and punch him in the face. "Sorry. I like to keep my gifts secret—safer for me that way." I give him a saccharine smile, batting my eyelashes. "You understand."

Jeffrey's calculating expression doesn't go away, and it gives me the creeps. I start to wonder if he's the reason my gut is still telling me I'm in danger.

"Some friend!" one woman shouts, drawing the room's attention. Her eyes are red rimmed from crying. "She got Maya killed! She pretended to like her and got her killed."

My stomach sinks, and I shake my head. "I *was* Maya's

friend," I say. It comes out too quietly, because I'm choking on guilt. "I didn't know until tonight that Maya was helping Daniel. I didn't know about their relationship. I never wanted to see her get hurt."

"Maya challenged your luna! She got herself killed!" Alpha Toth snaps, glaring at the upset woman and then casting his frown toward the whole group. "Maya and Daniel were traitors to this pack. They were stealing from you. They were cheating you out of your hard-earned money. They were lying to you and breaking pack laws. They were criminals who could have severely weakened this family and put us at risk with our neighboring packs."

That shut the crowd up.

"Nora not only agreed to help us at a great personal risk, she agreed to keep all of this secret for the safety of the pack, and she refused to take compensation for it. She helped us out of loyalty to Wulf and his family."

All eyes shoot to me and then to Rook. I blush under the speculative gazes. Some wolves look curious and others excited, while some wear knowing smirks. I want to flip them all off and tell them, again, that there's nothing going on between Rook and me, but it's pointless. The wolves are going to speculate no matter what.

"We owe her our gratitude, not our accusations," Alpha Toth continues. "Do not place your anger for this wrong on Nora's shoulders. It was not her fault. I had hoped to take care of this problem discreetly and without bloodshed." His eyes flick to the luna, who lifts her chin in defiance. Alpha Toth sighs. "But what's done is done, and that is the end of it. Let this be a lesson to anyone who thinks they can defy pack law and get away with it. Now, that said, though they were traitors, they were still wolves, and we will give them a proper burial. Jeffrey, see that it's done tonight."

Jeffrey's jaw clenches at the command, but he holds back a snarky reply and bows his head. He barks out several names, and wolves jump into action, removing the bodies. The motion breaks up the crowd, and people start to gather their families to leave. Guess the party's over.

Rook stays where he is, blocking me from the pack until the majority of the crowd is gone. Several wolves—mostly some of the stronger men I danced with tonight—linger like they want to talk to me, but Rook growls at any of them who comes too close, and they eventually get the hint. I don't comment on his possessive actions because I'd rather not deal with the curious wolves.

Alpha Toth and Luna Marie are the only people Rook lets approach. When they come over to us, Rook relaxes and moves out of my way. Alpha Toth is apologetic, while Luna Marie is wearing a stilted smile.

"That did not go as planned," Alpha Toth says. "I apologize that your involvement in this was brought to light."

I shrug. Honestly, it could have gone a lot worse for me. "It's okay. Shit happens. At least my powers were kept secret, and we figured out who was stealing from you."

"That we did." Alpha Toth holds his hand out to me. Again, I shake it, not wanting to disrespect him. His thoughts are of gratitude toward me and sadness for his lost wolves. He's upset that two wolves he liked so much betrayed him, but he's even sadder that their lives were forfeit. I like that. He's strong and harsh but also compassionate. He seems like a good leader.

"I, too, am grateful for your help," Luna Marie says, flashing me a beautiful smile. It turns rueful as she looks at her mate. "Though, I am upset I was not let in on this problem or the plan to involve Miss Jacobs."

Alpha Toth cringes. "I didn't want to worry you with the problem until I knew for sure what was going on."

"You went to an outsider before consulting me," Luna Maria says through clenched teeth. "And then you brought her here and still didn't tell me of her involvement."

Talk about marital issues. Alpha Toth, to use a horrible pun, is going to be in the doghouse with his mate for a while. But since I like him, and she seems a bit bipolar, I take pity on him and help him out a little. "Oh, that was all me," I say, covering for him as much as I'm able. I make sure not to tell any lies for Luna Marie to sniff out. "Part of our deal was that he tell no one about me."

Luna Marie narrows her eyes on me. I easily wave it off. "Sorry. It's just, I know how private packs are, and I knew the pack wouldn't like my getting involved. There was some danger to me in that respect. Plus, I keep my gifts a very closely guarded secret. Even Alpha Toth still doesn't know exactly what I do or how it works. The truth of my gifts getting out would make me a target. I made him promise it would stay between us if I agreed to help, or I wouldn't do it."

Luna Marie considers me a moment before sighing. "I understand. I'm not happy about it, but I do empathize with your need for discretion. And I am grateful to you for your help."

Luna Marie dips her head in gratitude and steps closer to her mate as some sort of show of solidarity, like she needs to prove to me that she's sincere and on her husband's side. Admittedly, it helps. I'm a little disturbed by the woman after watching how fast she put down Daniel and Maya.

I shrug awkwardly, wondering how to end this conversation so that I can leave. "Well, I'm glad I could help. I'm just sorry about Daniel and Maya."

Luna Marie gives me a soft, sad smile. "We all are, dear. Maya was beloved in the pack. And as much as I hate to say it, there will be wolves in the pack who harbor resentment toward you, the outsider, for her death. I know you are not responsible, but my wolves, who loved her, will be in denial for some time about her actions and will need someone to blame. You may want to be careful around here in the future."

Both Rook and Alpha Toth sigh at the truth in her words. I know she's right, too, considering there are several wolves still watching us, and not all of them look happy. And I still have the vague sense of being in danger, which means someone in the pack still means me harm.

"Perhaps," Alpha Toth says slowly, "it is best if you keep your distance from the compound for a while."

The real regret in his voice is surprising, and he can't help the way his eyes flick to Rook. I'm a little shocked. Was he hoping Rook and I would hook up as much as the rest of the pack? I guess it makes sense. He and Rook are best friends. He must want to see Rook happy almost as much as Wulf does.

I nod my understanding, though I'm disappointed. "I can do that." I frown at Rook. "I guess I won't be getting that training after all."

"I can still teach you," Rook offers. "I'll just have to come down to Wulf's home in the city. We can use his gym."

"Of course!" Alpha Toth jumps on the idea, his face brightening up again. "Anything we can do to repay you for your service to our pack. Plus, I'm sure it would be good for Rook to get away from the compound a little, and I know he'll enjoy seeing his brother a bit more often."

Rook nods his agreement, as does Luna Marie. "That sounds like a suitable compromise," she says.

They all frown at my grimace. I have to explain my hesitation, though I'm embarrassed to do so. I hate my weakness where men are concerned. "I would be uncomfortable training alone in a private gym," I tell Rook, face flaming. "That's why Wulf suggested we come here in the first place."

"Oh. Uh, okay." Rook looks like he doesn't know what else to say to this. Alpha Toth and Luna Marie keep quiet, too.

I feel like an idiot, and I really don't want to pass up the training, but I'm not entirely convinced Rook won't fall under my spell if we spend the time together. He's been flirty, and his wolf has an interest in me. He's proven that a couple times tonight. If only Terrance or Oliver could train me... "Oh, I know!" I blush again at my blurted excitement. "Would it be all right if we trained, but I invited a few people to come to the sessions so that we're not alone? Do you think Wulf would care?"

"I'm sure he won't mind at all."

Rook shakes his head, looking at me with understanding that's bordering on pity. I squash down my anger at the look, because I am pretty pathetic this way. Maybe once I can defend myself better, I won't feel so vulnerable with men. Hopefully.

"Great," I say, looking at the ground as I nod. "Thanks. I'll call you then, after I talk to Wulf."

Rook gives me a small smile. "I look forward to it."

CHAPTER
TWELVE

"Okay, here I come," Rook warns politely. "Are you ready?"

I give him a stiff nod and brace myself for the physical contact that I know is coming. Strong arms wrap around me from behind, locking me against a firm chest. For an instant, panic creeps into my thoughts, but I push it aside and try to focus.

Rook has been training me for two weeks now. This is our sixth session. I'm starting to instinctively trust him, and it's getting easier to have him touching me. It helps that he always warns me before he puts his hands on me, and that he's always so professional about it.

Rook's thoughts are similar to my own. *She's doing great. Relaxing. She hardly flinches anymore. We're going to have to start practicing without me warning her every time so that she can get used to being taken by surprise.*

I'm not looking forward to any surprise attacks, but he's right that I need the practice. It would be nice if I didn't practically jump out of my skin every time someone touches me.

Releasing a slow, calming breath, I brace my foot, drop my shoulder…and flip a six-two one hundred eighty-five pound man onto his back. His grunt as he hits the mat is highly satisfying. My small audience cheers and whistles. Okay, Oliver claps and Ren whistles. Cecile, Wulf, and Enzo aren't paying me any attention. They're too busy planning my stupid underworld coming-out party.

"Excellent job, Nora. You've already got it down," Rook says without a hint of a groan.

I'm envious of his werewolf genes. If I'd been slammed to the mat as many times in a row as he has now, I'd be sore for days. We've been at this for two hours, and I'm drenched with sweat and on the verge of collapse. He's got a sexy shine to his skin and looks like he's ready to run a marathon.

I hold my hand out, offering to help him up. "Great. Now if only I had a tenth of your werewolf stamina."

Rook accepts my hand with a laugh and easily climbs to his feet. Our hands clasp just in time for me to catch his internal response. *If only.* Before I can let go of Rook's hand, he gently tugs me to him. I stumble forward, and my hands fall against his chest. "You would be glorious as a werewolf," he murmurs in a low voice.

A shiver runs up my spine that I'm not quite able to hide. Rook cocks a brow, then laughs when I scramble to put a little space between us. I glare at him, and he gives me an impish grin. "Sorry. My wolf enjoys teaching you as much as I do," he admits. "He's a little closer to the surface during our sessions."

I'm always fascinated when Rook speaks of his wolf. It's as if they're one and the same and yet separate at the same time. I know what he means about his wolf rising to the surface, though. Something about Rook changes when his wolf is awake or whatever. He gets more confident, more forward, more *primal*. You'd think it would scare me, and maybe it does make me a little nervous, but there's also something undeniably sexy about Rook the wolf. Of course, Rook the man knows that, and likes to mess with me.

I roll my eyes. "Well, make sure you keep wolf Rook on his leash when we practice, because I can barely keep up with Rook the man."

"Aww." Rook playfully chucks his arm over my shoulders and leads me toward the small group of people who have agreed to hang out while we train. "You'll get in better shape the longer you work out—nothing comes overnight. But you do have some natural ability. Maybe you can't run three miles yet, but you're picking up these moves like you've been doing them in your sleep your entire life."

"And you look sexy doing it," Ren says, grinning at me. He turns his smile on Rook and adds, "And so do you. You sure you don't like men even a little bit?"

"I'm sure, Ren," Rook says with a grunt.

Ren frowns. "Such a pity."

"You're right about her ability," Wulf says to Rook, saving his brother from Ren's advances. He eyes me suspiciously.

"You're picking it up quickly, almost *too* quickly. You've really never had training before?"

I crash to the small bleachers, shaking my head. And yes, Wulf's home gym is big enough to have its own small set of bleachers off to the side of the room. It also has a track, a boxing ring, a pool, and all the workout equipment a person could ever need. The man renovated an old warehouse solely for workout purposes since he's a wolf living downtown and doesn't get the chance to go running in his beast form as much as he'd like. It's a great setup.

"I'm sure I've never had any training. I had to defend myself plenty of times growing up, but no one's ever even shown me how to throw a proper punch."

"Maybe it's one of your gifts," Rook says.

I shake my head again as I grab a towel and wipe the sweat from my body. Rook has been making me train in a sports bra and shorts while he's in a tank top and shorts because he wants me to get used to having to fight while being bombarded with thoughts. It's a smart idea, but exhausting as well. "My gifts are all psychic-based abilities. It's a mind thing. I've never had any physical advantages."

"You've never tried before," Wulf argues. "If you really, truly have some underworlder blood in you, then it's a good possibility you have at least a hint of physical superiority over normal humans. Most underworlders do."

"Whatever it is, I'll take it. I could use an advantage with as many people who try to attack me."

Rook and Wulf frown matching sexy frowns. Beside me, Ren lets out a soft sigh and releases enough of his incubus pheromones to make everyone in the room shout at him to knock it off.

"Don't worry, Nora," Rook says, still glaring at Ren. "Give me some time, and I'll whip you into a proper badass."

I'm still trying to catch my breath from Ren's little lust roofie, but I grin at the idea of me in some tight leather outfit, throwing punches and wielding a Katana sword like the heroines in all of those urban fantasy books. I wouldn't mind being a badass. Not that I'd go looking for fights, but they certainly have a tendency to find me.

"Every woman should know how to defend herself," Cecile chimes in, in her singsong voice. "But don't worry too much, Nora. Because after this party, everyone in the city will know and love you. You don't mind if we move the location from my penthouse to Terrance's club, do you?"

My eyes narrow at the sweet smile she shoots me. I don't believe her innocence for a second. "Why would we need to do that? You promised this thing would stay small."

She waves me off. "*Small* is a relative term, darling. There are a lot of underworlders in this city, and word about your party has gotten out. I've got people ringing my phone nonstop, asking for the details."

"Just tell them it's private."

Cecile cocks an eyebrow at me. "The point is to make people like you, and denying them invites to the party of the year would hurt their feelings."

I groan. "Ugh, whatever. I'll talk to Terrance about it."

Cecile beams a victorious smile. "Thank you, dear. And don't worry, you're going to love it. I promise."

"If you say so."

Oliver, who's once again sitting back letting the others do the talking, shares a secret smile with me, knowing I'm going to hate this party. I'm so glad he's promised to come. He said he'd hide out with me somewhere, but I know that's only wishful thinking. Cecile is never going to let me escape the spotlight. But I'm still glad Ollie will be there. Seeing him in the crowd, just knowing he's there if I need him—like right now—always calms me down.

I make my way to my quiet friend and bump his shoulder with mine when I sit down beside him. Since he knows how much I hate hugs and handshakes, shoulder-bumping in greeting has kind of become our thing. "Thanks for coming," I tell him. I've made sure to tell him thanks each time he's shown up. He's my only friend who's been at every single session. "You don't have to come to them all, you know. If it's too much…"

"I don't mind." He pats the computer in his lap. "I can do my homework from anywhere."

I eye the computer with doubt. "Homework? Or *Dragon Quest X?*"

He chuckles, flashing me the cutest guilty smile. "Always a little of both."

He closes out of his homework and sobers up. "What is it?" I ask, startled by his grave expression.

"I spent the week looking through FUA records for cases that sounded like your mom's."

My stomach leaps up into my chest. "And?"

His face falls. "I found nothing. I'm sorry, Nora. I looked

at everything over a five-year span, and there wasn't a single report about rogue vampire killings."

So much for that. I don't know what I expected anyway. Finding out the people who killed my mother were caught wouldn't bring her back. "Thanks for looking, at least."

A pained expression crosses Oliver's face, and he bites his bottom lip. "Nora…"

"No, it's okay. I've been dealing with not knowing for nearly twenty years now. I'll just have to make peace with it going unsolved. Maybe I really do need this vampire party."

"There are other ways we could look into this. I could hack the Detroit PD's database. Maybe there were other cases like yours, and the FUA just never flagged them. I mean, you fell through the cracks somehow. What's to say others didn't, too?"

I swallow hard. Part of me really wants to look into this deeper, but another part feels it's a hopeless case and a useless cause. Finding my mother's killers might give me closure, but it wouldn't make me fear vampires any less. "No," I say with a heavy sigh. "It's all right, Oliver. You're awesome for trying, but it's probably best just to move on. Case closed."

Oliver hesitates, but then gives up and nods. "If you're sure."

I hesitate, too. "Yeah. I'm sure. Thanks, though." I shake off my melancholy and force my attention to my small group of friends busily plotting my demise—or, my underworlder coming-out party, but it feels like the same thing. "So!" I clap my hands and smile with false cheer. "Who are all these decent vamps that I'm not going to be scared of?"

"Why look for others when you've got the best of the best, right here?" a velvety voice says.

I'm startled to see Parker walking toward me. What's he doing here, and who spilled the beans of my schedule to him? I want to ask, but the words stick to the roof of my mouth. All I can croak out is a small, "Hey."

Parker smiles hesitantly. "I *am* going to make it on the coveted guest list, right?"

Cecile's eyes light up, and she claps her hands together. "Of course you are! You were first on the list."

Parker looks almost relieved. Then he takes a seat on the bleachers in front of me, and his smile turns to a look of sheer determination. "I'm not letting you avoid me any longer."

I wince, and at the same time, my pulse reacts to his dominant alpha male act. Cecile interrupts our staring match. "Oh! Parker, darling." She snaps a couple times to gain Parker's attention. He looks her direction, and I suck in a deep breath. I hadn't realized I was holding it.

"Since we have you here," Cecile says, "would you be a dear and help me come up with a few more names to add to the guest list? You know most of the vampires in the metro area. The point of this party is to introduce Nora to as many nice vampires as possible, after all. We need to get our girl used to your kind."

Cecile winks at Parker, and he chuckles. "I'm sure I can come up with a few names for you, though…" He looks my way and pins me with another determined stare. "I know a better way for you to get used to vampires. Have dinner with me."

Everyone around us falls silent. Parker holds my gaze, refusing to let me look away. I want to say yes. I know I need to get over both my fear of vampires and of men in general, and I know Parker would be a good person to start with. He's a good guy, and there's no denying he makes me feel things I thought I'd never feel for a man, but he's Henry's right-hand man, and I *hate* Henry.

"I—"

"Please, Nora. I really need to talk to you."

His deep blue eyes are pleading with me, making it hard to stick to my plan—which was to never spend time with him again. The truth is, I'm scared of him. Or, I'm scared of myself around him. He lowers my defenses in a way I don't like. And he gets my blood pumping in a way I like too much.

"You're here," I say stubbornly. "Let's talk."

Parker sighs. "I need to speak to you privately. It's important, Nora. *Please.*"

I think I surprise everybody when I break down and agree. It's just that I don't think he would lie to me or try to trick me into hanging out with him, so whatever it is he wants to tell me, he must really think it's important. I'm intrigued. "Okay, fine. But dinner's on you, and I'm not dressing up."

Parker's mouth curves up into a smile that reaches his eyes. "I can live with that."

"Fine," I say again. "I'm going to hit the showers. Don't give Cecile too many names while I'm gone. This is supposed to be a small party."

I glare at Cecile, and she simply waves me off with a beautiful smile.

Once I'm clean, I change into the only clothes I brought with me—a pair of jeans, a long-sleeve T-shirt, and Rook's jacket that he told me to keep. It's not much, as far as date outfits go. I also don't have a blow dryer or any makeup. "Stop it, Nora," I chide myself when I realize I'm stressing over what I look like for Parker. "This is not a date." But I can't help thinking that the last time I went out with Parker strictly for business, it totally ended up being a date.

Parker likes to push my boundaries. On our not-a-date-date last month, he struck a deal for a kiss good night that I ended up not being able to follow through on. I'd nearly had a full-blown panic attack right there in front of the restaurant. I'd rather not have a repeat of that tonight, and at the same time, I can't stop thinking about that almost-kiss. "Get a grip, woman."

With a deep breath that I let out in a long puff, I zip up the track jacket that's too big for me and head back out into the gym, where Parker is still talking with Cecile. Ren and Enzo are involved in the conversation now, too, and Cecile is scribbling down notes in a notebook with a look of delight that makes me groan. "Small, Cecile!"

"Themed!" she replies.

I shoot Oliver a *help me* look, and he lifts his hands, palms out, as if to say *What can I do about it?*

"You ready?" Parker asks, rising to his feet.

I have to push down a bundle of butterflies when he offers me his arm like a true gentleman. As I accept it, I look over my shoulder back at Oliver. "You working tomorrow?"

He nods.

"Great. I'll stop in before I go to work and bring you dinner."

His face lights up at that. His eyes flick to Parker quickly, and he says, "It's a date."

I almost laugh when Parker's jaw clenches. Oliver, the rascal, only said that to annoy Parker. Usually, Oliver is sweeter than sugar, but he's not a big fan of Parker. Aside from having his own feelings for me, he doesn't like the way Parker pushes me until he gets his way—like with dinner right now. His attempt to be rude and overprotective is adorable. I find myself grinning and winking at him, even though I shouldn't be encouraging his behavior.

Parker takes the high road and doesn't comment as we head out into the small parking lot in front of Wulf's warehouse gym/home. He clicks his key fob to unlock his black Mercedes and quietly says, "Thank you for agreeing to dinner tonight."

"You're welcome." I huff into my hands, jumping from toe-to-toe. I didn't realize how cold it's gotten just in the last week. "It's freezing out here."

When Parker opens my door for me, I dive into the car and rub my arms while I wait for him to get in and turn up the heat. As soon as he's in and he shuts the door, instead of reaching for the heater, he breathes in a deep breath and wrinkles his nose. He eyes me for a long moment, chewing on his thoughts while I continue to warm myself with good old-fashioned friction. "Okay, I'm sure vampires must be impervious to the cold and all, but the human needs heat."

"Are you wearing Rook's jacket?"

"What?"

He's eyeing the jogging jacket I have on with distaste. My cheeks flush. I'd forgotten all about the jacket and the fact that I would smell like werewolf all night. "Sorry. It's the warmest thing I've got at the moment. I keep meaning to go buy a coat and just haven't gotten around to it yet."

"Right."

Parker finally turns up the heater and buckles his seat belt. When he heads away from downtown instead of toward it, I frown. "Where are we going?"

"Macy's."

"Macy's?"

"We're going to buy you a coat before dinner."

CHAPTER
THIRTEEN

HE'S TAKING ME SHOPPING? AWW. THAT'S REALLY SWEET OF him, even if he is only doing it so that I'm not wearing a werewolf's jacket on our second non-date. "Thanks, but, I can buy a coat another time. I'm really looking forward to food."

Parker slides me a sideways smirk. "Then it's a good thing Macy's is at a mall, where there will certainly be several restaurants and an entire *food* court."

"Haha. When did you turn into a comedian?"

"Maybe I've always been one, and you've just been too scared to get to know me."

He looks at me again, a long, meaningful look that makes my pulse spike and urges me to lecture him about keeping his eyes on the road. "Would you watch where you're going, please? Delicate human cargo, here, remember."

His gaze turns back to the road. "I remember," he

murmurs under his breath.

Why does everything he says somehow make me want to blush? I have to clear my throat in order to speak. "So what's so important you had to tell me in person and privately?"

He sighs, as if this is the last conversation he wants to have right now, but knows I won't talk about anything else unless we get it out of the way. He's right about that. "Do you remember, last month," he asks, "when we got kidnapped by those dark magic users, and you had to feed me your blood so that I could escape?"

I snort. "Yes. I remember that. Feeding a vampire your blood isn't exactly something you forget."

Actually, most times it *is* something a human forgets because the vamp sucking their blood compels them to forget, but Parker didn't compel me. I wouldn't have let him, and honestly, I doubt he'd want me to forget that experience. The feeling I got when he drank from me was…euphoric and orgasmic.

I turn red again, my entire body heating up at the memory of being so intimate with Parker. His lips twitch as if he's fighting a smile. He knows what I'm thinking about. That's so embarrassing. I huff in exasperation. "Yes, I remember. And why are we bringing this up now?"

"There's something different about your blood," he says quietly, staring out at the highway. "It's highly addictive. I've craved it since that day, and for the first two weeks I couldn't drink anything else. I had to have Henry compel me to go hunt someone else."

I rear back in shock, and a shiver races down my spine.

Not a good shiver. "Seriously?"

He grimaces. "Yes, seriously. You aren't human, Nora."

"What?" That isn't what I expected him to say.

"You don't just have a little underworlder blood in you; you *are* an underworlder. A very strong one. One I can't identify."

The news is so shocking that I realize I believe him. If I didn't, I'd be laughing right now. But I've always felt different from the people around me, and my gifts have to come from somewhere. It makes sense that I'd be an underworlder. I just have one small problem. "Every underworlder I've ever met has said I'm human, and underworlders can tell."

"You're wearing a glamour." Parker squints at me until he's forced to pay attention to driving again. "It's so strong that even now, knowing it's there and looking for it, I can't see it."

"If you can't see it, then why do you think I'm wearing one? What makes you think I'm not human?"

"Because of your blood. Glamours wrap around a person like a cloak. They hide you, but they can't change your blood. You *are* an underworlder, just one I've never had the pleasure of tasting before. I can't identify your species."

I sit back in my seat and digest this. I'm an underworlder. I belong in this crazy life I've stumbled into. But what am I? I don't seem to have the power that most other underworlders have. I have gifts they don't, and I'm physically weaker, like a human. I also don't have the built-in radar for knowing the difference between humans and others. "If I'm such a strong underworlder, then how come I'm so weak? Yeah, I have some strange psychic powers, but I don't exactly fit in with the monster crowd."

"A lot of underworlders are physically as weak as humans, Nora. But in your case, I believe your glamour is suppressing your power as well as hiding what you are. I think you're a lot more powerful than you realize. Your blood would suggest it, anyway. You can't share it with anyone ever again. No matter what."

I grind my teeth, not liking the tone in his voice. "Don't lecture me like I'm a child. It's not like I plan to make a habit of it. I only fed you because I had no other choice. I *stopped* Henry from biting me, and Josephine wasn't exactly my fault. I can't help it if your friends keep trying to kill me."

Parker sags in his seat, feeling like shit. My words were too harsh. I'm angry about the vampire attack, but I know it wasn't Parker's fault, and I know he feels terrible about it. "Nora," he croaks. "I'm so sorry."

Now he's apologizing for things that weren't his fault. Don't I feel like an ass? "Never mind. It doesn't matter. I've already forgiven you for taking me to Henry. What he tried to do, and what Josephine did, is not your fault. I don't blame you, and I'm not mad at you. Let's not fight."

Parker mulls over my words before slowly reaching across the console to drop his fingers on my forearm. I'm grateful he doesn't grab my hand. He knows how much I hate that. "You've really forgiven me?" he asks.

There's no mistaking the hope in his voice. I feel bad for putting it there. I hadn't meant to lead him on, but I'm probably the queen of mixed signals where Parker's concerned. It's not my fault my body and my head want different things in his case.

I shrug as indifferently as possible. "I forgave you the night I met Director West and she freed me from Henry. You were out trying to find your missing friend, and I was not only hanging out with your main suspect, but I was acting suspicious. You did what you had to. I get it. No harm, no foul."

Parker's murmured thank-you is so soft it quiets us both, and we finish the drive to the mall in silence. Parker keeps his hand on my forearm, and I don't move it. I should, because it's basically the closest thing I can get to handholding if I don't want to spend the drive in his thoughts, but I find his light touch comforting.

When we arrive at the mall, he parks in front of Macy's and leads me straight to the coat section. I don't even want to know how much the coats on these racks cost. Parker doesn't seem to care. He wastes no time heading into the clothes and holding out ones he likes. I'm not surprised the man likes to shop, considering he dresses immaculately and looks like a *GQ* model.

"Oh, this one is lovely."

He holds out a red coat that is, admittedly, very stunning. I give him a look as I shake my head. "If you can describe it as *lovely*, it's not the coat for me."

He waits a moment, then decides not to argue, and reaches for a white one. "White?" I laugh. "Are you kidding? I'd ruin it in a day."

He puts it back and reaches for the same coat in black.

When he cocks his brow, I still shake my head, pointing at the waist. "Nothing with a belt. That's just ridiculous. I belt my pants, not my coats."

He chuckles and wanders to another rack. I stand back, watching the man shop for me with amusement. He's got great taste, but he's completely missing *my* taste. He holds up a coat that would go to my knees with a hopeful expression. "Parker. No. That's a dress, not a coat."

He sighs. "It's called a skirted swing coat, and it's very nice, Nora. Have you ever owned anything nice?"

I laugh. "I grew up in foster care in Detroit, worked in a garage changing oil and tires, and lived in the slums. What do you think? I'd probably have been shot for a coat that nice where I used to live."

He puts the coat back but doesn't reach for another one. "Nora…" His face falls. "You deserve so much more than the life you've had."

His comment doesn't faze me. When it's the only life you've had, you get used to it. "A lot of people deserve more than they have. And plenty have more than they deserve." I shrug. "That's just life. No use dwelling on what could or should be. Best to learn to be happy with what you've got."

He holds my eyes with a steady gaze and says, "I admire you, Nora."

I have to look away when my cheeks flush. I'm not one of those women who can't take a compliment, but Parker has a way of taking intensity to the extreme. "Thanks," I mutter, grabbing the nearest coat. It's a puffy monstrosity that I'd never wear in a million years and actually recoil from when I realize what I'm holding. "Ugh. Who would wear this?"

Parker chuckles, and I'm grateful I've successfully relieved the tension between us. I can handle him a lot better when his mood is light. He picks up a stylish sleek black jacket next, and I sigh. "Don't they have anything…I don't know…badass? Something that says *stay back, before I cut a bitch?*"

Parker bursts into laughter. The sound shocks me. I don't think I've ever heard him laugh out loud like that. He's normally so reserved and serious. I'm kind of proud to have broken through his composure. "Sorry," he says. "I didn't take you for the tight black leather type."

"Ugh. I'm not. First, that's way too cliché, and second, I wouldn't want Nick to think I'm copying his style."

I roll my eyes conspiratorially, and Parker laughs again. Sadly, he's gone back to that quiet chuckle. It's nice, but not nearly as satisfying or sexy as his laugh. "I think you're the only person in the world that gets away with calling him Nick."

I smirk. "I am *not* calling him Gorgeous. That's just ridiculous, and the man hears it way more than is healthy for a guy's ego."

Parker laughs again—a second real laugh—and I can't help the proud grin that spreads across my face. I meet his smile with mine, and suddenly he's right there, all up in my space, stealing the breath from my lungs and making my heart beat erratically. His eyes lock on mine, filled with so much heat that I gasp. "Parker." I mean it as a warning, but I can't quite make it sound like one.

He moves in closer. "I want you, Nora."

Well, shit.

I gulp in some air and accidentally shiver. Our chests are touching now, but his hands are still at his sides, and he's being very careful not to touch my skin with his own. Our mouths are just inches from each other. He refuses to break our stare, and I can't. "I'm a desperate man," he whispers. "Ease my suffering."

He leans in. I don't move. I'm not sure if that means I'm giving him permission or if I'm just too frozen with nerves to back up. His lips hover, just for an instant, over mine, so close I can barely feel them. Instead of pulling away, my eyes fall shut, and then, suddenly, Parker devours me in a heated kiss.

It's the first kiss I've had in almost four years, and my body reacts as such. I push myself against him, and kiss him back.

His thoughts start out sweet. *Her lips are as soft as I knew they would be, but she tastes so much sweeter than I'd dreamed. I've wanted this kiss since the first night we met. I can't believe she's honoring me with it. I didn't think she ever would.*

He nudges my lips with his, and in my daze, I progress the kiss to an openmouthed one but don't open up enough to let him deepen it. I'm not ready for that.

Feeling me respond is enough to send Parker's thoughts in a much lustier direction. He can't help himself. He's wanted this—me—for too long. He really is desperate for me. He wants so much more than a kiss.

I see in his mind all the things he wants to do with me.

His thoughts quickly spin into intense fantasies. His body responds to the images in his mind. He wraps his arms around me and pushes the kiss deep, and suddenly I'm not kissing Parker, but I'm back in the arms of my one and only boyfriend—the one guy I ever risked giving my heart to. Only, he'd taken my body instead, despite my begging him to stop and my efforts to fight him off.

He'd been dazed afterward and claimed he didn't know what had happened. He said I put him in some kind of trance. I believed him, but he'd still hurt me, and I couldn't stand to be around him or even look at him anymore. After that, I figured because of my power—my curse, whatever it is—I'd never be able to be in a relationship. That was the day I'd sworn off dating forever.

Parker's arms around me now feel like a cage, and his tongue in my mouth makes me choke with fear. I can't breathe. I can't remember where I am. I just feel my ex-boyfriend pushing me down on the couch and taking what I'm not willing to give.

Panicking, I start to thrash and hit the person holding me. Parker releases me immediately, but it's too late. The damage has been done; I can't calm down. I scramble away from Parker, trying to regain some sense of security. I push my back against a wall and reach for the small, thin ash wood stake in the sheath attached to my belt. It was a gift from Terrance after Josephine attacked me. I've carried it with me at all times since he gave it to me, and it feels good to have it in my hands now.

"Nora?" Parker's eyes bulge as he notices the stake I'm

holding. He steps away from me with both hands up in surrender. "Nora, calm down. It's okay. You're okay. You can put the stake away. I'm not going to hurt you. I won't touch you again."

My eyes are still out of focus, and my breathing is so fast I'm on the verge of hyperventilating, but his low, steady voice breaks through my panic, and I start to calm down. It takes me a few minutes before I become fully aware again, and I'm shaking so hard my vision is blurry.

Parker, thankfully, doesn't approach me. His eyes are on mine, full of regret. I glance down at the way I'm clutching a weapon specifically meant to kill him, and I'm overwhelmed by remorse. "I'm sorry," I whisper. I put the stake back in its sheath. "I'm so sorry, Parker."

"It was my fault," he says. "I knew you had problems with physical intimacy. I pushed you too hard last time, too. I don't know what happened. I meant to be so careful, but when you kissed me back, I lost control. Nora, I am *so* sorry."

His words break my heart. "It's not you," I insist again. "It's my power. That's why I can't date. My allure is too strong. It makes men go crazy. Especially if I want what's happening."

I crack a small smile, letting him know that I purposely admitted to wanting him to kiss me. I'm hoping my acknowledgement will make him feel better, but it doesn't. He looks completely devastated. "At least you were able to stop yourself," I say. "The last guy I kissed couldn't. Not until the deed was done, anyway."

I look away from him, hugging myself as I remember,

again, my ex pushing me down. I'd been sexually abused before, but somehow what my ex did disturbs me the most because I had trusted him.

"What can I do?" Parker asks. His voice sounds strangled. "How can I help you?"

He can't. The only thing that could help me is figuring out what I am and learning how to control my power.

I take a deep breath and let it out slowly, trying to calm my still-racing heart. Parker's waiting for instructions. I don't know what to tell him, so I say, "Help me find a coat?"

He chews on this a moment before giving in with a nod. Turning back to the sea of clothes without a word, he pulls a moss-colored military-style coat off a rack. My face lights up. It's feminine looking but still hard-core. I love it. "That's the one."

CHAPTER
FOURTEEN

THE MOOD LIGHTENS, BUT PARKER AND I NEVER REALLY GET back the playfulness we had before our disastrous kiss. He keeps a good distance from me the rest of the evening, careful not to touch me at all or even get too close. I'm both relieved and disappointed at the same time.

When it's time to eat dinner, he asks if we can skip the food court and go to a place nearby that he really likes. "As long as it's not all fancy like the last place you took me to."

He grins. "Actually, it's a bit of a dive."

"Sounds like my kind of place."

We drive to the south end of Dearborn to a building that looks like a doctor's office. It's closed for the night, but Parker stops there anyway. "What are we doing here?"

"Look closely at the building." He smiles at my confused frown. "You're an underworlder. You should be able to see through a weak glamour."

"That building is glamoured?"

He nods. "To keep humans away. Let your eyes relax and pay attention to the feel of it, then wait a second. If you concentrate, you should be able to shake off the glamour and see the building beneath it."

I focus in front of me, trying to pay attention without really looking directly at the building, like he suggested. My eyes catch a glimpse of a ripple in the air, and when I look back there's a dumpy-looking motorcycle bar in front of me where the doctor's office was. "Holy shit!"

Parker laughs again. That's three times now I've made him laugh. This time he's laughing *at* me, but I don't care. I love the sound.

The place is busy but looks rundown. It's made of dirty old cement and has no windows out front. It's long and skinny, with a row of motorcycles parked along a wooden walkway lining the front of the building. Sadly, none of the bikes are half as nice as Nick's beauty of a machine. Eighties rock pours out the open door, and the neon sign above the place is half burned out, so instead of Skinny's it just says Skin. I snort, wondering if they haven't bothered to fix the sign because they find it amusing. "Classy place."

Parker grins. "I told you it was a dive."

"It's perfect…as long as I survive it."

Parker looks up at the place, considering. "You should be all right. Enough people know about the crazy little human now. Plus, you're with me. Even if we got jumped by everyone in there, I should be able to get you out."

I'm not sure if I want to comment more on the cockiness

of that statement or his use of the word *should*. In the end, my need for food wins out, and I choose to worry about neither. "Whatever. I'm hungry enough I'm willing to risk it."

Inside, the place is dim but surprisingly clean. A counter lines the back wall of the dining area, and a row of dark green vinyl booths runs along the front of the building. There's not much room for anything else.

The place is fairly busy with a variety of underworlders. Like with the club, a lot of them have dropped their human glamours and look like the creatures they really are. All conversation stops when I walk in. Some recognize me from the club and quickly go back to their meals. Others openly gawk. I shrug it off. After the last few weeks working at Underworld, I'm used to being stared at.

A tall man with gray skin that looks almost like stone grins at me from behind the counter. The smile is creepy, considering this man has the face of a goblin and several horns protruding from his head. He's also got thin, leathery wings tucked behind him and a set of razor-sharp claws on his hands. "Ah, Parker, you've brought me something new to cook."

I snort. His words are disturbing, and I don't doubt he'd probably roast a human if he could get away with it, but I can tell he recognizes me. I trust Terrance's reputation to keep me safe. Parker doesn't appreciate the joke, though. His arm slides around my shoulders in a protective grip. "Skinny, this is Terrance's human," he says by way of introduction.

"Ah. The crazy one who works at the club."

"Nora," I say, rolling my eyes. "My name is Nora. Not

Terrance's human, or the crazy human. Just Nora."

Skinny's smile spreads so wide it seems to pull his face out of proportion. A long, thin lizard-like tongue shoots out, licking his entire chin. "Sexy and feisty. I like it. Welcome to my joint. No fighting inside. If you're going to start something, take it to the parking lot. And eat my food at your own risk. Word to the wise: stay away from the fey and demon food."

"Do you serve human food here?" I ask, suddenly worried I'll starve tonight.

Skinny shrugs. "Enough. Shifters and magic users eat pretty similar. You'll be fine if you just stay away from the magic and the poison."

I nod and say, "Thanks for the heads up," even though I would have been smart enough to avoid those things anyway.

Parker ushers me to an open booth, and we slide in across from one another. Most people have gone back to their own business. Only a couple still stare. Parker ignores them, so I do, too.

"So…" I grab a laminated menu from the side of the booth. "What's good here that I can eat without turning into an animal or being cursed or whatever?"

"Stick to the burgers or steaks. Stay away from anything you can't pronounce."

"I'm always up for steak and potatoes."

"Then you'll be fine."

Skinny quickly comes to take our orders. I get the steak, and Parker, thankfully, doesn't order any blood, though it's on the menu. Conversation doesn't get awkward until after our food comes and I take my first bite. The steak is the best I've ever had, and I moan with pleasure. "Mm, this right here is worth all the shit I've been through since I got caught up in the underworld."

Parker smiles. "Has it really been so bad?"

I smirk. "Well, let's see. Aside from all the drama with Henry, Elijah kidnapped me and stabbed me. Then there was that faerie who strangled me. Oh, and of course Josephine tortured and nearly killed me. But I'm still kickin', and I got myself a nice new coat. So, you know, not too bad, no."

Parker looks horrified. I haven't really done much to ease the awkwardness. Oops. Guess I'm feeling unsettled because of our earlier kiss. When I'm out of sorts, I tend to get bitchy. I feel bad about snarking, so I backpedal and try to soften my attitude. "Actually, despite everything, I'm doing better than I have...well...ever. I've got a great new place to live, and I've got friends for the first time in my life. It's strange that I've finally found where I belong, and it took becoming part of the underworld to do it."

"Makes sense since I think you're really an underworlder. Plus, with your powers, even if you are human, you still fit in better with us than in the human world."

My smile becomes a little more genuine. "I'll admit it is very cool to not have to hide the fact that I'm different. Now if I could only figure out the why and how, and find a way to break my curse, I'd be all set."

Parker's brows draw low over his eyes, and he leans forward over the booth. "What curse?"

I cringe. I hadn't meant to bring that up. But since I

kissed him and then freaked out earlier, it's only polite to explain it to him. "It's not a curse, necessarily. I just draw people in."

Parker grins, and it reaches his eyes. "I've noticed."

I can't help returning his smile. "I'm serious. It's—"

I'm interrupted when someone steps up to our booth and clears his throat. Rage bubbles up inside me at the sight of Henry, Parker's clan leader and sire. "Well, isn't this cozy," he says with a pinched smile. After giving Parker a hard look, he smiles at me again. This one is real. "Hello, Nora. It's lovely to see you again."

I grit my teeth and manage not to cuss at the jerk. "Wish I could say the same, Henry, but I was kind of hoping we'd *never* see each other again."

Henry sighs. "We got off to such a bad start, Nora, and I would really like the chance to apologize. Not only for my own behavior, but also for the recent behavior of one of my vampires. Do you mind if I join you?"

I scoff and throw my hand out when Parker starts to scoot over to give Henry room to sit. "It was way worse than a *bad start*, and no, you can't join us. What are you even doing here? You need to quit stalking me."

Henry makes a face as if he's sucking on sour lemons. The ancient vampire has never found my temper endearing. (It's very unladylike.) Considering how bad it is, you'd think he'd be a little less obsessed with me. But he got a good look at all of my memories once, and it turned him into a possessive asshole. He wants to be my savior or something and protect me from all the bad men out there. That's ironic, coming from him.

"I am not *stalking* you." He makes another face. "I simply wanted the chance to apologize to you for Josephine's actions." His eyes narrow on Parker. "When I asked you to talk to her, I didn't mean for you to ask her on a *date*."

Ah, there's the possessive douche bag I know so well. "It's not a date," I say. "But even still, you're not welcome to crash it."

Henry sucks in a sharp breath through his nose. He opens his mouth to reply but stops. His head rears back, and he looks at me with wide eyes. "Why do you smell of werewolf?"

It takes me a moment to realize that I'd been wearing Rook's jacket earlier and there must still be some lingering scent on me. Damn. Vampires have better senses of smell than I thought. Before I can explain, a man sitting across from us at the restaurant counter spins around and grins at me. "Haven't you heard? She's dating Rook Winters."

Henry whirls on the man, while my jaw drops to the table. "I beg your pardon?" Henry asks.

"I'm not *dating* him. Sheesh." I eye the man. He isn't someone I recognize, but he looks wolfish enough for me to make the assumption that even if he isn't from Rook's pack, he's still a werewolf. "All you wolves gossip worse than a bunch of old ladies at a quilting club."

The stranger winks at me, then grins at Henry as if he's thrilled to burst the vampire's bubble. "I heard he took her home and cooked her a meal, then escorted her to his pack social. Males only cook for females that they're courting."

The blood drains from my face. "Is that true?" I ask Parker.

"As far as I know." He doesn't look any happier about this new information than Henry.

Well, no wonder all the wolves in Rook's pack have been acting so strangely. I'm going to kill Rook next time I see him.

"So you *did* allow Rook Winters to cook for you?" Henry demands.

His eyes are glowing a soft red that all vampires get when they start to lose control of their temper. That Henry cares so much pisses me off. "It's none of your damn business." I glare at the wolf sitting at the counter and add, "Yours either."

The man laughs. "Sorry, honey. Every wolf in Michigan knows about Rook Winters and how he lost his mate and won't look for another. The two of you are the biggest were-wolf gossip this century. Personally, I'm rooting for you. He could use a good woman again."

I groan, and the wolf chuckles. Henry and Parker are not amused. It's Parker I defend myself to. "I was low on my red count because Josephine nearly drained me, so he cooked me a steak to build up my iron. He's my trainer. We're friends. That's all. We're not *dating*."

I don't know why I'm so determined to set the record straight right now. It's not like I'm dating Parker, either. But he's been really sweet tonight, and I feel bad throwing my relationship with Rook in his face.

"Rook Winters is your trainer?" Henry asks, pulling me from my thoughts.

While I'm busy glaring at Henry, Parker—the traitor—answers him. "He's teaching her self-defense."

Henry perks up at this. "You wish to learn self-defense?"

"Seeing as how people keep trying to kill me, it seems appropriate."

"Nora, love, if you wish to learn to protect yourself, will you allow me to teach you instead of the wolf?" He ignores my laugh. "Wolves fight using their brute strength. Vampires use more finesse. I am a master in six different forms of martial arts and many weapons that would be well suited for your size and stature. I would be a better fit to teach you than Rook Winters, and I would be honored. Please consider—"

"The answer's no, Henry. I don't care if you're five hundred times the teacher Rook is. I trust him. I don't trust you. And I don't like you."

"I could change your mind about that. Give me one date."

I laugh again, throwing all the sarcasm and condescension I'm capable of into it. "Never going to happen, so stop asking. Even if I *were* to start dating a vampire one day, it sure as hell wouldn't be you."

My eyes flick to Parker, and he gazes back at me with so much hope that I can't look away.

Giving up, Henry hisses and then goes storming out of the diner. Once he's gone, the werewolf at the counter stands up and leaves some cash by his plate. He meets my eyes, chuckling, then tsks. "It's not wise to piss off a master vampire."

"And yet it can't be helped," I say, pushing my plate

away. I've lost my appetite.

Understanding my current mood, Parker signals to Skinny for the check and asks him to box up our food. As we're waiting, tingles shoot up my spine. "Shit!" I hiss.

Parker stiffens. "What? What's wrong?"

"Someone here means to do me harm."

Parker rears his head back. "What?"

"It's a thing I have." I slide out of the booth, glancing in every direction. No one in the restaurant looks suspicious. They're all too busy watching me like I'm a freak on display for their amusement. "My intuition always tells me when I'm in trouble. Right now it's saying get the hell out of here, quick."

Parker looks around the diner, same as I just did, and throws some cash down on the table. "Then let's go."

He takes me by the sleeve of my new coat and tugs me close behind him as he steps outside. Neither of us sees anything, but the warning of impending danger grows stronger. "There has to be someone out here."

Parker takes a deep breath, smelling the air, and snarls. "Werewolves. Quickly, Nora."

He doesn't wait for me to respond, but rather scoops me into his arms and dashes to his car so fast I want to vomit. "Ugh…" I moan as he unlocks my door. "Remind me never to—"

A huge werewolf comes out of nowhere and tackles Parker to the ground. "Nora, get out of here!" he shouts as three more wolves run toward us.

I dive into the car, locking the doors. I feel like a jerk

leaving Parker alone to face off with four werewolves, but I'm just a human with only a handful of self-defense classes under my belt. I can't fight them, and Parker would lose his focus if I were out there. He'd probably die trying to protect me.

I call the only person I can think of to help us. "Nick!" I shout when he answers the phone. "Parker and I are at Skinny's Diner. We're being attacked by were—agh!"

A fist smashes through the passenger window, and before I can duck, a huge man with a big scraggly beard and dark eyes grabs me by my new coat and pulls me out the broken window. "What the hell?" I shout as the broken glass rips my new jacket. "Let me go!"

"I don't think so." The man holding me pulls me close and breathes in deeply, scenting me. His eyes take on a faint glow, letting me know his wolf is close to the surface. "You'll make a very strong wolf," he says in a rumbly, gravelly voice that is more wolf than human. "You'll be an excellent mate."

Oh. Hell. No.

Rook says all it takes is one bite from a werewolf while they're in wolf form and I start the change. So when Mr. Needs To Trim His Beard flashes me his teeth and starts to shake as if he's about to shift, I quickly use one of the moves Rook taught me for getting out of someone's hold. I half expect it not to work, but the move performs as well on him as it did the hundred times Rook made me do it on him and Wulf.

Once I'm free, I jump-slide across the hood of Parker's car, putting the vehicle between us before Beard Man even realizes the weak little human got away from him. He snarls at this and goes to follow me around the car, but another guy quickly snatches me from behind. This one smells a little better and has a lot less hair on his face, but he's sniffing me and telling the other one that I'm his, so you know, he's still a douche.

Beard Man and New Guy start trading threats and insults. I'm lucky they have to be in wolf form to turn me, because this new guy's teeth are too close to my neck for comfort. I have another move Rook showed me to get out of a hold from behind, but I know that even if I escape, I can't outrun them. They'll wolf out to chase me, and then I'll be in real trouble. For now, I let them fight with each other and hope Nick shows up quickly.

Parker is now fighting two wolves while two lie on the ground dead or unconscious. Parker is a badass, but he's starting to slow down. He's got huge, bloody gashes across his chest, and the way he's blinking and wincing, I don't think he's going to be on his feet much longer. If only there were some way to help that didn't end with me sprouting fur and a tail.

Parker knocks a wolf away, and the wolf is slow to get up, but the second wolf gets the jump on Parker. Parker's jacket gets ripped to shreds, and he screams out in agony.

"Parker!"

I can't help my fearful scream. He's going to get killed. My shout gains the attention of the wolf, and he turns on me with a vicious growl. My heart leaps into my throat, and the feeling in my gut becomes so strong my knees buckle.

The man holding me keeps me from falling, but he makes no other move. He and the bearded guy have both lost the dominance battle.

I'm going to die. This wolf isn't interested in a mate. He's hungry for a kill. "Nice doggy?"

The wolf snarls. Guess werewolves can understand English.

The wolf slowly stalks toward me, growling and drooling from his bloody snout. That's Parker's blood on his muzzle. Parker's down on the ground now, and I can't tell if he's dead or alive. With each step the wolf takes, the man holding me from behind grips me tighter. The feeling in my gut intensifies.

Then, something else rises from deep inside me, a power that I don't understand. It's only happened once before. I got kidnapped by a sorcerer when I'd been searching for the missing underworlders. When he was about to kill me, I put him under a spell somehow. I don't know what kind of power it is, or why I have it, but I know it has to do with my curse. The one that makes men become obsessed. The sorcerer had eventually used his magic to fight me, but this guy doesn't have magic.

I embrace the power coming alive. Now that it's awake and I can feel it, I can sort of grab onto it and bring it all the way to the surface. Once I'm fully in control, I know that I'm stronger than the wolf in front of me. I'm stronger than the two holding onto me, too. I'm more powerful than all three of them together. If I want them in my thrall, they will be.

I focus my attention on the one in front of me, the one who means to kill me. When our gazes lock, he flairs his nostrils and his pupils dilate. I have him now. He's under my control. "Stop," I say. My voice sounds strange. It's lighter somehow. Almost musical.

The wolf stops moving.

"Sit."

He does.

"What the hell?" the man holding me from behind mutters.

I keep my focus locked on the wolf sitting before me. It whines and jerks forward, as if it desperately wants to come to me but doesn't want to disobey me, either.

"What's going on?"

"I don't know, man," says the guy with the scraggly beard, "but I'm getting out of here. This bitch ain't worth losing my mind."

The man runs off, but I don't break my gaze. "Turn back into a human," I order.

The wolf whines again and then morphs into a man right before my eyes. He's sitting on the ground, completely naked, and still staring at me with complete adoration. He looks so infatuated that I bet he'd do anything I ask him to right now, even kill himself if I ordered it.

The man holding me isn't gripping me tightly anymore. He's merely watching the scene in front of him with morbid fascination. "What have you done to him?" he asks. His voice is a whisper, and he sounds awed enough that I wonder if some of my power hasn't captured him as well.

The sound of a roaring motorcycle breaks my concentration. I look just as it screeches into the parking lot. The second I break the werewolf's stare, he shakes his head as if coming out of a daze, and then his eyes become hard. In an instant, he changes back into a wolf and lunges for me. Nick is faster. As the wolf jumps at me, Nick tackles him, stabbing him with a knife I can only assume is silver, judging from the way the wolf howls.

The battle is over in seconds, and the wolf will not be attacking me again. It won't be attacking *anything* again. Nick climbs to a stand with his kill at his feet and glares at the man still holding me. The man instantly lets me go and raises his hands in surrender. I almost do the same thing.

Nick isn't his normal self right now. He's in fight mode. He's radiating some sort of power that I think is meant to strike fear into his prey. It works, because both the werewolf and I start to tremble with terror. Nick's eyes have changed; his pupils are now vertical slits like a cat's. His skin is different, too. I can't see it well in the dark, but it's glinting in the moonlight as if it's shiny now. Like it's made of metal or something. Maybe armor? Or scales?

"Are you hurt?" he asks. His voice is rough, with a surprising amount of emotion, but it's also just deeper, more guttural. It's almost as if he's having difficulty speaking.

I shake my head, unable to stop staring. Just what in the hell is Nick Gorgeous? "I'm fine. Just shaken up."

He looks me over from head to toe. After deciding to

believe me that I'm not injured, he shakes himself out of his fury and seems to transform back into his normal self. It takes him a moment to collect himself. Then he flashes me a roguish grin and nudges the body at his feet with a snort. "Well, he's not going to be any good for questioning."

CHAPTER
FIFTEEN

WHILE NICK SECURES OUR ONLY REMAINING BAD GUY, I rush to Parker's side. He's conscious, but only just. His chest and side are both shredded, and his shoulder has been bitten. His face is green instead of its usual pale coloring, and he's sweating. I didn't know vampires could sweat. The poor guy looks awful. "Call Henry," he croaks, holding out his phone to me. "He should still be close. He can help me."

His eyes roll back in his head before Henry picks up.

"I asked you to talk to her, not buy her dinner!" Henry hisses in lieu of a greeting.

"Henry!"

"Nora?" His tone changes completely at the sound of my voice. "What's wrong?"

"We were attacked by werewolves. Parker's hurt. I think he's dying. Please come help him."

Over the line, I hear him make a screeching turn in his

car. "What about you? Are you hurt?"

"No. I'm fine. Just come help Parker!"

"I'll be there in two minutes."

Gravel crunches and Nick crouches down beside me, examining Parker's scratches and the bite. He checks for Parker's pulse and sighs. "He needs vamp blood. That's the only thing that will save him now."

I blink at Nick. Parker told me not to feed anyone anymore, but I'd feed him again if it meant saving his life. "Only vampire blood? I can't...?"

Nick shakes his head. "Werewolf saliva will turn a human, but it's deadly poison for most underworlders—vampires especially. He needs more vampire blood to strengthen him and flush out the poison. If he doesn't get some soon, he won't survive."

Henry's Mercedes pulls back into the parking lot, and I breathe a sigh of relief. This is the only time I've ever been—or will ever be—glad to see the vampire. I wave him over and he comes quickly, but his eyes are on me, not Parker. He grabs me by the arms and looks me over from head to toe. "Were you bitten?"

I wave him off with a huff. "Not me. Parker. Help him."

Slowly, reluctantly, Henry turns away from me and crouches next to Parker. While he's checking Parker's wounds, Nick pulls me aside. "What the hell happened here?"

I follow his gaze to the carnage around me and shake my head. "I don't know. They came out of nowhere. I think I was their target, and Parker was just collateral damage. They planned to turn me, though, not kill me. Well, all of them except the one you got. That guy was ready to tear me to pieces."

"Do you recognize any of them?"

I start to shake my head again, but then stop. I do recognize one of them. I point to one of the guys Parker took down. All three of them have shifted back into their human forms, and one of them has a very familiar face. "That guy was in Skinny's having dinner when we were. He was teasing me about dating Rook. I think he was trying to piss off Parker and Henry. He left before us. He must have called his buddies for help. But why they'd want to attack us at all, I don't understand. We didn't make him mad or anything."

Nick sighs. "They were rogues."

"What?"

"Packless werewolves." Nick points to the guy he killed. "I've had trouble with that one before. When rogues attack unprovoked, it usually means they were hired to do it. Rogues often work as mercenaries."

My stomach rolls at the implication. Someone hired rogue werewolves to turn me? Or possibly kill me? Why would someone want me dead now? And who would hire wolves to do it?

I come back from my thoughts when Henry hisses loudly. He's glaring at me with red eyes. "Why do I smell you on him?"

Um…because he kissed me, I think. But no way am I telling Henry that. He'd shit a brick.

"NORA!"

I don't like being yelled at and snap back. "It's none of

your damn business why!"

He growls at this and places his hands on Parker's head.
I wince. I'd forgotten he could just look at Parker's memories
if he wanted. His eyes stay open, but they gloss over and go
unfocused as he sifts through the night's events in Parker's
mind. When he gets to our totally hot and disastrous kiss, he
stiffens, snarls, and then digs his fingers into the wound on
Parker's side. Parker wakes with a jolt and screams in pain.

"Henry!" I rush over and try to stop Henry from hurting Parker, but he's too strong for me. I kneel beside him and
yank on his arm. "What are you *doing?*"

"Killing him," Henry growls. "Slowly and painfully."

His claws are extended, and he's deepening the wound
in Parker's side. I pull again on his arm and am unable to
move it even a millimeter. "Henry, stop! Please!"

"He deserves it," Henry says, but he pulls his hand back
and frowns at me.

Parker quickly sinks back into unconsciousness. I'm
actually relieved by that. His cries of pain are not something
I will forget anytime soon.

"He saved my life, Henry," I murmur.

Henry replies just as softly. "He kissed you."

"That's not a reason to kill him."

"He betrayed me." Henry sounds devastated by that.
He stands up and looks down at Parker with sad eyes. "I
warned him. He has wanted you from the very first night he
brought you to me, but *I* claimed you. You were supposed
to be *mine.*"

"And what I want doesn't matter?" I scoff.

Henry meets my eyes with a solid gaze. "It should not matter to him. I am his *master*. He is supposed to obey me with unwavering loyalty."

His gaze falls to Parker again. His remorse shocks me. Parker's actions have genuinely crushed him. "He was my best vampire," he murmurs. "My favorite." Shaking his head, he looks at me and his expression turns bitter. "For you, I won't kill him, Nora, but his life is in your hands now." He starts heading back to his car, wiping his hands with a handkerchief he pulls from the pocket of his suit. "Let him know, if he wakes up, that he is dead to me. He is no longer a member of my clan."

I jump to my feet. I'm actually thrilled that Parker is out of Henry's clan—though he'll probably be upset by that—but I can't believe Henry is just walking away. "You're just going to let him *die?*"

Henry shakes his head. "He has hurt me deeply, Nora. I will not save a traitor. I will not kill him, but I won't spare his life, either." His bitter smile turns scornful and hateful. "Good luck saving him in time. He's got maybe minutes left."

With that, he sends a quick glare to the disapproving Nick and heads for his car. Tears of anger well in my eyes as I follow him. "You selfish bastard!" I scream as I kick his stupid tires.

Henry sighs at my immaturity. "Do call me if you ever need anything. Perhaps you'll give me a chance once Parker is out of the picture."

The nerve of the man! Riled with rage, I kick his side

passenger door, leaving a dent that is going to cost him a pretty penny to fix. "Never, you asshole!"

Henry makes his displeased, pinched sour-lemon face and says, "Good-bye, Nora," as he climbs into his car. Hopefully it's the last time I ever have to see him. I flip him the bird as he drives off and then rush to Parker's side. His heartbeat is so faint.

"Help will be here in ten minutes," Nick tells me, crouching down beside me. "The FUA has a few vampire friends in other clans besides Henry's."

I shake my head. "Parker doesn't have that long, and you know it."

I look into Nick's eyes, and his face falls. "I'm sorry, Nora. I wish there was more I could do."

"You're not a vampire, are you?" I ask jokingly, trying to cover a sniffle with a laugh. It doesn't work.

Nick manages a small smile. "If I was, I'd have fed him already."

"Then, what are you?"

The question pops from my mouth without thought. I have no tact when I'm distressed. Nick chuckles and puts his arm around me. "Nothing that can help him right now," he says quietly. "I'm sorry."

Nick has given up on Parker. The defeat in his voice, fuels my determination. I can't let Parker die. "Do you have a knife?" I ask.

I'm not surprised when Nick pulls a knife from his cowboy boot, nor that he hands it over to me without question. I hold it against my wrist. I know I don't have vampire blood, but any blood makes a vampire stronger, and Parker said my blood was different somehow. Maybe it's strong enough to help him last until Nick's vampire backup gets here. It certainly helped him last time he drank it.

Parker's warning that I should never feed anyone my blood again runs through my head, but then I look at his pale face. "Screw it."

I drag the blade across my skin, wincing at the sting. I cut deep, and red begins to pour from my wrist. I quickly hold my arm over Parker's mouth, but he's unconscious, and the drops drip down the side of his face. Nick helps, holding Parker's mouth open so I can drip the blood down his throat. "Thanks." I sniffle.

"You realize this probably won't work, right? He needs vampire blood to purge the werewolf saliva out."

"I know. But maybe it'll give him the strength to last until we can get him some real help."

As the words leave my lips, Parker swallows. I give him several more mouthfuls before pulling my arm back. Nick tears a piece of his T-shirt for me to cover my wrist with. He smirks as he ties it in place for me. "This was a Mötley Crüe T-shirt. That's got to be good luck somehow."

I bark out a surprised laugh and sniffle again. "I'm sure it is. Thanks, Nick."

"For you, beautiful, anytime. Oh, and hey! We caught ourselves a werewolf. Once we get him back to the Agency, you want to help me interrogate him?"

A smile creeps across my face. "Aw, shucks, Gorgeous. You know just what to say to make a girl feel better."

Nick laughs, but surprisingly, he's not the only one. Parker has regained consciousness and chuckles, though it sounds like it hurts him to do so. "Is that what a guy has to offer to get you to like him? I've been doing this all wrong."

"Parker!" I throw my arms around him, and he groans. "Sorry." I let him go and sit back. "You're awake! How is that possible?"

"It shouldn't be," Nick says, gaping at Parker as if he's some sort of living miracle.

Parker nods his head toward me. He's still too pale, but he's awake. "It's her blood. It's so strong."

He coughs again and lies back with a groan. His eyes close again, but he's not unconscious. "I told you never to feed anyone again," he moans.

His voice is weak. He doesn't have much time left, but maybe he has enough now.

"Your blood is different. If people knew..."

"Different how?" Nick asks.

I glare at Parker, though his eyes are still closed and he can't see me. "You were going to *die*. And Nick's not going to say anything."

Nick is too busy frowning at me to confirm my trust in him. "How is your blood different?"

"It's magical," Parker says. "It tastes like immortal blood. Like a vampire's, or one of the stronger fey. Stronger than even yours would be. And it's highly addictive. I'll need to be compelled to not crave it."

Nick eyes me skeptically. "What are you?"

I smirk. "I believe I asked you that question first."

Nick's eyes narrow, but his mock irritation doesn't stick because his lips twitch, and there's laughter in his voice when he says, "What do you think I am?"

I easily turn the question on him. "What do you think *I* am?"

The playful banter breaks between us as Nick's gaze becomes thoughtful. "I have no idea. You seem human, but humans don't have your gifts, and their blood definitely doesn't have magical or immortal properties. You have to be something else. But what?"

Parker shakes his head, eyes still closed, and says, "I don't know, but we need to keep this to ourselves." He coughs again, and a little trickle of blood drips from the corner of his mouth. "Her blood is like vampire heroin. I've never tasted anything like it. If others knew, they'd kill her just to taste her."

A dark look crosses Nick's face. "I'll end anyone that tries."

I'm touched by Nick's loyalty, though not wholly surprised by it. My curse affects everyone, to some extent. Nick doesn't seem too horribly influenced, but I have noticed he's friendlier toward me than to others, and he's as protective of me as Terrance is.

He turns his glare on me as if it's my fault people would want my blood. "Parker's right. You can't use your blood anymore. It's too dangerous. This secret can't leave the three of us."

I bristle. "If it can help the people I care about, then I'm willing to take the risk. And I won't keep it from Terrance or Ollie. Terrance would kill me if I kept a secret from him that puts me in danger, and Oliver might be able to help me figure out the mystery."

Both men are glaring at me, when Nick's backup finally arrives. Parker sighs, and Nick gives me a curt nod. "Fine, but no one else. We'll talk more about this later."

"Fine."

A heavy silence falls between us as Nick and I back away to let the vampire help Parker. We walk back to Parker's car—where Nick has shoved the handcuffed werewolf in the back seat. The wolf's eyes lock on me, as if he's trying to figure me out. *You and me both, buddy.*

I stare right back, refusing to let him intimidate me. Honestly, I'm more freaked out by the fact that I brought his buddy down with some kind of magic than I am upset over the attack.

After a few minutes, Parker is back on his feet. He looks like death warmed over, but he's up and moving around. Damn. Now, that's some healing power. I'm so happy to see him alive and sort of well that I throw my arms around him. Parker is shocked by the hug but quickly returns it and doesn't let go right away. I let him hold me for a second, because he feels safe and I'm so tired of people trying to kill me.

The moment he runs his hand over my head and down my back, caressing my hair, I catch his thoughts. *She feels so perfect. I could hold her like this forever.* It's both sweet and frightening at the same time, so I break the hug and step back. I can't stand his loving gaze on me with so much hope in his eyes, so I turn my back on him and grab my arms to hug myself.

"Oh, Nora…" Parker brushes off my back with a sigh. "I hate to tell you this, but you've ruined your new coat."

"Figures." Glancing over my shoulder, I can just make out some tears in the fabric made from glass and werewolf claws. "Speaking of bad news…" I hesitate a second before passing him Henry's message. "Henry saw you kiss me in your memories. He *freaked.*"

Parker winces. "I knew it must have been something like that." He leans back against the side of the car and trains his attention on the FUA crew, which is now cleaning up the dead werewolf bodies and putting them in the back of a large van. "He's severed the sire connection," he says quietly. "I'm no longer part of his clan."

I was happy about that a few minutes ago, but seeing the disappointment on Parker's face, I feel bad for getting him kicked out of his home. I want to comfort him, so I place my hand on his arm. "I'm sorry."

When he moves to cover my hand with his, I quickly pull back. I really don't want to be inside his head at the moment. Parker flinches at the rejection but quickly shoves his emotions away and gives me a small smile. "Don't worry about me, Nora. There are other clans I can pledge to if I wish, or I may just join the FUA. They've been trying to recruit me for decades, but I refused to leave my clan for them. My loyalty to Henry was always too great."

I lean back against his car as well and watch Nick direct the FUA agents in the cleanup process. He's rather efficient.

"Why would you have to leave Henry to join?"

"FUA requirements." Parker shrugs. "Anyone who becomes a member can't have strong ties to outside clans, covens, or packs. You have to be impartial."

I frown. Does that mean Oliver doesn't have a coven? And Ren doesn't have a...whatever incubi families are called? "Sounds lonely."

Parker shrugs again. "Not necessarily. When you join, the FUA usually becomes your family. It's made up of a lot of outcasts."

The puzzle pieces start to fall into place. "Like a gay incubus, or a sorcerer who won't use his magic?"

"Exactly. Or a human girl with psychic powers." Parker grins. "Don't tell me they haven't tried to recruit you, too."

I laugh. "They try all the time, but I'd feel horrible quitting on Terrance. Now that I know I'd have to abandon his clan, too, there's no way it'll ever happen. I couldn't do that to him."

Parker's grin falls away. "And that is why I have never joined. I couldn't leave Henry. But now..."

Guilt swamps me again. I have to swallow back a lump of emotion. "I'm sorry."

Parker turns to face me, leaning against the car on his side instead of his back. His ice blue eyes get intense again as he pierces me with a meaningful gaze. "It's okay, Nora. It was my choice. I knew there would be consequences for pursuing you."

He risks tucking a strand of my hair behind my ear. Our

kiss is now in the forefront of his mind. He thinks it was worth it, though he hates that it ended up upsetting me. He's not the only one who feels that way. I have to clear my throat in order to speak, and then my damn traitorous voice comes out shaky. "Pursuing me, huh? Is that what you're doing?"

I laugh weakly, but Parker responds with complete seriousness. "Yes. And I will continue to do so until you tell me to stop."

He pauses, as if he expects me to say stop right this second. I should. Part of me wants to. But I stay quiet, and Parker's lips curve up into a tiny smile. "You do me a great honor, Nora."

I gulp. My heart is suddenly pounding in my chest. "I can't promise anything. I'm really messed up. I have a complicated past."

"I understand, and I thank you for at least giving me the chance to try."

Nick walks over to us, unknowingly breaking the tension. I'm grateful for the reprieve. "We're ready to head out," he says. "You guys want to follow us back?"

Parker hesitates and then sighs. "You should take her with you."

I'm so shocked I rear my head back. Parker grimaces. "It's not that I don't want to, but...I'm exhausted." He lets out another weary sigh. "If someone were to try again, I don't think I could protect you in this condition."

Parker swallows hard, as if admitting his weakness kills him. Which is ridiculous. He was outnumbered four to one, and he still came out alive.

In a rare moment of seriousness, Nick places a hand on Parker's shoulder and says, "You saved her life tonight."

Their gazes meet, and something passes between them. It sort of makes me wish I could hug them both. Nick gives Parker's shoulder another squeeze. "Go home and get some rest, friend. I'll look after her."

It takes Parker a moment to accept defeat, but then he nods. Nick lets him go, and he sucks in a deep breath while raking his hands through his hair.

Nick catches the longing look Parker casts my way. His lips twitch, and I know he's reached his serious quota for the day. He jerks his head my direction and smirks at Parker. "Well, go on. Kiss our girl goodnight. She owes you one for saving her."

My eyes bulge, and my jaw drops. "NICK!" I punch him in the arm, and I swear it hurts me worse than him. It takes everything I have in me not to stomp my foot like a petulant child. But there is no stopping the blush that creeps into my cheeks.

Nick somehow manages an innocent shrug and heads toward his bike, whistling a cheerful tune. Jerk. I glare lasers into his back until Parker blocks my view. Suddenly he's *right there*, so close I can smell his cologne and feel him invading my personal space. My heart rate kicks up so fast a ghost of a smile crosses Parker's face. His gaze falls to my mouth, but he quickly lifts it again. "You going to be okay?"

I pry my tongue off the roof of my mouth and whisper,

"Thanks to you."

I'm rewarded with another almost-smile.

Parker lifts his hand and I think he's going to tuck my hair behind my ear, but he cups my cheek instead. His eyes fall shut, and he sucks in a deep breath. *Have to be patient. She needs time. She'll trust me eventually.*

His thumb brushes my cheek so softly my eyes flutter shut, and I shiver. The air around me shifts, and then Parker's soft lips press against my forehead. "Good night, Nora."

I'm speechless and frozen in place, until Parker gets in his car and drives off. I watch him go, unable to reconcile the warring emotions inside me. I don't know what I'm doing with him. He's too intense, and I know part of him is under the same spell everyone else is under. I know he's drawn to me more than he should be. But for some reason, I can't help encouraging him. I like him, but I'm playing with fire, and I always get burned.

I yelp when a hand clamps down lightly on my shoulder, and Nick chuckles. "Come on, little spitfire. Let's go back to the Agency and beat a confession out of a merc."

I snort but follow him to his bike. He stops before climbing on and grins at me. "You know...I also saved your life tonight. I think I deserve a kiss, too."

He's joking. But at the same time there's something in his expression I've never noticed before. A hint of, I don't know, a dare? I narrow my eyes at him. Just what is he playing at? When his lips twitch and I realize he's only messing with me, I have the overwhelming urge to punch him. "You know what you can kiss, Gorgeous? My *ass.*"

Nick bursts into laughter and climbs onto his motorcycle, patting the seat behind him after the bike roars to life. "Come on, Nora. Let's go interrogate our perp. I'll let you be the bad cop."

Damn him for making me laugh.

CHAPTER
SIXTEEN

THE INTERROGATION ROOM AT THE FUA LOOKS THE SAME as it does in the human world. Small. White walls. One-way mirror. Single table. The main difference is that it's warded to be magic suppressing. By the time I follow Nick into the room, my new werewolf friend is bitching about his silver handcuffs being too tight. The guy stops complaining when he notices me. "What's she doing in here?" He almost sounds scared. Nervous, at the very least. "She's not a cop."

Nick winks at me. "Nah, but she's cute, though, isn't she?"

I roll my eyes. Wolf Man scoffs.

"So...Dennis," I say, reading the rap sheet sitting on the table in front of Nick and me. "No priors. Attempted murder is a pretty serious first offense. Money must be tight for you to take that job." I meet his blazing yellow eyes. "It *was* a job, wasn't it? Or did you just try to kill Parker and me for the fun of it?"

Dennis snarls at the accusation. "It was a job, but I didn't try to murder anyone. I didn't go near the vamp, and we were only paid to get you out of the picture—employer wasn't specific as to how. Turning you and mating with you would have done that just fine, and you're only human. That's not against the law. I'm allowed to claim a human mate."

I grit my teeth and glare at no one in particular. "There really should be a law that you can't just take humans at will."

Lack of that law is the whole reason Henry originally took me and why I'm neck-deep in the underworld now. But, underworlders aren't big fans of humans as a whole, so I doubt that law is getting passed anytime soon, even if it would make my life infinitely easier.

"Fine," Nick says to Dennis, shrugging casually. "You're allowed to claim a human mate. Nora is exempt from that because she has underworlder blood, but you probably didn't know that, right?"

Dennis vigorously shakes his head, staring at me with wide eyes. "I didn't know. I swear."

Nick cocks his head to the side, considering something, then nods once. "Fine, you didn't know." Can he smell lies, like a werewolf? I wouldn't put it past him. "Tell us who paid you, and we'll let you go."

"Seriously?" I shout.

Nick shrugs. "Unfortunately, he's right. Claiming a human mate isn't illegal, and, technically, he didn't go after Parker."

"But he was an accessory! And he was hired! Isn't there some kind of law against being a mercenary?"

Nick leans back in his chair and folds his arms across his chest. "Not if the job isn't for something illegal." When I scoff, he sighs. "I know you're pissed, but he's not really the person we're looking for. Small fish, you know? We need him to talk."

Who knew I really would be the bad cop of our strange little duo? I start to lose my patience. I want to know who paid these guys to come after Parker and me, and I have a better way of getting that info than making deals with this jerk. "Screw it."

Dennis's hands are shackled to the table in front of him with silver cuffs. He can't move them, so I lean across the table and rest my hand on top of his. "Who paid you to come after me?"

His thoughts go exactly where I want them to. He can't help it. When I hear the answer, I pull my hand back so hard I nearly fall out of my chair. "It was Huron River pack money?" My heart plummets into my stomach at the betrayal. "But why? I *helped* them!"

Nick's staring at the wolf, incredulous. "The Huron River pack hired you?"

Dennis doesn't answer. He's too busy gaping at me in horror. "You're a *mind reader?*"

The door to the interrogation room opens, and Madison West, the Director of the Detroit Division of the FUA, strolls in wearing either a smug or impressed smile. I can't tell which. "So it's true, then?" she asks. "It was the Huron River pack who ordered the hit?"

"It wasn't a hit," Dennis growls.

"Technically," I grumble. I turn to Director West. "Was that confession enough for you?"

"It's unconventional." She glances at Nick.

He shakes his head. "There was no lie in her words."

So he *can* sniff out lies. I wonder if he's a shifter of some sort.

Director West thinks for a moment then nods. "The truth from you about what you heard in his mind is still the truth." She smiles at me like a cat who's caught a canary. "Nora, we really must discuss, again, you coming to work for us. Think of all the good you could do."

I can't think of anything right now except for the fact that the pack I'd just helped put out a hit on my life as thanks. "Sorry, Director West, I have a more pressing issue at the moment than my current employment." I turn my gaping gaze back to Dennis. "Was it really the Huron River pack? Or was it just someone in the pack working individually? Who, exactly, paid you?"

"Garrett paid me," he snaps. "You know, the wolf your buddy here killed?" He jerks his head in Nick's direction.

I snort. "Yeah, I don't feel bad about Nick sending him into his next life. He was about to do me the same courtesy. You know he was."

Dennis's glare softens a little, as if he feels bad about that. "He wasn't supposed to," he mumbles, looking away from me. "It was a mistake to hire him. He's always been bloodthirsty."

"That's probably *why* he was hired," Nick says. He narrows his eyes in thought and taps his lips with a finger. Slowly, he nods his head. "Yeah, that makes sense. If you want someone dead but you don't want to be guilty of ordering their hit, you hire the most unstable, bloodthirsty mercenary to do the job and give him loose orders not to kill. Very smart." His eyes flick back to me. "Technically, whoever paid them is not really guilty of being anything more than a jerk."

"Of course not." I roll my eyes at the complete crap penal system of the underworld. "But guilty or not, the fact is, someone in the Huron River pack wants me dead, and I need to know who before they try again."

I turn to Dennis with a sugary sweet smile and bat my lashes. "Dennis, sweetheart, who in the Huron River pack paid Garrett to not kill me?"

Dennis clenches his jaw, mouth shut tight as he glares at me. I glower right back. "Fine. We'll do it my way again."

When I reach for him, he thrashes in his chair, straining so hard his wrists get scraped raw and start to bleed. "Stay out of my head!"

"Then tell me who in the pack paid for the job."

My fingers graze his skin, and he frantically shouts, "I can't! I'm a lone wolf. The Huron River pack is large, strong. If I betray them, I'll be killed."

I lean over the table, coming closer to the wolf so I can look him directly in the eyes. "Newsflash, buddy, you've already told us it was them. You've already betrayed them. Now tell me what I want to know, or I'll steal it from your head. I don't like doing that, but I will because I need to know who wants me dead."

When I reach for his hand again, he blurts out the answer I'm looking for. "It was the luna!" He deflates as the words leave his lips, and he slumps over in a resigned heap. "Luna Marie of the Huron River pack paid us."

Both Nick and Director West gasp, but I'm a lot less surprised than I should be. I'm also relieved it wasn't Alpha Toth. That betrayal would have stung deep.

"The luna?" Madison asks, blinking in disbelief.

I'm not surprised she's upset that a luna—a pack's most respected and honorable female—would do something so underhanded. Of course, she wasn't there to see how fast Luna Marie murdered Daniel and Maya.

I freeze, the blood chilling in my veins as I piece together a bit of truth I'd missed before. "It was Luna Marie," I murmur.

Everyone frowns at me like I'm insane, since we'd already established that fact, but I'm not talking about the contract on me anymore. It was Luna Marie who had stolen the pack money. Or, she'd been blackmailing Maya and Daniel to do it, anyway. She must have known about their clandestine relationship and used it against them. Then, she killed them both so quickly to keep them from spilling the truth. And now she's trying to tie up loose ends with me. She can't know for sure how much I know, or how I figured out the secret in the first place. She knows I have powers that helped me solve the mystery, but not what exactly those powers are. I'm a wild card that she can't afford.

"All right," Director West says, breaking the quiet that

has fallen over the room. "Gorgeous, you may uncuff him. Since he has broken no law by trying to claim a human mate, and he has given us the information we needed, he is free to go. Bring in the luna of the Huron River pack for questioning, though. She may have technically broken no law, but she clearly has ill intentions toward Ms. Jacobs. We need to figure out why and make sure no more attempts to harm her are made."

I know the answer to that, but I've sworn secrecy to Alpha Toth, and I don't know if he'll want the FUA knowing pack business, so I keep quiet. I need to talk to Alpha Toth, but before I do, I need to take care of one more thing. "Hang on one second," I say to Nick when he moves to release Dennis. I grab Dennis's hand once again and ask, "What's your biggest secret?"

The question was asked so randomly and so suddenly that he doesn't have time to try and distract his mind before his thoughts betray him. I get a picture of a young face in his mind's eye. His daughter. He keeps her hidden in the human world. She's about eight years old, and she's half sorceress. She is the reason Dennis wanted to claim me as a mate. He wants her to have a mother, and he wants a strong partner to help keep her safe. The underworld isn't always kind to mixed breeds, sorcerers especially. That's why he abandoned his pack and became a lone wolf—to protect her. But being a lone wolf is dangerous, so when he heard of me and how dominant I would be if turned, and that I had special abilities and strong ties to the FUA, he wanted me on his side.

I pull my hand away in surprise. He gapes at me in

horror. "Why?" he rasps. "Why did you do that?"

"Insurance," I whisper. "You know what I can do. Mine is a dangerous gift to have. People might try to kill me or use me because of it. I don't like that you know about it, and I don't trust you. So you keep my secret, and I'll keep yours."

His face turns green. He doesn't trust me, but he doesn't see how he has a choice. If the sorcerer community learned of his daughter, she would be in danger, and he will do anything to protect her.

My face softens, and I grab his hand again to give it a squeeze. "You have my word. I'll never tell a soul, so long as you do me the same courtesy."

My compassion surprises him. He's shocked that I didn't just want to use his secrets against him to get revenge, since he's being let go. "I won't," he swears. "I'll never tell anyone."

"Then neither will I."

I feel bad for the guy. Not enough to become his mate, of course, but enough to scribble down my phone number onto a piece of paper and hand it to him after Nick lets him out of the handcuffs. He stares at it, confused. "Just in case you ever need my help," I explain.

His jaw falls open, and his eyes bulge. I give him a smile. "Good luck."

"Thank you."

Getting back to the matter at hand, I look away from Dennis to find Nick and Director West watching me, as if waiting for something. Curiosity burns on all their faces. I shake my head. "It's not illegal and will bring no harm to anyone. It's his secret to keep, so don't ask."

Madison's lips twitch up into a smile. "Of course not. We're just impressed with how you've handled this entire situation. Perhaps you would join me for dinner?"

"So you can try to recruit me some more? Sounds like fun, really, but wouldn't you know, I already ate? And besides, Parker said I'd have to leave Terrance's clan if I joined. Is that true?"

Director West sighs. "Yes, that's true. But you don't really belong there anyway."

I bristle. Terrance's place is the first place I've ever felt I did fit. "Maybe it's not conventional, but Terrance *does* want me there."

Director West holds up a hand to placate me. "That's not what I meant. I know exactly how Terrance feels about you. He considers you clan. But the fact is, you are human. And some day Terrance will expand his clan. He'll take a mate. Have children. How will you feel when that happens? Will you be able to live in a den of trolls?"

I squirm under her stare. I hadn't thought about that. Terrance is one thing, but a bunch of others? And none so welcoming or understanding as Terrance? "He's the first real family I've ever had," I say, though my voice lacks conviction.

Director West's answering smile is small and calculating. "What about Oliver? Do you not consider him family as well? You know how happy it would make him if you joined us."

Ooh, she fights dirty.

Her smile turns smug. "Just think about it."

When I narrow my eyes and ball up my fists, Nick

chuckles and grabs my shoulder to lead me out of the small interrogation room. "Come on, little spitfire. Why don't you come with me out to the Huron River pack instead, since I know you're heading that way anyway."

I grin at his rueful smile, not feeling the least bit ashamed. "You betcha, cowboy. Any chance you own something other than the motorcycle, though? As much as I love it, it's freezing out there, and the human doesn't have an internal heater."

Nick's grin turns wicked. "Would you rather take the Porsche or the Lotus?"

CHAPTER
SEVENTEEN

Werewolf gossip. There's really nothing like it. By the time Nick and I get from the guard shack to the parking lot park in front of the pack's clubhouse, word of our arrival has already spread. Half the pack is out there to greet us. Both Alpha Toth and Rook are in front of the masses.

While Alpha Toth extends a formal welcome to Nick, Rook grabs me, sniffs hard, then growls. His eyes start to glow. "Why is your hair a mess? Why is your coat ripped up? And why the *hell* do I smell strange wolves all over you?"

He doesn't says so out loud, but as he inspects me for any kind of injury or bite, his thoughts keep repeating, *My human!*

Rook the man doesn't seem all that affected by my curse, but his wolf grows more attached to me every time we meet. I know it's the wolf acting like a possessive douche right now, so I don't call him out. That would only give all the gawking wolves something more to talk about.

"I was attacked by rogues tonight," I say, stepping back out of Rook's grasp. "Parker nearly died trying to protect me."

Rook snarls again and pulls me into a tight embrace, squeezing me so hard I can barely breathe. "Whoa! Down, boy!"

"Hold very still, Nora," Alpha Toth says quietly. "Rook's wolf is in control right now, and it appears he considers you his. Any sudden movements and he may very well shift and turn you so that he can claim you as a mate."

"I thought Rook never dates," I say as I wait out Rook's embrace.

"*Rook* doesn't. But his wolf must be ready to take another mate. I'll have to talk to him about suppressing his instincts. As you can see, it can get dangerous to deny our wolves their primal needs."

"How do I get him to stop?"

"Talk to him. Hug him back. Your voice and your physical touch will settle his wolf."

Right. That's not awkward or anything.

The wolf is on the surface, so it's him I talk to. "Hey, big guy," I say as I rub soothing circles on his back. "Think you can settle down for me? I know who ordered the hit on me, and I need Rook's help to catch 'em. Think you can do that? Can you let Rook back out to play?"

Rook's wolf growls, and he buries his face in my neck to sniff deeply. He lets me go but takes my hand and laces our fingers together. When he steps back, Rook is in control again. Though, his wolf must still be close to the surface, because he tugs me against his side and slips his arm around my waist as if he needs the physical touch. When I try to break his hold and put some distance between us, he tightens his grip. "I'm sorry about this, Nora, but I need you to stay close for now. My wolf really doesn't like smelling strangers on you, and if you get too close to another male right now, I might lose it."

I sigh. I can't be angry with him. We've spent so much time training together over the last two weeks that this was bound to happen. I need to figure out how to break this damn curse. "I'm sorry, Rook. This is my fault. I told you it might eventually be a problem. I guess we're going to have to stop the training sessions now." When his jaw clenches and his eyes start to glow again, I quickly add, "But hey, I totally used the moves you showed me on one of those rogues tonight, and it worked. I felt like a real badass." *Until I got caught again, anyway.*

Rook squeezes my hand and gives me a crooked smile. "Good girl."

"You in control enough now?" I ask. "Nick and I really need to speak with Alpha Toth privately."

He clenches his jaw and growls again. "I'm coming with you."

I roll my eyes and look to Alpha Toth for permission. Alpha Toth nods curtly and leads us inside the building, ignoring all the gaping werewolves. I want to flip them all off, but I can hardly blame them when their ex-alpha is acting like I'm his property.

Once we're in Alpha Toth's office, I quickly give him the rundown of tonight's events. Alpha Toth leans far back in his desk chair, looking pale-faced and fifty years older. "After everything you did for our pack, my own mate tried to have you killed? You're sure?"

"As sure as the guy who abducted me was sure. He didn't take the money personally, but there was no hesitation in his thoughts when I asked where the money came from."

Alpha Toth digests this, then looks to Rook. Rook thinks on it long and hard. "Why?" he finally asks no one in particular. "What motive could she possibly have?"

I cringe inwardly. If Alpha Toth didn't take the last news so well, he's definitely going to freak out with this. "Don't you see?" I ask them both. "It was Luna Marie who was stealing the money."

Rook's eyes widen, and Alpha Toth rears back with a soft gasp.

"Money?" Nick asks.

Alpha Toth glares at him. "Pack business."

Nick rolls his eyes, then raises a curious brow at me. I ignore him and give Alpha Toth a pained smile. "It's just a theory. I haven't proven it yet. Hopefully, I'm wrong."

Alpha Toth grinds his teeth so hard I can hear him from my seat across the desk. Rook, pacing the office behind Alpha Toth, suddenly comes to a stop. He rakes a hand through his thick brown locks and grimaces. "Okay, what's your theory?"

"Maya and Daniel."

Both current and former alphas' eyes flash to me. The

intuition sparks in both of them, but I continue my explanation. Mostly for Nick's sake. He's out of the loop right now, and his irritation is growing. He's twitching in his seat and bouncing a knee. But he's being patient and was a really good sport when I made him swear to let me talk to Alpha Toth first before he barged in demanding to question his luna. "Maya and Daniel had a secret unsanctioned relationship."

More teeth grinding from Alpha Toth. He really didn't like that betrayal.

"My guess is either Luna Marie found out about them and blackmailed them into stealing the money for her, or they went to her for help and she manipulated them into taking it for her, promising to help them leave the pack. She killed them awfully quickly once they were found out. And that was only after Daniel started to speak."

"She was keeping them quiet," Rook mutters. He stops his pacing and leans against the back wall, as if needing the support to stay upright.

I nod. "Remember Maya's reaction after Luna Marie killed Daniel? She was defiant to the end and said she wanted to rid the pack of its real problem when she challenged Luna Marie."

"Marie was tying up loose ends when she ordered the hit on you," Rook says.

I nod again, keeping my steady gaze locked on Alpha Toth. "She knew we were onto the missing money. She knew I'd discovered Daniel and Maya by using gifts she doesn't understand. Obviously you didn't know the truth, but she wasn't sure how much I knew, or if I'd piece together the rest."

The room falls silent. Nick must understand what's really going on now—he's awfully intelligent, despite the fact that he insists everyone call him Gorgeous—but he knows better than to comment right now. This is pack business, and unless Alpha Toth asks for help, or it starts threatening the underworld as a whole, it's his right to take care of it without the FUA stepping in. Alpha Toth is hanging by a thin thread, and any interference, no matter how well meant, would send him over the edge.

"It makes sense, boss," Rook says quietly.

Alpha Toth knows it does. His eyes have started to glow. He's accepted the truth, and his wolf is starting to surface.

Suddenly, Alpha Toth slams to his feet and flips over his desk with a mighty roar. Nick, moving a lot faster than I could, sweeps me out of harm's way. His arms lock tightly around me in a protective grip.

For a minute I'm not sure if Alpha Toth's mad at Luna Marie, or mad at me for making such an accusation against her. "My own damn mate!" He shouts with so much force spittle flies from his mouth with each word. His chest is heaving, and his body is shaking with rage. He storms toward the door, but Rook stops him, placing a gentle hand on the alpha's shoulder. "Easy, Peter."

"I'll kill the bitch!"

"We'll take care of this, but you must calm yourself first. You want to act honorably and with a level head. You don't want your pack to watch you kill your mate in a fit of rage."

Alpha Toth sucks in a sharp breath through flared nostrils, then rolls his stiff shoulders.

"Let's talk to her first. Give her the chance to explain herself. We still have no idea why she was taking the money. Maybe she had a good reason."

Whoa. Wrong thing to say. Alpha Toth's head snaps to Rook, and a snarl rips from his chest. "A good enough reason to steal from my pack and kill two of my wolves who may have been guilty of nothing more than asking their luna for help?"

Nick steps in front of me, blocking me from view of the alpha wolf. It's a protective gesture, because Alpha Toth is losing the battle with his wolf. If he shifts in this temper while locked in this room, he's liable to attack the messenger. Since that would be me, I'm more than happy to let Nick protect me.

When Alpha Toth starts shaking so badly he falls to his knees, Rook moves in front of him. "Calm yourself, Peter!" he snaps with all the force of a very powerful werewolf. I wince at the sting of the command. Rook's so easygoing it's hard to remember that he's more dominant than Alpha Toth. Right now it's clear as day, though. Alpha Toth trembles under the command and lowers his head, exposing his neck as a show of submission.

Rook eases up, and I take a deep breath. Even Nick shudders once the tension in the air is gone. Alpha Toth remains on his knees a moment, staring at the ground while he sucks in huge, gulping breaths. Once he's calm, he looks up at Rook with sorrow and gratitude in his eyes. The two say nothing but exchange a long glance that needs no words. Rook holds out a hand to his alpha. The large, broody man rises to his feet and pulls Rook into a tight hug. "I'm sorry, Peter," Rook whispers.

Alpha Toth finally pulls back with a long sigh. "I've always known she's ill fit to be the pack luna. She's too power hungry, and she's got a dark side to her that has to be kept in check. But her wolf is so dominant none of my other females could ever win a challenge against her. When she beat Isabella for the right to be my mate, I accepted her because I knew she'd never stop causing trouble if I didn't. I thought I could keep control of her if she were my mate."

All the fight seeps out of Alpha Toth. He seems more resigned now than anything. Self-pity's never a good thing, especially not if you're an alpha, so I risk speaking up. "Don't dwell on the problem, Alpha Toth. Fix it."

Alpha Toth's head snaps my direction, eyes hard after the reprimand, but I stand my ground. "You can't do anything about past choices, so focus on the present. Change what you can."

He glares a moment longer, but then his eyes soften. "That's sage advice."

I shrug. "My past is ugly. If I worried about the what-ifs, I'd go crazy. With my gifts, there's a lot I can't control in my life, so I focus on what little I *can* do something about."

Alpha Toth gives me a long, searching look, then places a hand on my shoulder. "You are an amazing woman, Ms. Jacobs. Thank you for all you've done to help my pack. I'm so sorry that my luna put you in danger."

Uncomfortable with all the emotions flying around, I step out of the alpha's grip and shrug again. "Don't worry about it. Not your fault. I don't hold any ill feeling toward your pack. However, if you want to mete out some punishment on Luna Marie, well, I'm not going to stand in your way."

Alpha Toth barks out a surprised laugh and shakes his head as if I bewilder him. "Very well, Ms. Jacobs." His voice turns hard again. "Let's go find my mate and right the wrong she's done."

. . . . .

Luna Marie is not on the compound, nor is she answering her phone. "Could she know we're on to her?" I ask once we've searched the entire place under the guise of giving Nick a tour. We've ended up back in the parking lot next to Nick's car.

Alpha Toth isn't happy about Nick staying. But since Director West ordered Nick to bring Marie in for questioning—and because Nick refuses to leave my side until we're sure no more attempts will be made on my life—he allows it. Toth feels much better after Nick promises he'll let Toth handle the situation however he sees fit. Meaning if Toth wants to hand Marie over to the FUA, Nick will take her off his hands, but if he wants to give her the same sentence she gave Maya and Daniel…well, that's up to him, and Nick will stay out of it.

Alpha Toth and Rook both frown in thought, but Nick speaks up. "It's likely she knows. Mercs usually get half payment up front and half when the job is completed. If no one checked in because the job was botched, she'll know something went wrong. There was a whole diner full of witnesses who saw Nora walk away from the attack and saw us take Dennis into custody."

I wince. "She may have bolted, knowing Dennis might talk during interrogation."

Nick nods, agreeing with me. He looks at Alpha Toth and Rook. "Any idea where she might go?"

The two share a grim look and say together, "The apartment."

Nick heads for his car while I ask the million-dollar question. "What apartment?"

Alpha Toth sighs. "We've been trying to trace the missing money since Maya's and Daniel's deaths. Maya rented a small apartment out in Ann Arbor. It's mostly safe from rogues because it's surrounded by three really strong packs who all use it as neutral territory—us, the Waterloo pack out in Chelsea, and the Island Lake pack up in Brighton. Rogues generally keep to Detroit. We figured the apartment in Ann Arbor was where Maya and Daniel were going to try to make a go of it as packless wolves."

"Wouldn't Luna Marie know you'd look there?" I ask.

Both Rook and Alpha Toth grimace. "We haven't told Marie we know about it," Alpha Toth says. "It's just easier to keep her out of stuff."

Yeah, that's not hard to imagine. She's a real piece of work. I smirk. "Can't blame you there, and it works in our favor." I clap my hands together in excitement. "All right. Who's up for a drive to Ann Arbor?"

CHAPTER
EIGHTEEN

WHEN WE GET TO THE APARTMENT COMPLEX IN ANN ARBOR, Nick flashes something that looks like an FBI badge, and the manager hands over a key. The apartment is a modest one-bedroom. I'm sure it's very standard for middle-class suburban living, but it makes my old dump in Detroit seem like third-world living. Luna Marie must have stolen a *lot* of money from the pack.

The apartment is empty. Though, judging by the growls of Alpha Toth when we enter the place, Marie hasn't been gone long. "She wasn't here alone."

"Do you recognize the scent?" Rook asks.

He, Nick, and Alpha Toth all wander around the open living, dining, and kitchen area, sniffing the air. "It's definitely wolf," Alpha Toth says, shaking his head. "And male. But he's not pack."

His eyes are glowing again. We all know what Luna

Marie being here with another male wolf means, and Alpha Toth's wolf does not like being cheated on.

"It's a little familiar," Rook says, taking a deeper whiff. "But it's too mixed with Marie's scent for me to get a good read on it."

Nick looks up from a small stack of mail he's sorting through. "You got anything for us, little psychic?"

I wander the room, running my hands over everything from the kitchen table to the TV remote. When I pick up nothing, I groan. If this was Luna Marie's secret love nest, chances are there is only one kind of vision I'm going to get from this place. At my grumble, all three men look my direction. "It's nothing," I tell them with a sigh.

I head for the bedroom, and Rook follows behind me, chuckling when comprehension sinks in. Alpha Toth walks into the bedroom, takes a deep breath through his nose, and then roars. "That cheating whore!"

He grabs the nearest thing he can find, which happens to be a dresser, and smashes it thoroughly with his fists before throwing it into the bedroom wall, putting huge holes in the drywall. He sheds his clothes and shifts into wolf form, moving to shred the mattress next. Rook stops him. "Wait, Peter!"

The wolf growls and his chest heaves, but he turns his glowing eyes to Rook and waits. "Nora needs the bed. Let her do her thing, and then you can tear this entire apartment to pieces. Promise."

Alpha Toth snarls but plops his butt on the ground with a huff. He looks at me, and for a moment I forget to breathe.

I'm trapped in a room with an angry wolf, and he's barely containing his temper. In this form, the dominance rolls off him in thick waves. I want to fall to the floor and curl up in the fetal position, but werewolves appreciate strength, so I pull back my shoulders and glare at the alpha wolf. "Stop it," I say. "I get that you're pissed, but I can't do my job with you in here being all alpha I-will-rip-you-apart wolf. Calm down or get out, because I can barely breathe with all the testosterone you're throwing at me."

I point toward the bedroom door, showing him which option I'd rather he take. The wolf narrows his eyes and growls a warning at me, but I don't so much as flinch. He huffs again, but he follows my orders and leaves the room.

"Nicely done, Nora," Nick says, clapping.

Rook doesn't join in. He's frozen in place, watching me with a proud and hungry gleam in his eye, as if his wolf really likes my display of dominance. I stare him down next. "Do I need to kick you out, too?"

Rook's eyes flash, but he quickly shakes his head and stamps down his wolf. "Sorry. You're just so dominant. My wolf can't help himself. I think if you ever turned, I'd have to take back my no dating policy. I think my wolf would claim you whether I wanted him to or not."

And my curse strikes again. It's impressive that Rook the man is holding out even if his wolf is struggling with my allure. He must have loved Lilly so much. "You in control now?" I ask, even though I know he is. "I don't want you to bite me while I'm under. This imprint might take a while."

Rook smirks. "I'm good."

"I've got your back," Nick adds, stepping up beside Rook. "You do your thing. I'll watch out for you."

That makes me feel better, but I spare the bed another wary glance. The sheets are still a mess. I start at the foot of the bed, hoping to pick up something without having to actually crawl into the place where the dirty action happened. Thankfully, I luck out. I run my hand across the foot of the bed and am immediately sucked into the imprint.

I fall right into the middle of the show. Luna Marie is busy taking her lover for a ride when a cell phone rings. The man is definitely a wolf—his eyes glow faintly, the same way Rook's do when his wolf is close to the surface—but I don't recognize him as one of Alpha Toth's pack. He isn't one of the rogues who attacked me, either. This man is new, and very dominant.

I've never been a fan of these kinds of visions, because the only experiences I've ever had with sex have all been horrific. But I have to admit, if I have to sit back and watch this show, at least Mr. Alpha Wolf makes for a great view.

"Leave it!" the man snarls when Marie leans over the foot of the bed.

Marie doesn't listen. "I have to know if the job is done. I need that nosy bitch taken care of."

She climbs off the bed, and the vision ends.

I come to, and my head spins. Rook, having seen me at work before, is right there to catch me as I almost fall off the bed. "Find anything useful?"

"Not yet." I groan.

This whole sucking up multiple imprints in a row thing really sucks. But there's a good chance I'll get that phone conversation if I can just find the right spot on the floor where she answered it. She was bound to be pissed as hell when she learned I got away and one of her rogues was taken into custody. I get down on my knees and smooth my hand over the carpet in front of the bed until I'm sucked into another vision.

Marie crawls across the floor and snatches up her phone. "Is it done?" she demands. She listens a moment, then goes rigid. "What?" she shouts. She sits up on her knees. "You incompetent fools! No. I'll take care of it. And you'd better leave town, because if I ever find you, I'll rip you to pieces for being such a useless idiot."

She hangs up the phone and throws it across the room, screaming in a fit of rage. Her lover chuckles and joins her on the floor. Her tantrum has done nothing to kill his mood. "I take it the job didn't go well?" he asks as he starts kissing her neck and shoulder.

"No." She huffs, leaning her head to the side to give him better access. "Not only did Nora get away, one of those idiots I hired got taken into FUA custody. If he's not already singing like a canary, he will be soon. Nick Gorgeous has ways of making people talk."

"Doesn't matter," her lover insists as he pushes her onto her back and climbs on top of her. He kisses her deeply, then says, "We stick to the plan."

"But I have to disappear now, Axel," Marie demands. "Peter will kill me when he finds out I paid rogues to attack his precious little pet, Nora." She spits my name with bitterness and loathing. The feeling is totally mutual.

Axel growls, his impatience growing. "Then stay at my safe house for now," he snaps. "And forget about the human girl. She's of no consequence. We stick to the plan."

Marie snarls at Axel, but it only makes him smile. "You're so hot when you're pissed. Stop worrying and make dirty love to me, you naughty bitch."

Something flashes in Marie's eyes, and she attacks Axel with the full force of an angry wolf. Lots of screaming and clawing and biting ensues. I try to escape the vision, but like always, I have to wait it out.

By the time I come back to the present, my head is pounding so badly I can't see. There are too many black spots in my vision. I'm also going to lose my dinner. "Bathroom," I groan.

Rook needs no further explanation. He scoops me up and places me in front of the toilet just before I puke my guts up. The sweetie even holds my hair back for me.

"Damn, girl," Nick mutters from the entrance of the bathroom. "At least you didn't get my boots this time."

I flip him off while I heave some more, and he laughs. Once I'm done throwing up, I lie down on the floor and press my cheek against the cool linoleum. "You okay?" Rook asks, gently rubbing my back. The touch feels soothing, for once. "You were out cold for half an hour."

"Half an hour?" I groan again. "That has to be a record. I've never witnessed such passionate, angry sex before. I was lucky they decided to take things back to the bed after getting too many rug burns, or I might never have escaped them. I'll never question a werewolf's stamina."

Rook chuckles at the stamina comment but quickly stops when Alpha Toth growls. Oops. I should be a little more sensitive when talking about his mate sleeping around on him. "Sorry. If it helps, I know who it was. Well, I have a name."

"WHO?" Alpha Toth demands.

I start to move, and Rook helps me sit up without my having to ask. The room spins again. "Whoa. No more imprints for me for a long time."

Alpha Toth takes a deep breath, attempting to calm himself. "Can we do anything to help?"

I appreciate the concern when I know all he wants is to know who's banging his mate so he can go kill him. "Pain-killers?" I say. "And maybe some tea, if there's any around?"

Alpha Toth heads for the kitchen, while Rook helps me to my feet. He guides me to the sofa in the living room. Nick brings me some aspirin, and Alpha Toth hands me a glass of juice. "Sorry. No tea," he says gruffly. It'll have to do.

The three of them wait until I've swallowed down the pills and can sit up without feeling dizzy. "What can you tell us?" Alpha Toth asks as I sip the rest of my juice.

I applaud his patience up to this point, but I still don't quite trust his temper. "You're not going to kill the messenger, right?"

Alpha Toth and Rook exchange a look that's way too serious. Alpha Toth moves across the room, and Rook shifts into a sort of ready position, like he's going to pounce if Alpha Toth does lose his temper and attacks. "Well, that's comforting."

"You'll be safe," Nick promises. One glance at his face, and I believe him.

I meet Alpha Toth's angry gaze. "His name is Axel."

Alpha Toth's eyes bulge. "Axel Day? Are you sure?"

"I never got a last name, but he had sandy blond hair, blue eyes, and was more ripped than any man has a right to be."

"That's Alpha Day, all right," Rook mutters.

I nod. "Yeah, this guy was definitely an alpha. Which pack is he?"

"Island Lake," Alpha Toth bites out. He's got his arms folded tightly across his chest, and he's clenching his jaw so tightly the muscles in his neck are pulled taut.

"Are they a strong pack?" I ask.

Alpha Toth's eyes narrow. "Not as strong as mine, but they aren't weak. Why?"

I think he knows what I'm about to say, because his eyes start to glow again. "He kept saying they had to stick to the plan. It seemed pretty important. And nefarious, I might add."

"A takeover?" Alpha Toth growls. "Is he planning to attack my pack?"

I shrug. "Could he?"

Alpha Toth glares at the ground and then looks at Rook. "With enough help and no warning, he might be able to pull it off."

"Or, he could just be planning to take Marie off your hands," I suggest.

Rook sighs. "That's the same thing. If he challenges Peter

for Marie, it's a fight to the death, and the winner inherits the other's pack. But if he's plotting in secret, he's not talking about a fair challenge."

"Maybe they just want to run away together, like Maya and Daniel did." I know it's a bogus suggestion, but I can't help trying to make him feel better.

"Alphas don't run off," Toth says, as if personally offended by my suggestion. "And they never desert their packs. No. Whatever he's planning, it has to be a takeover. What else is there?"

"He must think he can win, or he wouldn't dare attempt it," Rook says.

The two share another long look.

"Could Island Lake and Waterloo be teaming up?" Alpha Toth asks.

"To what end?" Rook shakes his head. "They're not going to merge packs, and splitting ours wouldn't give either of them any advantage."

"You're right. Day has to be working alone. Rogues?"

Rook nods. "It's possible. They did pay some to go after Nora."

Alpha Toth sighs. "We need more information."

Rook nods. "Where, when, allies, numbers…"

"And whether any of your own pack is involved," I say.

Both men growl at me for that one. I grimace but stand my ground. "Look, we know Luna Marie is in on it, and Jeffrey seemed really certain at the social that he was going to take over the pack. The way his thoughts were, it was like he was sure. Like he had a specific plan in place."

Alpha Toth loses his temper again. This time it's the coffee table that suffers his wrath. His fists come down on it, and the thing gets smashed to smithereens. "Damn it!"

"Easy, Peter," Rook says, pulling me off the couch and away from the raging shifter. "We'll get him. We just need to figure out his plan."

"How are we supposed to do that? I don't have time to send in a spy, and if they're in league with rogues already, we won't be able to hire any ourselves."

An idea sparks in my mind. "What about me?"

All three men freeze and wait for me to continue. "What if I invite him to my party? I could read him the way I did the people at your social."

They all think about it. Nick nods and Alpha Toth starts to, but then shakes his head. Rook shakes his as well. "Too suspect," he decides. "Marie has already told him you're digging around. They'll know you're up to something if you invite him now."

"But he won't know what. Marie's not aware of what my gifts are. They'd never know I can pick the thoughts right out of their heads."

"What if we invite all three pack alphas?" Nick suggests. He meets the gazes of Rook and Alpha Toth before continuing. "If we invite you, Axel, and Lucian of the Waterloo pack, you'll show for sure, and there's no reason for Lucian not to show."

Alpha Toth's eyes light up. "There's no way Axel would miss it if Lucian and I were both going. His pride wouldn't allow it."

"Plus, it makes sense to invite you all. I mean, Cecile is inviting all the vampire clan leaders and prominent fey. She may have already added you all to the guest list. I'll invite the lunas and betas, too, and then maybe we can see what Jeffrey knows."

Nick, Alpha Toth, and Rook all fall silent, each thinking about this plan. The wheels turn in each of their minds as they run through the pros, cons, logistics, risks, and so on. "Works for me," Nick says.

Rook nods, too, and they both look to Alpha Toth. He hesitates. "Are you sure you don't mind?" he asks me. "It's your party, after all. And it could be dangerous."

I snort. "It's Cecile's party. I'm just required to show up. Having a case to work on will make it interesting. And I'm already in danger. Marie wants me out of the picture. The sooner we stop her and Axel, the sooner I'll be safe."

Alpha Toth sighs. "All right." His demeanor changes in an instant, turning very somber. "Thank you, Nora. My pack is indebted to you in a way we might never be able to repay."

Oh man, again with the gratitude. "It's all good, alpha man. I'm happy to help." I rub my hands together and grin. "Okay, then. Let's go party and catch us some cheating lovers."

CHAPTER
NINETEEN

I'M SITTING AT THE BAR IN UNDERWORLD WHILE CECILE AND a team of people get ready for the party. My party, I guess, though it feels more like Cecile's since she's done everything to organize it.

The DJ stand is gone for the evening, and in its place on the stage a band of faeries is setting up musical instruments. The dance floor is covered with red rose petals, and the whole room glows faintly from hundreds of magically burning candles. She's even had large white columns brought in and placed around the edges of the room, making the place feel like some kind of ancient Greek palace. She's really outdone herself.

My mouth falls open when her sorcerer friend turns the ceiling of the club into a clear night sky. I blink up at what appears to be an endless sea of stars and a beautiful full moon. "Wow."

Beside me, Oliver chuckles. "Pretty cool, huh?"

I shake my head, amazed. "It's beautiful. And it looks so real."

Oliver smirks. "That's the point of the illusion."

I just can't believe what I'm seeing. "Magic is cool." I nudge his shoulder playfully and say, "It's probably a good thing you don't use magic. I'd make you hate me, asking you to do tricks for me all the time."

Oliver laughs, but then clears his throat. "Actually, I've been meaning to tell you that I've started seeing a therapist about that."

I peel my gaze away from the sky and look at Oliver. "Really?"

Ollie nods. "Remember back when we were trying to find those missing underworlders, and you got into a fight with Gorgeous about me not using my magic?"

"I wouldn't call it a fight."

Oliver's look turns wry. "An argument, then."

I concede to that one with a small smirk. "Okay, yes, I remember."

Oliver's smile vanishes, and he looks at his lap as he shrugs his shoulders once. "I'd never considered that it might be some kind of post traumatic stress that was keeping me from using my magic. Or, at least, not that it was something treatable. You mentioned you'd gone to therapy after it happened, and I figured it couldn't hurt. Director West knows a werewolf who works as a therapist for shifters who refuse to shift because they've lost control in their animal form, or had traumatic experiences. She figured I'm not a shifter, but the problem is basically the same."

Oliver looks strangely vulnerable right now, so I place my hand on his thigh and lean my head on his shoulder. "And how's it going?"

Oliver wraps his arm around my shoulders, pulling me tightly to him without touching any of my skin. "I've only had a few appointments with her so far, but I'm hopeful."

I give his thigh a pat. "I'm sure you'll get there. You'll be the most badass sorcerer in the Midwest in no time."

Oliver chuckles again, shaking his head softly. His hug grows tighter, but instead of pulling away from him, I soak up the physical affection with a sigh of contentment. It's getting easier for me to touch Oliver. He's so understanding and considerate of my condition. For some reason, my curse doesn't affect him the same way it does others. It's almost like he's not affected, and just cares about me like a normal person would. I don't understand it, but I trust him not to lose control and hurt me the way others have done in my past.

We sit together in peaceful silence until Cecile glides over to us like a Grecian goddess in a flowing blue gown. "Well?" She looks around the room with a proud smile. "What do you think?"

I give her the truth. "It's beautiful, Cecile. Thanks for moving the date up sooner."

Cecile sighs. "It wasn't easy, but it came together nicely enough, and you had a point. The sooner everyone meets you, the sooner they'll stop attacking you."

Or more of them will start attacking me. I don't voice this thought. There'd be no point. Cecile will still make me go upstairs to her suite and change into that dangerous gown she's picked out for me to wear. "Let's hope," I say.

Cecile gently pats my cheek. "Darling, everyone is going to love you. You'll see."

"That's what I'm afraid of."

Oliver's grip tightens again as he hugs me supportively. "Your friends will keep you safe," he murmurs. "Cecile, me, Ren, Terrance, Parker, Gorgeous, Wulf, Rook…we'll all be here keeping an eye on you. And I promised not to leave your side all night."

I'm stunned by his words, though, not because I find it hard to believe they'll look out for me. It's just finally occurring to me that I have real, genuine friends. I've been alone for so long that having so many people who truly care about me seems impossible. But somehow I've managed to build a family of sorts. And with a crazy group of underworlders of all different races. They may be supernatural misfits, but they're my friends. My family.

My eyes mist over, and my voice comes out raspy when I smile at Cecile and say, "Thank you for doing all of this for me."

Cecile's face softens. "You're welcome, dear." She claps her hands together, breaking the tender moment. "As adorable as the two of you are right now, it's time for you to go get ready. Oliver, your tux is in Terrance's private suite."

The way Oliver cringes at the word *tux* is hilarious. "Oh, come on," I tease him. "You wear a suit to work every day. A tux can't be that different. And besides, since you're my date for the evening, I need you looking extra hot so that no one will notice me."

Oliver snorts. "Right. You could wear sweats and throw your hair in a ponytail, and you'll still be the most beautiful woman in the room tonight."

He grins, proud of his cheesy line, and yet laughs about using it at the same time. After rolling my eyes at him, I shoot Cecile a hopeful look. "*Can* I wear sweats and a ponytail?"

Both Oliver and Cecile laugh.

Cecile herds us upstairs, shooing Oliver down to the end of the hall to Terrance's room. "You'll come get me, right?" I ask Oliver, my heart suddenly in my throat. "I won't have to make my big entrance alone?"

"Of course not," Cecile assures me as she ushers me into her suite. "A debutante always needs an escort."

Relief floods me, but I still frown. "A debutante?"

"Why not? You're coming out into underworld society. Is that not what a debutante is?"

"Honestly, I have no idea."

Cecile follows me into her suite, laughing her light, tinkling laugh. She's glowing with anticipation when she sits me at her vanity and begins to do my hair. After curling it into big, loopy curls, she piles all of it up on my head and fastens it with a pearl and diamond wreath thing that can't decide if it's a headband or a crown.

After applying my makeup—which she goes very heavy on, calling the eyes smoky—she hands me a pair of earrings that match my hairpiece and drapes a pearl and diamond necklace around my throat. The jewelry is the nicest thing

I've ever worn, and I'm scared to move for fear of breaking it somehow.

Cecile smiles at me in the mirror. "Stunning."

I can't argue. I've never looked so beautiful in my life. And I'm not even wearing the dress yet.

She looks me over one more time, then turns her head toward the door as if listening. I'm not sure if succubi have better hearing than humans, but even I can hear the growing crowd mingling below us. "Can you manage the dress?" she asks. "I really should head down and greet the guests."

When I nod, Cecile grabs my hands and pulls me to my feet. "Wait for me to welcome everyone, and then you and Oliver can come downstairs, all right? I'll speak into a microphone. You'll hear me. Promise you'll wait for me to introduce you."

I sigh. She's determined for me to make a grand entrance. "All right. I'll wait."

Cecile's face brightens, and she waltzes out to the room, blowing me air kisses. Once the door is closed behind her, I slowly make my way to the garment bag lying on the bed. I haven't seen the dress yet. Cecile had my measurements taken, then insisted she surprise me. She had the dress made by a faerie seamstress and said she wove magic into it, so I have no idea what to expect.

The first thing I notice when I unzip the bag is that it's white. I free it from the bag and gasp as I lay it carefully on the bed. It's *gorgeous*. It looks like a wedding gown.

It's easy to slip the dress on. It's got thin straps lined with pearls and a low-cut back. It clings to me as if it were specifically designed for my figure. I suppose it was. It hugs my body and drapes from my hips to the floor, and has a small train. The whole thing is covered in delicate white lace with pearls woven into the fabric. It's elegant and whimsical all at once, and definitely looks like something a faerie queen would wear.

I feel the slight tingling of magic. It's different from the sorcerer magic around the club and at Terrance's place. This magic is lighter somehow, airier, like a gentle summer breeze. I don't realize what the magic does until I look in the floor-length mirror and see the soft sparkles making the entire dress shimmer. My breath catches. I've never seen anything like it.

I stand in front of the mirror, staring at the beautiful stranger in front of me, until a soft knock startles me. "Nora?" Oliver calls out.

"Come in, Ollie!"

I turn, just as Oliver steps in the room and shuts the door behind him. His breath catches when he sees me. "Nora…"

He shakes his head as he struggles to find words. I've rendered him speechless. "You don't look so bad yourself," I say, willing my cheeks not to blush.

Oliver looks as if he was born to wear designer tuxedos all the time. I've never seen him more striking. His light-brown hair is sculpted stylishly for once, making it look a little darker. It really brings out the honey color of his eyes. And his tall, lean figure fills his tux perfectly. He's positively dashing.

"Nora…" he whispers again. "You look…"

"Like I'm ready to walk down the aisle?" I tease.

He takes my hands. I'm instantly filled with his thoughts and feelings. I think he's choosing to let me hear his thoughts right now because he can't put into words how beautiful he thinks I am.

His feelings are overwhelming. My chest constricts, and my face heats up. I've never felt so adored. No, *cherished* is maybe the right word for it. And again, Oliver's feelings ring with a sincerity that no man has ever accomplished. I don't have an ounce of fear with him. I'm not sure why, or how, but Oliver will never hurt me. Just like with Terrance, I know this. I can feel it. "Thank you, Oliver," I mutter. My voice cracks with emotion.

His gaze suddenly falls to my mouth. It's the briefest flicker, but it sparks something inside me. I suck in a breath, and my heart flutters. When my mouth goes dry, I realize that I *want* Oliver to kiss me.

I'd wanted Parker to kiss me, too, but my chest had pounded with anxiety the whole time. It was as if my intuition knew he was under the influence of my curse and wouldn't be able to control himself. I have no such fear with Oliver. All that's in me now is desire. It's not a lustful want, but a hopeful curiosity. Can I kiss him? Would I be able to without breaking out into a panic attack?

The tension in the air becomes thick. As if Oliver knows what I'm thinking about, he finds his courage and steps so close our bodies meet. I don't back away. I place my hands on his chest and meet his steady gaze with a shy one. When he speaks, his voice is so soft it's almost a caress. "Is this okay?"

I can't seem to find my breath. My emotions are spinning wildly out of control. I can't look away from him. All of my strength is in those amber eyes. "I'll stop you if it isn't," I say. It's the best answer I can give him, because I honestly don't know how this will go down. All I know is that I want to try.

Sucking in a breath, Oliver wets his lips. His gaze falls to my mouth again, and he lifts his hand to gently cup my cheek. He pauses a moment, giving me time to make sure I'm okay with his actions. When I don't protest, he leans his face down to mine.

Our lips meet in the lightest of touches. His kiss is feather light. He very delicately presses our mouths together. Desire flares through me the moment we touch, and I lean into him, wrapping my arms up around his neck. Following my lead, Oliver slides his hands around my waist and pulls me closer. He parts his lips to make it an open-mouth kiss and hesitantly seeks out my tongue with his. It's sweet, and delicate, and just demanding enough that it's breathtaking. It's a perfect kiss.

And then, without me having to end it, Oliver pulls back. He's smiling softly, but there's a question in his eyes. I know what he's asking, but I can't answer him. Not vocally, anyway. I'm too choked up. When my eyes mist over, I bury my face in his shoulder. He gently holds me while I try to compose myself. "You okay?" he asks.

I nod, still refusing to let him go, face still buried against his shoulder. "More than okay. Thank you, Oliver."

His hug tightens, and he brushes his lips against the side of my head. "You're welcome, sweetheart."

With one more deep breath, I pull myself out of Oliver's embrace and smooth out my dress. I've managed to stop any tears before they could leak from my eyes. I'm afraid to look at him, afraid it will be awkward, but when I meet his gaze and he looks at me with such an understanding smile, a weight lifts off my chest. He's still Oliver. He's still my best friend. He glances toward the door. "You ready?"

I pull my shoulders back with a sigh and stand up straight. "As I'll ever be."

Through the door comes Cecile's muffled voice, welcoming everyone and thanking them for coming. I know that's my cue, but I'd rather stay here. Oliver knows exactly what I'm thinking, and he smirks. "You'll survive."

"Maybe."

"Come on. Your public awaits."

Oliver has to drag me from Cecile's suite. When we reach the stairs that lead down into the main room of the club, the first thing I notice is that I am the only person in the entire club wearing white. Everyone else is in dark or bright colors. I stand out big time. I'm sure that was Cecile's plan. The second thing I realize is that no one is moving or talking as I make my way down the stairs with Oliver. All eyes are trained on me, my guests watching me enter with reverent awe. It's quite the entrance. Cecile certainly knows what she's doing. "I'm going to kill Cecile," I grumble as Oliver and I descend the stairs arm in arm.

He chuckles. "Just don't trip down the stairs, and you'll

be fine."

"Don't jinx me."

Terrance is waiting at the bottom of the steps, with a scowl on his face. He looks me over from head to toe and grumbles, "I'm going to kill Cecile."

I take that as a compliment and laugh. "You and me both. Stick close by and fend off any extra enthusiastic admirers tonight?"

He grunts, but he's trying to hide pleasure behind his scowl. He loves playing my surly bodyguard.

Cecile finds me next and greets me with an air kiss. "Nora, darling. Come. There's someone I want you to meet."

Yeah. I just bet there is. Like every single person at this party, which has to be a couple hundred people. So much for small. I try not to groan as she grabs my wrist and drags me into the crowd. It's going to be a long night.

C H A P T E R
TWENTY

I drop onto a barstool with a groan. It's been hours, and I haven't had a second to myself all night. I'm exhausted, my head hurts, and my feet are about to stage a revolt. Wulf appears on the other side of the bar. He's in a tux as well, but I think he's spent the majority of the night serving drinks despite the fact that there are other employees who've been hired to do his job for the evening. Truth be told, even though he's one of the most social guys I've ever met, I think he's more comfortable back there. "Need something to drink?" he asks me.

Gratitude and relief wash over me at the mere thought. "Yes, please. Something with caffeine."

"Make that two," Oliver says. He squeezes my hand and adds, "I'm going to hit the restroom. Think you can manage a few minutes without me?"

His smile is teasing, but my answer is serious. "It'll be

difficult. Hurry back?"

Oliver's answering smile is a sympathetic one. "Two minutes."

I watch him as he hurries off, warmth spreading through my chest. Oliver's been such a lifesaver tonight. Just like he promised, he hasn't left my side all evening. He's stood quietly beside me through every introduction, content to be my arm candy. Having him with me has been my saving grace.

"How's your night been so far?" Wulf asks, sliding two Cokes across the bar. I take a huge swig of mine before answering.

"Chaotic. It's been nonstop introductions, and I still haven't met half the people here. I haven't met any of the people I was hoping to meet yet."

Wulf frowns. He knows who I'm talking about. Rook and Alpha Toth let him in on the plan so that he could be added security for me should Axel or Marie try something. So far, all has been quiet. "Hmm. Well, don't go too far, and I'll see if I can find a few friends of mine."

He's not gone two seconds before a new voice startles me. "Looking good, little spitfire."

I open my eyes to see Nick and Parker standing in front of me. When had I closed my eyes? "Just good?" I tease. "Don't you mean *gorgeous?*"

Nick smirks. "I'll start calling you gorgeous when you start returning the favor."

I laugh. He winks. I shake my head at his silliness. It's pretty much par for the course with us. Then he goes and surprises me by saying, "Seriously, though. You look beautiful tonight."

"Thank you."

When he turns to order a drink from one of the bartenders, Parker uses the opportunity to snag my attention. "Good evening, Nora."

"Hey, Parker."

I take a moment to look him over. Like Oliver, Parker seems as though he was born to wear a tux. He's so James Bond. He looks *good*. As always, he gives me a tiny, knowing smile, as if he can tell how much I'm attracted to him.

He takes my hand in his and leans forward. I think he's going to kiss my hand, but he surprises me by going for my cheek instead. "You look positively enchanting tonight," he whispers.

Goose bumps blanket my skin, and I have to suppress a shiver.

He starts to pull away, but then he freezes and his body goes rigid. He takes a deep breath, inhaling my scent. When he finally leans back, he's frowning slightly. His eyes seem to have a million questions in them. It takes me a moment to realize what upset him. I don't get it until Oliver reappears and Parker's frown deepens. Parker can smell Oliver on me. He must know that Oliver kissed me. The two men eyeball each other warily and force strained smiles at each other. All I can do is wonder how in the world I got myself into this position, and more importantly, how am I going to fix it?

"Well, this is an interesting development," Nick teases, smirking at Oliver and Parker.

I shoot him a nasty glare, which he returns with a wide

grin. "My money's on the wolf."

Startled, I glance behind the bar. Wulf has returned, and though he's grinning as if this conversation is the most entertainment he's had all night, he holds up his hands in surrender.

"Not that wolf," Nick says.

He casts his gaze to my left. Oliver, Parker, and I all follow it to the group of people walking toward us. Rook is leading the charge. Oliver sighs, and Parker's jaw clenches. Wulf and Nick both chuckle. I flip them both off with a sweet smile, which makes them burst into laughter.

"Sounds like good times over here," Rook says. "Nora, you look stunning tonight."

"Thanks."

"I'm sorry I haven't had the chance to spend any time with you yet this evening. You've been a popular lady."

"Blame Cecile."

He laughs. "Well, I've got your attention now, and that's what counts, right?"

He pulls me from my stool and into an embrace that is a little more intimate than I expected. His thoughts are jumbled as if he's fighting his wolf. *...have such a strong reaction to her. Get it under control, Rook. She's not yours. But it's getting harder to ignore her.*

He inhales deeply, and then, just as Parker had done, he stiffens when he smells Oliver on me. Actually, he probably smells both Ollie *and* Parker on me now. His grip on me tightens just a fraction, and his thoughts simplify. *Smell other men on her. Must claim what's ours...*

"Rook," Alpha Toth says sternly, causing Rook to flinch. He finally lets me go, but he does the same thing he did last week and pulls me close to his side as he introduces me to the people with him. I flash a pleading look to Alpha Toth, but he subtly shakes his head, telling me to just let Rook do what he needs.

Rook's jaw is still tight, and his eyes still have a faint glow in them. I look to Wulf next, but all I get from him is a smug grin. Oliver and Parker both seem stunned. I suppress a groan and curse my stupid curse. I have got to find a way to control my allure like Cecile does, or I'll never be able to keep my friends. They'll kill one another over me.

"Nora, this is Lucian Williams, and his mate, Isabella," Rook says. "They're the alpha and luna of the Waterloo pack."

I shake each of their hands, and then Rook points to two other men. Both of them are familiar, one surprisingly so. The man is one of the underworlders I rescued back in September. He'd been sickly then, dying slowly from silver poisoning. He looks so much healthier now. Young and robust, even. I smile brightly for him and say, "I know you. You look a lot better than the last time we met."

The man grins. "Thanks to you." He holds out a hand for me to shake. "The name's Evan Fuller. It's good to finally meet you. Properly."

"You too."

A throat clears, and Evan immediately steps back, letting the man from my vision in Marie's apartment step forward. "Nora," Evan says, "this is my alpha, Axel Day."

"Many thanks for saving my beta," he says as he shakes my hand. His thoughts are running a different direction. *No wonder Marie is so crazy over this woman. She's the most beautiful creature I've ever seen, and her dominance is so much stronger than Marie's.*

"I'm just glad I could help," I say, breaking Axel's grip. To Evan, I add, "I'm glad I got to see you again. I didn't think I was going to, and I was worried. You were in such bad shape that night." I check out his physique and give him a crooked smile. "I see you've recovered well enough."

Evan laughs while a rumble starts in Rook's chest. The growl is so low I feel it rather than hear it. While I'm busy glaring at Rook, Evan steps forward again. "I'm glad I got to see you again, too. I've wanted to thank you. Perhaps you'll allow me a dance?"

This is perfect. I haven't danced much tonight, and I was wondering how I'd hear anyone's thoughts. Having a few minutes alone with Axel's beta will really help. And maybe it will prompt Axel to ask me to dance next. It wouldn't surprise me. Wolves are so competitive. "I'd love to."

I step forward to join him, but a hand clamps around my waist and Rook growls louder. *"Rook!"* I snap.

Stupid territorial wolves. I shoot Alpha Toth a meaningful glare. I need this. Rook has to let me talk to—and possibly flirt with—Evan and Axel both. I need to find out what's going on.

Alpha Toth understands my plight and steps beside Rook. He clamps a white-knuckled hand on Rook's shoulder. "Rook. Let the lady have a dance. Evan only means to show his gratitude. He'll behave himself."

Evan's surprise is obvious, but he recovers quickly and holds up his hands in surrender. "I would never dream of moving in on your female. Forgive me. I didn't realize you had a claim on her. I meant nothing by the invite. I simply wanted the chance to thank Nora for saving my life."

No! No, no, no! He's backing off! Damn it, Rook!

"Of course you can have a dance with her," Alpha Toth says, squeezing Rook's shoulder so hard Rook grimaces. "Rook's just feeling a little overwhelmed with so many people expressing interest in Nora tonight. But he doesn't mind. *Do you, Rook?"*

"Sure," Rook grinds out. "Just keep it friendly."

I elbow Rook in the ribs, and he finally lets me go. Then I force a smile at Evan and push him toward the dance floor. He follows reluctantly. "I'm sorry for causing trouble. I had no idea you and Rook were more than friends."

Me either, buddy. "It's…complicated, but don't worry. I've danced with over a dozen men tonight. I think it's just different with you because you're the first wolf who's asked me. But don't worry about Rook. He knows the point of this party is for me to get to know other underworlders."

We reach a clear spot on the dance floor, and Evan glances once more at Rook. He's standing off to the side, scowling at us, with Alpha Toth and Terrance standing on either side of him, as if ready to hold him back. I shoot him another look, then step into Evan's space, forcing him into action. He gently places one hand on my waist and takes my hand with his other.

For a moment, I simply read him as he leads us into a waltz. He's shocked—more than shocked—that Rook has finally taken a mate. What I like about him is that he's not disappointed I'm spoken for, he's excited about it. *They'll be a good match. Rook deserves someone like Nora. If they're going to be mated, I wonder if he'll try to reclaim the Huron River pack. I wish he'd challenge Axel instead. We could use a good alpha pair. I'd be honored to be Rook's second.*

Interesting. Evan really doesn't think much of his alpha. That counts as points in his favor. He seems like a good man who just wants what's best for his pack. "So," I say, searching for something that might bring up the topic of Axel without sounding obvious. "You didn't bring a date this evening? No mate?"

Evan gives me a roguish grin. "I'm still in the market for the right one."

I snort. Wolves. "How about your alpha? I didn't see a woman with him, either. I thought wolves couldn't be alphas without having mates."

Evan sighs. "It's uncommon. Axel is..." *an abusive jerk who the women in our pack fear and loathe.* "...very dominant. He won't take anyone but the strongest female as his mate, and there aren't any in our pack that satisfy him in that department."

"Sounds very...shifter-ish."

Surprised, Evan laughs. "I suppose that's true, though not all wolves are created equal." *Not all of us are monsters like Axel. I'm glad Nora got to know Toth's pack first. Toth is a good man, and Rook is one of the best.*

"I'm sure they aren't. Just like with any group of people. I've seen the worst of the human race all my life, but I know there are good ones out there. As for wolves, well, I admit I quite like you guys. Aside from the rogues that attacked me, I've had a great experience dealing with your race."

Evan smiles proudly. "I'm glad to hear it. And, might I add, if you do decide to make the change, you'll be a wonderful addition."

I don't know how to answer that. How can I explain Rook's possessiveness without explaining my curse? It's not something I want to get into tonight with a man I just met. "Thank you. That's sweet of you to say."

The song comes to an end, and Evan lets go of me with a playful sigh. "I suppose I should return you now. But seriously, Nora…" His smile vanishes, and his face grows somber. *"Thank you."* I start to protest, but he shakes his head. "No. You saved my life. I am in your debt. If there is ever anything I can do for you, all you have to do is ask."

Arguing is futile, so I force a smile and nod. "I'll do that."

Evan walks me back toward Rook, but Axel steps in front of him, his hand outstretched to me. "Think you have one more in you?" he asks.

His smile is more of a leer and makes me feel dirty, but I force myself to stay pleasant. "Of course."

"So…" Axel says on the way to the dance floor, "you're the woman who saved my beta. Evan talked about nothing but you for weeks."

We reach the spot where Evan and I had just been

dancing, and Axel pulls me into his arms. Unlike his gentlemanly beta, Axel lifts my arms around his neck and slides both of his hands low around my hips, pulling me closer to him than I care to be. I grit my teeth and force my smile to stay on my face.

"He said you're special, not the average human."

"I have my gifts," I say vaguely. It appears Axel and I have the same purpose for this dance—to feel each other out and glean as much information as we can.

I wonder what her powers are. She's so dominant, and if she's as powerful as rumors claim, she would be a great luna for my pack. Much better than Marie. She's so much more beautiful, too.

"You definitely have your gifts," he agrees. It's completely suggestive, and he squeezes my hips a little to emphasize his point. I want to gag.

I'll have to get Marie out of the way. Easy enough to tip off Peter to her location. He'll take care of her himself. Rook's going to be a problem, though. "So what's the deal with you and Rook?" he asks.

Again, I'm not sure how to answer him. I can't decide if it's better to let him think Rook and I are together or fake an interest in him. I decide to go with the first option, because wolves can smell lies and it would be very hard for me to fake any interest in Axel. "It's complicated. We're very good friends, but it seems Rook's wolf is demanding more. I think he's claimed me."

Axel's brows reach for the ceiling. "Then you two aren't dating?"

Again, I decide truth and vagueness are the way to go. I shrug. "He cooked me dinner and escorted me to his Pack's social."

Hmm. It's more serious than I thought. I'll have to get Rook out of the picture before I turn her. That means I'll have to take care of his brother also. I'll have to order hits on them both before we attack Peter's pack. I can't have the Winters brothers fighting with Peter. They're too powerful.

"Well, my congrats to the happy couple, then," Axel says, without missing a beat. "I have to admit, I didn't think Rook would ever choose another mate."

I chuckle. "Neither did he. We were both quite surprised when his wolf started acting so possessively of me. Alpha Toth was plain shocked."

"I can imagine." *He's probably worried Rook plans to take the pack back. Perhaps letting Rook live a while longer is a good thing. He's probably an excellent distraction for Peter. I'll have to ask Jeffrey what he thinks about it. He just can't mate with Nora. He'll be so much stronger then, and she'll be that much harder to force into submission.*

I shudder at that last thought and try to focus on what he said about Alpha Toth's beta. So Jeffrey *is* in on the plan to attack. At least, in some capacity. He's spying for Axel, at the very least.

The song comes to an end, and Axel stops spinning me in slow circles. He doesn't let go of me just yet, though. He pulls my hips so close that our bodies press together, and he leans down to sniff my neck. After a deep inhale that has my skin crawling, he nuzzles me, as if deliberately trying to wipe his scent on my skin. "It was lovely meeting you, Nora," he whispers.

Across the room, there's a fierce snarl and we both look over to see that Alpha Toth and Terrance are holding Rook back. He looks like he wants bloodshed. Nick, too, for that matter. Axel chuckles and lets me go, but he takes my hand and brings it to his lips. "Until we meet again." *By Christmas, you'll be mine.*

I don't think so.

I somehow manage to force one last smile, then quickly escape the creep. He must realize he pushed Rook too far, because he doesn't escort me back to my friends, but rather, melts into the crowd heading toward the exit.

I hurry back to my safety net of friends, trying to shake off the heebie-jeebies Axel left me with. "Well," I say when I reach the group. "That was unpleasant." *But informative,* I try to add with my eyes and a subtle nod.

Rook scoops me into his arms, eyes lit up like torches and chest heaving. I freeze, knowing this is his wolf I'm dealing with and that he's extremely unhappy. Alpha Toth, Nick, Terrance, Parker, Wulf, and even Oliver all look ready to jump in and save me even though there's no way Rook would hurt me like this. Hurt anyone else who gets too close, yes, but me? He'd protect me with his life.

He buries his face in my neck and snarls again when he smells Axel on me. His entire body starts to shake. Terrance doesn't like that sound and matches his snarl with a protective growl of his own.

Uh-oh. My troll and my wolf are going to lose it on

each other if I can't get this situation under control. "Calm down, you big, possessive brute," I say to Rook. "He didn't hurt me."

When I meet his scowl with an unwavering glare, Alpha Toth gently says, "With finesse, Nora."

"Finesse?" I scoff. "Look at him. He's not going to respond to finesse. He needs to be put in his place. He's not my damn mate!"

Rook's eyes flare brighter, and when he growls at me, there's a low rumble that sounds more like a purr.

"That's why you need finesse. Your dominance right now will only make it worse."

"I don't see how. Aren't you supposed to be firm with shifters?"

"You're *exciting* him, Nora," Gorgeous explains dryly.

"Oh." I meet Rook's eyes again and finally notice that the heat is definitely not about being mad or wanting to protect me. I wince. "Oops."

Nick snorts. I shoot him a glare, then offer Rook a gentle smile. "Hey, buddy. Can I have Rook back now?" Of course he growls at this. I sigh. "I'm okay. He didn't hurt me."

"He *touched* you," Rook snaps. "He left his scent on you."

I roll my eyes. "I'll go up to Cecile's room and wash it off, if you hate it that much. You can even replace it with your own scent, if you need to. You just have to calm down for me, okay? You're making Terrance nervous, and we don't want the troll to lose control."

"Yes," Rook says gruffly. "Wash it off."

He grabs my hand and starts dragging me toward the stairs. Damn bossy wolf.

"Nora," Parker calls. "He's not safe like that. You shouldn't be alone with him. He could be pushed over the edge and decide to turn you."

The vampire has a point. I can't entirely trust Rook like this. His wolf is lost to my curse. I don't want to be alone with him. I meet Alpha Toth's gaze, and he steps forward to follow without question. That's perfect, because I need to talk to him anyway. Nick follows, too. Double perfect. We can just all have a little powwow in Cecile's suite while I wash Axel's stench off me. That should be fun.

CHAPTER
TWENTY-ONE

When we get up to Cecile's suite, Rook marches me straight into the en suite bathroom and starts to remove my dress. He gets the zipper all the way down before I can stop him. "Oh, whoa! Whoa, whoa, whoa! No way. You are not undressing me."

Rook's eyes flash fiercely. He means to get his way. I don't care if defying him turns him on; I am standing my ground on this. *"No."*

I zip my dress back up, then reach for a hand towel and turn the water on in the sink. Rook watches my movements with narrowed eyes, and when I move to squirt some hand soap on the towel, Rook snatches the soap away from me. *"No,"* he grunts.

I cock a brow, and he glares at me. Then he moves to the tub and starts rifling through a large basket of soaps. He sniffs several and finally hands me one. "This one."

My jaw falls slack. I turn to Alpha Toth and Nick, who are both watching with amusement. *"Seriously?"*

Nick laughs and Alpha Toth bites down on his lips, doing his best not to join Nick. While I gape at my non-helpful friends, Rook grabs me by the waist and lifts me onto the counter. "What the—*Rook!*"

He grunts in response and takes the towel from my hands. Then, to both my horror and fascination, he wets the towel in warm water, lathers it with the sweet-smelling soap, and gently begins to wash my arm. His face softens as he works, and he starts to calm down.

I'm speechless. Rook is *washing* me. The moment is completely surreal. It's humiliating that he's washing another man's scent off me, but at the same time, it's a little exciting to have this kind of attention. Most men just want to rip my clothes off and take my body. And while Rook did try to undress me, he's trying to take *care* of my body. There's a huge difference.

Unexpected warmth spreads in my chest. Warmth that shouldn't be there. I send a pleading look to Nick and Alpha Toth. They share amused smirks, and then Nick says, "Why don't you tell us what you figured out?"

Both men snicker. Assholes.

Alpha Toth grabs a bath towel and winks at me as he drapes it over me to protect my dress from getting dripped on. He then looks at me as if waiting for me to start talking. I guess we're really doing this while Rook gives me a freaking sponge bath. With a sigh of defeat, I say, "Well, Evan is completely innocent. He seems like a really good guy, and he pretty much loathes his scumbag alpha. He's actually hoping Rook will challenge Axel because he thinks Rook has claimed me and he'd much rather Rook and I be his alpha pair."

Rook's eyes snap to mine.

"Down, boy. I'm not ready to turn furry and have your pups."

He does that rumbly purr thing in his chest again.

I huff, exasperated, and move the conversation along because he likes the idea of pups way too much. "*Anyway.* Evan is not part of some grand plot to overthrow your pack."

Rook rinses off my arm and goes to work on the other one.

"What about Axel?" Toth asks. "What did you find out about him?"

"Oh, he gave me a lot. He's definitely planning a take-over. It sounded like he and Marie were the brains behind the operation, but he's had a change of heart. He plans to leak her whereabouts to you so that you'll take care of her for him."

"Why?"

My face falls flat. "He's got his sights set on a new mate now."

And, predictably, Rook snarls. I ignore it.

"He's debating whether he should have Rook killed now or wait a while, because he also thinks Rook and I are going to be mated, and he thinks it will be a distraction for you." I shoot Rook a glare that says I'm not impressed with his public displays of possession. "He wonders if Rook plans to take over your pack once he has a mate. He mentioned talking to

Jeffrey about it."

"*Jeffrey?*" Alpha Toth repeats. Now I have two wolves growling at me. Great.

"Yup. Your boy's in on it. I'm not sure what he expects to get out of it, but he's definitely in league with the enemy. At the very least, he's a spy for Axel."

Alpha Toth's hands clench into fists.

"I didn't get anything of his plan, except that he for sure means to get rid of both Rook and Wulf before he attacks. He thinks you'll be too powerful with them. And he definitely plans to not let Rook claim me. He also said that by Christmas I would be his."

"Christmas?" Nick repeats. "Six weeks? He must not have all his ducks in a row yet."

Alpha Toth seems to relax a little at this. "That's good. We've still got a little time."

While Nick and Alpha Toth share a speculative glance, Rook moves his ministrations to my shoulder and neck, where Axel had rubbed his face against me. "Mine," he says, while he makes long, soft strokes with the warm, wet towel down my neck.

I send another pleading look for help and still get nothing. Both Alpha Toth and Nick smirk again. Grrr! "Okay, I get that you guys think this is funny, but seriously, what am I supposed to do? Letting him do this feels like encouraging him. It's only going to make him want more."

The smile falls off Alpha Toth's face. His expression is gentle but serious. "Would that be so bad?"

I close my eyes and let out a sigh. *Would* it be so bad?

Would it be so awful to date him? Or Oliver or Parker, either? A month ago I would have said yes, but I swear I'm not sure anymore. My defenses are breaking down, wall after crumbling wall.

Rook rinses his towel, then gently pushes my head to the side and runs the warm, wet edge over my neck and shoulder to wipe off the soap. Goose bumps rise on my arms, and my eyes roll back in my head. His touch is slow and sensual, and his body is so close I can feel his heat. I like this so much more than I should. I swallow a moan only because there are two other men in the room, and I so do not want them knowing how much I'm enjoying this.

"It's not real," I murmur as much to remind myself as to explain to the others. "It's just my curse taking hold of him. Rook doesn't want a mate. You *know* that."

Alpha Toth shakes his head. "You're changing him, Nora. You're healing him. Wulf was right to bring you to him. You were exactly what he needed."

"So what if you have some kind of natural allure?" Nick adds. "It's not some all-encompassing love spell. Rook and his wolf didn't choose you on sight. They're falling for you."

My face pales. Could that be true? Could Rook's feelings for me be real? At least, in some part? Or Parker's? And Oliver...I have no doubt that his feelings for me are real. I've never questioned that.

I groan in frustration. I have no idea what to do about any of this. Thinking that their feelings could be real, that they may truly be invested in me, makes me feel that much worse. I've got three amazing men all vying for my attention,

258

and for the first time in my life, I want to date them. The problem is, which one? How could I choose? And how could I keep Rook or Parker from losing control if I give them the okay? They may be only slightly affected by my curse, but they'd still lose themselves to it if things got too intense. Like Parker with his kiss. They just wouldn't be able to help themselves.

"No." I shake my head again and meet Alpha Toth's gaze. "Maybe it wouldn't be the worst thing in the world if I knew what I was or why I have this effect on people. If I could control it, maybe I *could* date. But until I figure it out, it's just not smart for me to get involved with anyone. People lose control of themselves, where I'm concerned. Case in point." I wave at the werewolf, who has put his washcloth down and is now sniffing me again.

Rook, satisfied that I don't smell of Axel anymore, runs his hands up and down my arms and nuzzles my neck, marking me with his scent the way Axel had before. "Much better," he whispers, his lips brushing my ear.

His voice sounds so normal that I gasp and push him back. There's a mischievous twinkle in his eyes, but no glow. "You're *you* right now!"

He chuckles and steps back. "Have been for a while. I was just enjoying the moment."

I gasp again and slap his chest. He catches my hand and holds it to him. "Maybe Peter's right. Maybe you're good for me." I try to pull my hand away, but he keeps a hold on it. "Maybe I'm good for you, too. For a woman who abhors most physical touch, you just let me put my hands all over you, and you barely thought about it."

Not true. I thought about it a lot. I just didn't hate it. He has a point, though. I did let him touch me. A lot. I let him *wash* me. And I had no reservations about it. No fear, anyway. I didn't panic or feel the slightest bit of anxiety. Maybe he, Parker, and Oliver are helping me as much as I'm helping Rook.

"It's something to think about," Rook says softly, finally releasing my hand and stepping back from me. "For now, we have something more important to focus on."

Change of subject! He's throwing me a life preserver. I can almost forgive him for being a possessive brute. "Yes!" I jump on the topic. "We still need to figure out who will be attacking with Axel. I didn't get any idea about numbers or what kind of outside help he plans to use.

"From the way Evan made it sound, I'd bet most of his pack doesn't have a clue what's going on. It sounds like they all fear him. Maybe we could tell Evan what Axel is planning and have him sniff around for us. He said I could ask him for anything since I saved his life. And the way he hates Axel, he'd probably love to help us. He could probably rally half his pack to take our side in the fight."

All three men exchange meaningful looks. "That could work," Toth agrees. "If we let Axel's wolves—the ones who aren't loyal to him—know what's going on, and we offer them clemency if they fight for us when the battle comes, we could trick Axel into thinking he's got the numbers he needs and then surprise him when his own forces turn on him."

"Evan would have to be very subtle, though," Nick says.

"We can't tip Axel off at all. We don't know what kind of outside forces he'll have or how many of his wolves are loyal to him. We'll need surprise on our side."

"Evan can handle it," Rook says. "I used to be pretty close to him before Lilly died. I know him well. He's a very intelligent wolf who cares a great deal for his pack. He'll know who the loyalists are, and he'll be willing to help."

"You're sure?" Alpha Toth asks. His brow is creased with anxiety.

Rook nods, and so do I. "I'm positive Evan will be on our side," I say.

The men grow quiet again, thinking about the upcoming battle. After a minute, Nick shakes his head. "There are still too many unknown factors. You'll want to be ready for the attack. You'll need to know the time and place, if you want to ensure the least amount of casualties."

My brain trips on the word *casualties*. I know we're talking about a hostile takeover, and I know they're talking about a fight, but I guess I didn't think it would be a fight to the death—except for maybe Axel and Jeffrey. My stomach churns at the idea of Alpha Toth, Rook, and Evan fighting for their lives. And if this involves the whole pack, how many other innocent people could be caught up in it?

Rook startles me from my worries when he blurts out, "A mating ceremony!"

All eyes turn to him. "We want to control the time and place, and we sure as hell don't want to give Axel until Christmas to solidify his plans and gather his allies, so we force his hand."

Alpha Toth's eyes light up with an eager gleam. "He doesn't want the two of you to be mated."

"Exactly," Rook says.

All three men turn their excited gazes on me. My stomach rolls. I know exactly what they're thinking, and I don't like it. "You're the one who told us everyone's already thinking it," Nick says when I start to shake my head.

"Yeah, but that doesn't mean I—"

I yelp, startled, when Rook's hand slips into mine. "We won't really have to go through with it."

He says that, but his thoughts beg to differ. His wolf really likes the idea. I can feel his longing. I can also feel Rook's conflict. He knows I don't want to, but he's starting to like the idea as much as his wolf. He doesn't want to be alone anymore, and he knows he can't ignore his wolf's instincts forever. He's getting tired of fighting it, and he thinks I'd be a good mate. He thinks I'm beautiful, I'm dominant, and he enjoys my company.

I tear my hand away from Rook's, not wanting to hear any more. He flinches at my rejection, but soon realizes I've been listening to his thoughts. He smiles sheepishly and shrugs. "All we have to do is fake it long enough. Axel will never let it happen. He'll attack before the ceremony can take place."

"Make it soon enough, and he'll be forced to attack at the actual ceremony," Toth says. "When the whole pack is together and has their guard down? It'll be too tempting."

Once again, all three men look at me, waiting for an answer. Nick smirks. "Come on, little spitfire. Don't wuss out on us now."

He has a point. There's really nothing to be afraid of. I won't really be mating with anyone. It's just a ploy. And it'll help Alpha Toth's pack so much. Both he and Rook are staring at me with such pleading, hopeful expressions. How can I refuse? "All right." I sigh. "Let's do it."

Alpha Toth lets out a huge breath of relief and takes my hands in his. "Once again, I owe you everything. My pack will forever be in your debt, Ms. Jacobs. Anything you need. Ever. If we can help, we will. We are your allies—your friends—for life."

I wait out his handshake and force an awkward smile. At least he didn't try to hug me. "Thanks. I'll remember that."

"We should get back out there," Nick says. "We don't want Axel to think we're plotting something, and no doubt the guest of honor is already being missed."

I groan. This has been such a nice break. "All right, back to the stupid party."

All three men chuckle as we head for the door. Before I can exit the room, Rook pulls me close to his side. "Showtime." He slides me a sideways glance and a crooked smile. "You ready?"

"You look a little *too* ready," I say flatly. "You do understand that this is fake, right?"

He shocks me then, by grinning and letting his wolf surface. His eyes start to glow faintly, and he growls a low, rumbly purr that makes the hair on my arms and neck stand up. My heart speeds up when he locks his eyes on mine. His smile turns predatory. He leans in, takes a deep breath, and nuzzles his cheek against mine. "I consider it a delicious challenge," he whispers. His lips brush my ear, sending a violent shiver down my spine.

Seeing my reaction, his smile turns smug, and he tangles my fingers in his. "I have a week to convince you," he murmurs, dragging me back down the stairs into the crowd.

We make our way to the bar, where Parker and Oliver are still talking to Wulf and, no doubt, waiting for me. Panic seizes my chest when all three men's eyes fall to my hand in Rook's. "Rook," I whisper so softly I can barely hear myself. "What about Oliver and Parker? And Terrance?"

A soft growl escapes him, and his grip on my hand tightens ever so slightly. "What about them?"

I elbow him. "We have to let them know what's going on."

He lets go of my hand and slides his arm low around my waist, pulling me tightly against his side. "I think they can see just fine what's going on."

"ROOK!"

If he's going to act like such a possessive ass, I'm not going to go through with this crazy plan. It would devastate both Parker and Oliver, and I refuse to do that. I care too much about both of them.

As if he can read my mind—or maybe he just senses my rage—Nick murmurs, "I'll talk to them, Nora. I'm sure they'll understand."

"Talk to who? Understand what?" a smug voice chirps from behind us. We all turn to see Jeffrey. His smile is more of a sneer. He zeroes in on Alpha Toth. "You all were gone for quite a while. Pack meeting I missed? Something I should know about?"

"Actually, there is." Alpha Toth puffs out his chest proudly. "Nora has agreed to a mate pairing with Rook."

Both Oliver and Parker both gasp. I can't meet their gazes. If I do, I'll give myself away, and Jeffery is standing right here, gaping at Rook and me. We need him to believe us. Out of the corner of my eye, I see Parker step toward us, but Nick grabs his arm, holding him back.

"You're taking another mate?" Jeffrey blurts, blinking wide-eyed. Before Rook can answer, he turns his stupefied gaze on me. "You've agreed to be turned?"

I can't find my voice. Rook, however, has no such problem. "My wolf didn't really leave us much choice. He's already claimed Nora."

"Nora, you don't have to do this," Parker says. It looks like Nick is really holding him back now. I hate seeing the worry on his face.

Oliver's expression is even worse, because mixed in with the worry and heartbreak there's also a loving smile. "Are you sure?" he asks.

For some reason, I want to cry. It's all fake, but I'm hurting him. Hurting them both. I need Jeffrey to leave so I can explain it to them. "Do you trust me?" I ask. I direct the question at Oliver, but glance at Parker, too.

Parker's eyes are pleading, begging me not to do this. I can't look away from his stare until Oliver whispers in a small voice, "Yes. I trust you."

My heart hurts. Oliver has so much faith in me. He's so

loyal. Though he's never told me he loves me out loud, he's thought it before, and it's plain as day on his face. What's surprising is that I feel the same way. Oliver's found his way past my walls and into my heart so much that I don't think I could ever live without him.

I meet his gaze again and try to convey how much I love him and am grateful for him. "Then trust me, okay?" My voice is soft and pleading. I have to choose my words carefully, because I'm trying to convince Jeffrey, and, as a wolf, he can sniff out any lies I tell. "This is the right thing for me to do," I say. "I'm sure of it."

Truth. Helping Alpha Toth is absolutely the right thing to do.

Oliver studies me for a moment and then slowly nods, accepting my decision. "I just want you to be happy. If Rook is the man who does that, then I'm happy for you."

My eyes start to burn. He's going to make me cry. "Thanks, Ollie."

Parker still hasn't said anything. His jaw is clenched tight, and his hands are fisted at his side. My heart does another somersault in my chest. For all that I love Oliver, I care about Parker, too, and this is hurting him. When he meets my gaze, there is fear in his eyes. Fear of losing me. There's also need. The man gave up his clan for me. "You don't have to do this, Nora. Just because his wolf has claimed you doesn't mean you have to accept him."

Rook growls and earns himself a nasty glare from Parker. "Are you really so selfish?" Parker asks. "You know Nora isn't ready for a commitment this big. Would you really push her into something she's not ready for? Ask her to give up her humanity?"

"Parker." I say his name so softly his eyes snap to me. He takes one look at me and deflates. I offer him a smile. "Thank you for looking out for me, but he's not making me do anything. I promise."

"You really want to become a wolf?" Jeffrey asks.

I have to stop myself from glaring at him. I don't like the way he's looking at me. He's too eager. I don't know how to answer his question without lying. Thankfully, Rook steps in. "My wolf has accepted her as she is now, so there is no need for Nora to jump into such an important decision without taking as much time as she needs to consider it."

Jeffrey's eyes bulge, and he looks at Alpha Toth. "And you're okay with this? With Rook mating a human?"

Alpha Toth places a hand on Jeffrey's shoulder and gives him a placating smile. "Rook is my dearest friend. He deserves his happiness. And I'm hoping that, given a little more time to think about it, Nora will choose to be turned and join our pack."

I notice Alpha Toth didn't directly answer Jeffrey's question, either, but I am a little surprised that he said he hopes I join them. It can't be a lie. I'm touched that he thinks so highly of me.

Jeffrey seems to be waiting for me to say something, so I return Alpha Toth's smile and say, "Like you said. That's an important decision. But I thank you for the offer, and am glad that you find me worthy of joining your pack."

Jeffrey gapes at the three of us. His eyes dart back and

forth in a frenzied sort of panic. They quickly still and narrow in a calculating way. He pulls his shoulders back and gives us a smarmy smile. "So when's the big day, then?"

"Next weekend," Alpha Toth says. When Jeffrey's eyebrows climb up his forehead, he adds, "You saw how Rook was when Nora danced with Evan and Alpha Day, right?"

Jeffrey's jaw clenches, as if he didn't particularly like me dancing with them, either. Considering he wants me for himself, I'm not surprised. "I saw," he admits through clenched teeth.

Alpha Toth shrugs. "This is a volatile situation. The sooner we get it taken care of, the better."

"Agreed," Rook says. "Next Friday would be perfect."

"Why not?" I add, because Jeffrey is looking to me to say something. "I don't know how mating ceremonies work, but I don't need anything big and fancy, and I already have the perfect dress, don't you think?"

I pull at the skirt of my dress, forcing Jeffrey's attention to my outfit. His eyes rake over me, and his gaze fills with heat. Rook's jaw clenches at the sight of Jeffrey's leer, and he pulls me just a little closer to him.

"It is a lovely dress," Jeffrey admits with a smug smile that seems unjustified. He sweeps his gaze over Rook and me, then nods to Alpha Toth. "Next weekend, then. I look forward to the ceremony." He dips his head in a bow to me and flashes me another unnerving smile. "If you'll excuse me, Ms. Jacobs, I believe it's time for me to say goodnight. It's been a lovely party. I appreciate the invite."

"Of course. Thank you for coming."

I force myself to shake his hand without cringing. His thoughts are on Axel. He's running off to tell him about the mating ceremony and thinking of the wolves he'll have to get ready in less than a week.

Once he's out of earshot, I tug Rook to a more secluded corner of the room. I'm not surprised when Alpha Toth and all my guys follow us. They gather around me, waiting for me to speak like I'm the quarterback in the team huddle. I give Rook, Nick, and Alpha Toth a knowing look. "He's running off to tell Alpha Day right now. You'll want to watch him like a hawk this week. He was thinking about wolves he'll have to get ready this week. He must have a few in your pack loyal to him that are in on the plan."

Alpha Toth's jaw clenches, but he nods calmly. "Thank you, Nora. Rook, please reach out to Evan. Discreetly. Let him know everything, and warn him he only has a week."

Parker can't hold back any longer. "What's going on?" he demands. "What are you guys up to? Because there is no way Nora agreed to be mated to Rook so suddenly."

Rook's eyes narrow, and he balls a hand into a fist. I elbow him lightly. "Oh, calm down, Rook. He's not insulting you. He just knows me."

Oliver steps forward, eyes wide. "So you're not being mated? I didn't want to believe it, but you said to trust you."

Rook huffs again, but I can't help pulling Oliver into a tight hug. His thoughts are full of hope and relief. "Thank you for trusting me, Ollie." My voice cracks from emotion, and I squeeze him as tightly as I can. "I promise I'll explain later."

CHAPTER
TWENTY-TWO

As I sit on the couch in Rook's house, waiting for Rook to get dressed, my eyes start to close. I'm exhausted all the way to my bones. It's been a very long week, and though I'm apprehensive about the mating ceremony and impending fight, I'm just glad it's almost over.

To say that Parker and Terrance were pissed when they learned of my involvement with Alpha Toth's pack would be a gross understatement. Oliver, amazing man that he is, was proud of me and only worried for my safety. Once they all settled down and realized they couldn't talk me out of the fake mating ceremony, they demanded they be in attendance in order to protect me. Normally, a mating ceremony is strictly a pack thing, but Alpha Toth agreed, happy for the extra help. He said their presence would be easy enough to explain because I wasn't pack yet, and of course I'd want my closest friends to see me mated.

To keep up with the ruse, I spent most of the week on the pack compound with Rook. He personally introduced me to almost everyone. I vetted as many wolves as I could and helped Rook and Alpha Toth figure out who were Toth's most loyal supporters and who I thought might be in league with Jeffrey. I've never used my abilities so much in all my life.

I pull my eyes open and rub my face when Rook clears his throat and says, "You about ready?"

He looks damn good in his suit, and he's shaved off his normal five o'clock shadow for the occasion. It's almost a pity this isn't a real mating ceremony. I look at the garment bag lying over the arm of the couch and sigh. I'm supposed to meet with the top-ranked women in the pack and let them get me ready for the ceremony, sort of like bridesmaids in a human wedding. I'm not really looking forward to it. "Can't I just get ready here?"

Rook smiles and holds a hand out to me. "It's tradition," he says, pulling me to my feet. Once I'm standing, he slips his arm around my waist and pulls me to him. "You'll break their hearts if you don't go," he murmurs, combing his fingers through my hair.

I gulp. He's acted so differently this week. His wolf has been calmer, but *he's* been more aggressive. I can't decide if he's doing it on purpose because he likes me, or if he's just losing the battle against his wolf's desires. I asked him that very question yesterday, and he told me the two things are one and the same.

I can't deny the connection I feel to him. There's

something about him. Aside from the fact that he's one of the hottest men I've ever seen, he's spent so long guarding his own heart that he knows where I'm coming from. He feels like a kindred spirit of sorts.

He untangles his hand from my hair and holds it to my cheek. I'm graced with his thoughts and am surprised to hear he's having doubts about the plan. He pulls his fingers away from my skin when I frown, and explains. "My wolf doesn't want to let you go out there today. It goes against my instincts to put you in harm's way."

I break his hold and take a much-needed step away from him. "I'll be fine. Axel doesn't want me dead, and I'll be surrounded by Wulf, Nick, Oliver, Parker, and Terrance, anyway. Besides. Unless he brings every rogue in the country, he's going to be sorely outnumbered. The fight is hardly going to be a fight at all."

Over the week we only found maybe ten of Alpha Toth's wolves who planned to side with Axel. They're some of the strongest, but they don't know Alpha Toth's wolves are expecting this fight and know they plan to turn on them. Alpha Toth has secretly spoken to all his faithful wolves already and coordinated the proper defense strategies. It also helps that Evan has been spreading the word to his loyal wolves that Toth is granting clemency to those who don't fight for Axel. Axel has only half the numbers for this fight that he's expecting, and Toth has twice as many.

Rook sighs. "You're right. I know. Still. My wolf knows there's going to be trouble, and he doesn't want you in the thick of it. *I* don't want you there."

I resist the urge to roll my eyes only because I really don't want to be there, either. I know my guys will keep me safe, but the thought of being in the middle of a bunch of angry wolves ripping each other apart is unsettling. I'm still having nightmares about watching Daniel and Maya die. "I'll tell the guys to get me out of there the second the fighting starts." I pick up the dress bag and smirk. "Unlike you wolves, I've got no problem standing aside while you all fight."

He can't stop the small smile that breaks out on his face. "Good. Still, I've got something for you, just in case."

He walks into his kitchen and pulls a sheathed knife from a drawer. "This is pure silver. It's werewolf Kryptonite," he explains, kneeling in front of me. He lifts my pant leg and straps the knife just above my ankle. "I know you don't know how to use it, but if anyone gets near you, just swing with it. You probably won't manage a killing blow, but any slice you can give with this will slow them down a little."

"I'm sure I won't need to use it, but thank you," I say as he tucks my pant leg over the knife and rises to his feet.

We bundle up in our coats, hats, and gloves—it finally snowed this week, and it looks like the freezing temperatures of winter are here to stay—and head across the compound to a house close to the clubhouse.

Two women answer the door with bright smiles and giddy squeals. They're sisters, both tall and lean with more muscle definition than I'll ever manage. One has blonde hair and the other brown. "Nora!" Rhea, the older of the two pulls me into a hug. "Finally. Come on, we've got a lot to do and not enough time."

Rook starts to follow us in after the sisters shuffle me into the house, but Lila, the younger sister, stops him. "No way, mister. You go away. You can't see her all dressed up until the ceremony starts."

I don't have the heart to tell them that he already saw me all done up in the dress at my party last week.

"Go," Rhea insists with a stubborn stomp of her foot, pointing toward the clubhouse where the ceremony is being held.

Rook frowns at me, and Lila throws her arm over my shoulders. "You'll see your mate soon enough," she says.

Rook preens at how she refers to me as his mate and finally smiles. "All right. Just hurry up. And take good care of my mate." His eyes shift to me and hold steady. "Be safe. I'll see you soon."

The two women coo over his gentle warning of safety as they shut the front door. "Ah, he's worried about leaving you. That's so cute," Lila says.

Rhea smiles, too, but hers is sad. "I can't blame him after losing his last mate." She sucks in a deep breath and shakes off her melancholy, flashing me a bright smile. "I'm so glad he's finally found a new mate."

Lila nods enthusiastically. "For sure. No one deserves to be happy more than Rook, and the way he smiles at you..." A lovesick sigh slips past her lips. "You guys are so cute together. You're going to be so happy. I can tell."

Guilt stirs in my stomach. The only people we've told the ceremony is a sham are the wolves we know are loyal and are ready to fight. Everyone else thinks it's real so that Jeffrey and his spies won't suspect we know about the attack. I'm afraid the news that the mate pairing isn't really happening is going to hurt a lot of the pack. They love Rook too much and are so excited to see him happy.

"Come on," Rhea says, shaking me from my thoughts. She leads me through the house to the master bedroom. "Okay, let's see the dress."

"Yes, put it on, I'm *dying*," Lila adds.

They leave me alone to change into my dress, and I tighten the knife around my ankle. Rook's right: I don't know how to use a knife, but I do feel safer with it on. Once I have the dress on, tingles shoot up my spine. That familiar warning of impending danger raises the hairs on my arms and neck. It's strong enough that sweat breaks out on my forehead and my stomach rolls. The dread in my chest is almost paralyzing. Someone wants me dead, and they want it violently and immediately.

Grabbing the silver knife from the sheath on my ankle, I tiptoe into the hallway and freeze when I hear Luna Marie's voice.

"Luna?" Rhea asks, voice laced with surprise. "I thought you were out of town."

Out of town... In hiding... I suppose those are the same thing. That was the downside to this plan. In order for us to keep the surprise, we couldn't let on that we know of Marie's treachery. The pack just thinks she left town for a while on vacation.

"You ladies head on over to the ceremony," Marie says. "I'll help Nora get ready. I'd like to have some one-on-one time with her."

Yeah. I'll just bet she does.

Rhea and Lila comply so quickly that I don't bother calling them back. It's clear that even though they don't know what's going on, their loyalties lie with their luna. Obeying her is ingrained in them. I'm not sure they won't side with her when she attacks, and I don't need to take on three wolves. I can only hope that Rhea and Lila get to the clubhouse fast and tell Rook about Marie showing up.

I sneak back into the master bedroom and lock the door behind me. I grab my phone and send off a quick text to Terrance that Marie is here and I need help. Then I head for the window. It's my only means of escape at this point. Before I can escape, the bedroom door crashes open and Luna Marie grins at me with a smile that's pure evil. There's a hungry gleam in her eyes.

"Well," she says, looking me over. "Isn't that a pretty dress? It's a shame I'm going to have to ruin it."

I have no idea what to do or say. I have no idea how to fight a werewolf.

"I'm going to enjoy ripping you apart, you little human bitch. You've taken everything from me. You bewitched Peter somehow and forced me out of my pack, and now you've taken Axel. I know he plans to mate with you instead of me."

I roll my eyes at her jealous, villain-esque monologue. "You forced yourself out of the pack when you betrayed your alpha, and as for Axel…" I shrug. "Peter knows he's coming, and the pack's ready for him. He'll be dead by the end of the evening."

Marie's smile widens. "That's what you think. It's not just Axel's pack—"

"You mean your little lapdog Jeffrey? Oh, Peter knows all about him, and the wolves he's managed to talk into mutiny. They won't be any trouble. The pack's itching to take them out first."

Surprise flashes in Marie's eyes, and her face becomes hard.

"Oh," I add. "We've also been working with Evan Fuller all week. Most of his pack hates Axel and have agreed to turn on him and fight with Alpha Toth. Axel is sorely outnumbered, and he has no idea."

Marie's face turns red from rage, and her eyes begin to glow. Her entire body begins to shake, and for a moment I think she's going to turn, but she gets it under control and shrugs. "No bother. Peter and Axel can kill each other all they want. I don't care. I have the means to disappear." Her feigned nonchalance isn't fooling me. "Seems to me the best revenge I can take is getting rid of you—their precious Nora. I don't know what it is about you that everyone loves so much, but I'm going to enjoy killing you."

Without warning, Marie shifts into a wolf and lunges forward. I barely have enough time to raise my hands to cover my face. I manage to keep my throat from being ripped out, but Marie's teeth sink into my shoulder, and her claws drag down the front of my body. She rips my dress to shreds and leaves gashes in my thighs. I cry out in pain, but she howls, too, and stumbles back. Blood leaks from a gash on her chest, and I suddenly remember I'm holding Rook's silver knife.

I fall to the floor, my wounded legs no longer able to hold my weight. My shoulder is on fire, and my head is beginning to fog over.

Marie regains her composure and snarls at me. She's on me in seconds, and her teeth tear into my arm. I scream in pain and give one last, desperate shove of the blade toward Marie's underbelly. She doesn't see it coming. She's arrogant and not expecting me to fight back. The knife plunges into her body, buried hilt deep, and she howls in pain as she falls over.

She's not dead, but she's definitely down. Hopefully long enough for help to arrive. I wish I could enjoy my small victory, but the fire in my arm is spreading through my whole body. It's becoming harder to think straight, and black spots are clouding my vision. I'm starting to float in and out of consciousness, when the front door is smashed open. I can't even tell who's come to rescue me. I can't see anymore. My entire body is burning.

"I've found her!" I think the voice is Parker's, but I can't be too sure.

Cool hands brush the hair out of my eyes. "Don't worry, Nora, we've got you."

There's a mighty roar, and then someone else yells, "Peter! She's dead already! Get a grip!"

Rough hands brush my cheek next, and a gruff voice says, "She's been bitten!"

"MOVE!"

The hands bringing me comfort disappear, and new, calloused fingers grip my face and prod at my shoulders.

"Is she going to change?"

I know that voice. I try to croak out Oliver's name, but I can't get the word out. I can only manage a small whimper.

"Hang in there, Nora. We've got you. We're going to get you fixed up."

"I'm sorry, son," a deep voice says. "She's been bitten. There is no stopping what will happen next. But don't worry. She'll be welcome in my pack. We'll take good care of her."

"*MINE!*" a rough voice snarls.

"Easy, Rook."

The voices in the room are hurting my head. I want to pass out, but the pain is keeping me awake. My whole body is on fire.

"She's not turning." The quiet, almost musical voice is soothing. I know it, but I'm too far gone now to remember who it belongs to.

"Nora is not human. She's an underworlder wearing a strong glamour. She's not turning right now; she's being poisoned."

"*What?*"

"You're sure?"

"I've tasted her blood. I'm certain. I don't know what she is, but she's strong, and I believe she's immortal."

"I'll call Enzo."

"What do we do? We don't know what kind she is. We don't know what kind of blood she needs."

"She may be strong enough that she'll burn it out on her own, but still call Enzo. He'll be able to help some."

"On it."

"It'll take him too long to get here."

"Guys. She's really strong. She'll be okay."

"Give her some of mine, just in case," Terrance's low, rumbly voice says.

There's a shuffle and a growl. It's answered with a snarl. "Guys! Not now! Rook, let Terrance have her."

Before they can move me, the pain reaches an all-new intensity that I can't even begin to describe. Pressure starts to build in my chest, my head. I feel something dripping from my nose and ears, and then, with a pop, the tension shatters. It hurts so badly a bloodcurdling scream rips from my lungs.

Several gasps ring out in the otherwise silent room.

"Shit."

"Well, damn."

"Didn't see that one coming."

"It can't be."

I have no idea what they're talking about, and I don't care. With the pressure gone, the pain has dulled to a tolerable level. I welcome the blackness when it overtakes me.

CHAPTER
TWENTY-THREE

I WAKE TO THE SOUND OF HUSHED VOICES. "HOW'S OUR little seductress doing? Any change?"

"Her fever broke, and she has some color back. I don't think she'll sleep much longer."

"I'm awake," I say. My throat is so parched it comes out in a croak, and I start coughing.

"Here, sweetheart."

Cool fingers comb back my sweat-crusted hair. I open my eyes to see Parker sitting beside my bed, holding out a glass of water. Terrance is sitting in a chair on the other side of the bed, glaring, arms folded across his chest as if he's been playing watchdog the entire time I was out. I'm sure he has. He swallows when I meet his eyes, and his face softens. "You scared the shit out of us, Trouble."

He clears his throat when he chokes up, and then glares at me as if it's my fault he can't completely hide his emotions.

My heart melts at the sight. "Sorry, T-man. Won't do it again. Promise."

"Damn right, you won't."

I grin at my surly troll, then cast my eyes around the room. It's one I recognize. I'm in the guest room at Rook's house, and the sun is shining brightly through the sheer curtains. Nick is standing at the foot of the bed, grinning like the devil. "Good to see you're not dead, spitfire."

Parker holds out the glass of water again, and as I sit up to take it, I gasp. My arms don't look right. My skin looks pearlescent. It's shimmering. "What the hell?"

"Relax, Nora," Parker says, placing the glass in my hand. "Everything's going to be okay."

I accept the water from Parker and gulp it down. Once I find my voice, I frown at Nick. "What's going on? What's wrong with me? Why do I look like this?"

"Nothing's wrong with you," Parker murmurs. "You're absolutely stunning like this."

Panic begins to claw its way up my throat. "But what *is* this?"

"It's you," Nick says. "Your true self. The werewolf saliva burned through your glamour."

I jump out of the bed and head for the bathroom. I gasp at the face staring back at me in the mirror. It's me, but it's somehow more. If I was pretty before, now I'm striking. It's as if my features were blurry, and they've suddenly been sharpened into focus. My skin is that shimmering pearlescent color all over, and there are bright blue, purple, and teal swirls around my eyes, as if my face has been beautifully decorated with paint. Natural makeup. My hair is also fuller, with more body, and it's streaked with pink, purple, and teal streaks. It looks windswept and wild but still controlled, like you'd see on a model in a magazine. I hardly recognize myself.

My arms feel smooth and a little cool, and the subtle swirls of color shimmer as I shift them in the light. It's beautiful in a way, but it's not human, and it's freaking me out. I turn to the men all gathered in the hallway outside of the bathroom. I'm scared to ask, but at the same time, I've wanted to know the answer to this question my whole life. "What am I?"

Terrance pushes Parker and Nick out of the way and smiles proudly. "You're one of my kind. You're fey."

"More specifically, a siren," Nick adds.

"A siren." I look at myself in the mirror again, and I can totally see it. I'm beautiful now in an ethereal way. I remind myself of a mermaid.

I shake my head in disbelief. I'm a siren. Trying to wrap my head around the idea, I think over everything I know about sirens. They were mythical creatures that lived in the ocean and lured sailors to their deaths.

"Am I dangerous?" I frown at my friends, worried that I might have some crazy affect on them. I would hate myself if I ever hurt them. "To you guys, I mean?"

When none of them answers right away, panic rears its ugly head again. *"What?"* I demand.

Parker takes my hand and gently tugs me out of the bathroom. "Let's take this out into the living room. We'll wake up Oliver. He always calms you down."

"Oliver's here? He's sleeping? What's wrong with him? Was he hurt?"

I push my way past everyone, without waiting for answers. Oliver is passed out on Rook's couch, wearing the suit he put on for the mating ceremony. It's wrinkled all to hell, and he looks pale with dark circles under his eyes. "What's wrong with him?" I demand in a whisper, not wanting to wake him.

"Nothing," Nick says. "He's fine. He's just tired."

"He refused to leave your side for two days straight. We finally convinced him to crash out here when he fell out of that damn chair by your bed."

Sweet Oliver. That sounds just like him. I comb my fingers through his soft waves. The poor man is so exhausted he doesn't stir. "I've really been out for two days?"

Nick nods. "Closer to three now."

"You had a rough go of it," Terrance says.

"Wake him up, and I'll call Rook. He'll want to be here for this discussion."

I frown at Nick. What discussion? When Parker and Terrance nod solemnly, I start to get a really bad feeling. "What's going on?"

I practically shout that question, and Oliver finally wakes up. His eyes pop open, and he bolts upright. "Nora!"

He throws his arms around me. He's shaking as he squeezes me like his life depends on it. My worry melts away, and I hug him back. "I'm okay, Ollie."

"You weren't. We almost lost you. Again."

I comb my fingers through his hair. "It's a good thing I'm tough, then, huh?"

He pulls back and looks into my eyes. His whole face softens. "Strongest person I've ever met," he says. "You sure you're okay?"

I take a mental inventory and nod. "Actually, I feel really good. Stronger, healthier, energized..."

He nods. "Not surprising. Your glamour was suppressing your power. That can be hard on the body."

Oliver sinks back into the couch, and I move with him, tucking my feet up under me and curling up next to him. Terrance grins at us, but Parker watches Oliver and me with a pained expression. I can't stand the look on his face, so I hold my hand out to him and pat the couch on my other side.

Surprise washes over Parker. He glances at Oliver again and frowns. "Just come sit down," I tell him.

Oliver stiffens but relaxes when I pat his leg. Parker reluctantly moves to my other side and sits beside me. I give his leg a pat, too. "Thank you both for watching over me."

Each of them murmurs quiet responses that make me smile. I can't help winding my arms through each of theirs. I lay my head on Oliver's shoulder, but pull Parker close against my side. He resists at first, but quickly relaxes and lets out a quiet sigh.

My heart seems to swell having them both right here with me. I close my eyes and take a deep breath, enjoying the sensation of being cared for, loved even. I let the air out of my lungs slowly and shudder, feeling better than I have in...well...ever, really.

When I open my eyes, Nick and Terrance are both watching me. Terrance's look is contemplative, while Nick's smirk is bigger than usual.

"What?" I ask, voice dry as the desert.

Nick opens his mouth to say something, but before whatever obnoxious retort he has can escape his lips, Rook comes bursting through the door, followed by his brother and Alpha Toth. Rook's eyes wildly scan the room until they fall on me. He's across the room in two strides and sits down on the coffee table in front of me. He places both hands lightly on my knees, and I realize for the first time that I'm wearing a pair of sweats and a T-shirt that I swim in.

"Are you okay?" he asks. His eyes aren't glowing, but his voice is rough with emotion.

I give him a soft smile, touched by his concern though not surprised by it. "I'm fine. How are you?" I shift my gaze to Alpha Toth. "How is the pack? Did Axel try to attack? Was anyone hurt?"

Alpha Toth swallows loudly and clears his throat. "Things went exactly according to plan. Thanks to you, he never stood a chance. We had a few scrapes and bruises, but we didn't lose a single loyal pack member."

"More than half of Axel's wolves turned on him and fought with us," Rook adds. "The fight was over within minutes."

"Axel and all of his wolves have been taken care of," Alpha Toth says.

Taken care of. Does that mean what I think it means?

"Axel's dead, then?"

Alpha Toth nods. "He went after Rook first. Rook killed him in self-defense. All of the wolves who fought for Axel were killed, including about ten rogues that Axel hired."

I nod. It's strange that I'm not as upset about all the death as I should be. Perhaps I'm finally getting used to the underworld and its violence.

My heart skips a beat. I've learned enough about pack life in the last few weeks to know what it means that Rook killed the alpha of the Island Lake pack. "So, you're going to be the new alpha for Island Lake?"

I'm proud of him, but a surprising ache throbs in my heart thinking that he's going to move to Island Lake and become their alpha. He won't have time to train me anymore. I'm going to miss him.

As if he can sense my sadness, Rook gives my knees a squeeze. "I didn't accept," he says softly. "I handed the position over to Evan. It's his pack anyway. He loves those wolves and has been looking out for them, trying to shelter them from Axel as much as he could for a long time. He deserves the pack and will make a great alpha."

I bite my lip, trying to hide my relief. It makes me feel selfish to want to keep Rook away from a position he was born for. "Is that what you really want?" I ask.

Rook lifts his hand to my face and tucks my hair behind my ear. "I think you know what I want," he murmurs.

My face flames, and I look away, unable to meet his gaze. "Rook..."

"You're not ready," he says. "I know that. But I'm not

willing to let you go, either. Not now that I know what I want. You might not have been turned, but my wolf has still claimed you. Whether you accept me or not, I am yours." He clears his throat and sits back. "I'm leaving my pack and moving in with Wulf."

My eyes snap back to him, and I gasp. "Rook! Why would you do that?"

He pins me with a determined stare. "To be closer to you."

My heart stutters in my chest. "Rook, they're your pack. You can't give that up just to—"

"I shouldn't really be in the pack, anyway," he interrupts. "I have no place in the hierarchy if I'm not going to be alpha. I know it, Peter knows it, and the pack knows it. I'll be fine in the city with my brother."

I shake my head. "You weren't before. You told me yourself that the last time you went to live with your brother, you missed your pack and needed to come home."

"It's different now," he says quietly. I don't ask what he means. It's obvious in his stare.

I can't believe he's doing this. I'm both thrilled and terrified by it. I want him to be closer to me. I love his company, his friendship, and I know he's good for me. My relationship with him has been healing me. I've come so far with my fear of physical touch since we started hanging out. Werewolves are so affectionate. He constantly touches me, and when we're training, he has to touch me. And I allow it, because, deep down, I trust him. I need him. I just worry that he's sacrificing too much, and that I won't be able to give him everything he wants in return.

"It'll be okay, Nora," he promises. "You're going to need me, anyway. With your glamour gone, you're going to need all the protection you can get."

His statement completely derails my train of thought. "What do you mean? Why?"

All the men in the room exchange serious looks. It's Nick who decides to be the bearer of bad news. "Sirens… in history…have been…hunted." My eyes bulge. *Hunted?* "They were hunted to extinction. Or so we thought. You may very well be the only one. Your mother was, no doubt, in hiding. Her death may not have been random, either."

I gasp. Could my mother have been killed by rogue vampires because of what she was? Had they been hired to kill her? My chest burns at the thought. "Why?" I croak. "What's so bad about being a siren?"

"You're strong, Nora," Terrance says. "Very powerful. One of the most powerful kind of fey there is."

"Many fear your kind. Men, especially. They say there's nothing more powerful than a siren's song. You have the power to control minds. You can capture men with a single look."

My blood turns to ice in my veins. *That's* what happened before. When that sorcerer kidnapped me, and again when the rogue wolves attacked me, I had used my siren's song on them to save myself. The wolves were terrified of what I was doing, and the one I'd captured in my thrall was so angry he tried to rip out my throat. Nick's right. I'm dangerous.

"It makes so much sense," I whisper. "The way men have

always been attracted to me..."

"It'll be worse now," Parker says. "Your glamour was suppressing your gifts. Only a fraction of your power was escaping. Now you're..."

He looks me over with admiration, and dread washes over me. "Oh, shit." I look around at the group of men surrounding me, and my stomach churns. "I've done it to you guys, haven't I? I've captured you or whatever."

"You drew us to you, maybe," Rook says. "But you've never taken our will. We're here for you because we want to be."

"We're not hopelessly in love with you, either," Nick says and grins. "Well, at least not *all* of us. Magic boy over there is a goner, but you haven't ensnared me."

Oliver blushes, and I glare at Nick on his behalf. Nick chuckles. "Don't worry about us. We all have the power to leave if we want to."

"But we won't," Parker insists. "You'll learn to control your gift, and we'll keep you safe while you do."

I take a deep breath and try to accept what they're saying. They don't seem worried, but I have doubts. I don't want to hurt them. I'm starting to love each of these men in their own ways. They're my friends. My family, even. I don't want them in my life because I've put them under some kind of spell. As I look at all the determined faces around the room, I gather up my own resolve. I will do whatever it takes to learn to control my curse.